More praise for William Bernhardt, *Primary Justice*, and *Blind Justice*

"Bernhardt skillfully combines a cast of richly drawn characters, multiple plots, a damning portrait of a big law firm, and a climax that will take most readers by surprise."

—*Chicago Tribune*

"An insider's view of corporate lawyering. Cynical, suspenseful, and fast-paced—a fun read."

—*Lia Matera*

"An unexpected treat, one of those non-stop reads that hold ̲ ̲ ̲hing for everyone ̲ ̲ ̲

"Enthral ̲ ̲ ̲ ... with a likable ̲ ̲ ̲ ̲ot, and a fascinati ̲ ̲ ̲ ̲ ̲ view of corporate law."

—*The Armchair Detective*

Also by William Bernhardt
Published by Ballantine Books:

PRIMARY JUSTICE
BLIND JUSTICE
THE CODE OF BUDDYHOOD

DEADLY JUSTICE

William Bernhardt

BALLANTINE BOOKS • NEW YORK

Library of Congress Catalog Card Number: 93-90073

ISBN 0-345-38027-4

Manufactured in the United States of America

First Edition: July 1993

for Joe and Barbara

When men are pure, laws are useless; when men are corrupt, laws are broken.

Benjamin Disraeli (1804–1881)

Lawyers, I suppose, were children once.

Charles Lamb (1775–1834)

* Prologue *

The black van pulled over on the south side of Eleventh Street. The driver rolled down a smoked glass window and smiled. He was a handsome man, especially when he smiled.

"Are you the one?" he asked.

The girl on the street corner stopped chomping her gum. "That depends on what you're looking for, pal."

"I'm looking for you."

"Then I guess I'm the one." She returned his smile, adding a raised eyebrow to complete the message. She was wearing a turquoise tube top, black spandex pants, and a black leather jacket with fringe dangling from the sleeves. "What exactly did you have in mind?"

"Peace. Contentment. An end to suffering."

"That's a tall order. Probably will cost you extra."

He shrugged. "Cheap at any price."

"Who's cheap? Are you calling me cheap?"

"Of course not." He flashed his winning smile again. "Step into the light, fair maiden. So I can see you."

She hesitated a moment, then approached the van. The neon signs of the massage parlors and sex shops flashed about her, bringing her features into sharp focus.

The man examined her carefully, from her swirling bleached-blond hair down her long coltish legs to the tips of her pink-painted toes. Clothes and makeup could not conceal what her thin flat figure betrayed: she was in her mid-teens, sixteen at the most.

1

The man checked the Polaroid photo he held out of her line of vision. Yes—she *was* the one.

"Let's go for a ride," the man said.

"Not necessary." She felt less skittish, now that she could see his honest, handsome face. "I have a room upstairs."

"What, some closet rathole in a house full of ratholes, with a different couple pumping like pistons on every square foot? I think we deserve something better than that." He popped open the door. "Get in the van."

"I can't." A worry line creased her brow. "We're not supposed to leave with anyone. Two girls have disappeared from The Stroll in the past week. I knew the first one. Her name was Angel."

The man appeared surprised. "What happened to her?"

"No one knows. But some of the rumors I've heard . . ." Goose bumps suddenly appeared on her neck and shoulders. "I just hope they're not true."

"When did you see her last?"

"The day she disappeared. It was her birthday. Trixie gave her a necklace, a gold heart broken into two pieces. It was real nice—cost Trixie a whole night's pay. She's always doing sweet stuff like that."

"Perhaps Angel moved on," the man said in a comforting voice. "Perhaps she found her own slice of paradise."

"Yeah, maybe. Still . . ." She leaned forward and touched his arm. "Why don'tcha come upstairs? You'll be glad you did. Everyone says I'm real good. I'll do almost anything. Some of it costs extra, though."

"Sorry. I don't like crowds."

The girl pushed away from the van. "Then you'd better move on. I'm not supposed to talk to anyone who's not a customer."

The man took out his wallet, removed five hundred-dollar bills and laid them end-to-end on the dash. "I've got a room at the Doubletree, just ten minutes from here. If you'll come with me, all this will be yours."

The girl stared at the money, her mouth gaping. "How ... long?"

"You'll be back by midnight," he lied.

"I don't know. . . ."

"Come on now. Do I look like someone who would hurt a poor working girl?"

The corners of her lips turned up, almost involuntarily. He didn't seem dangerous; on the contrary, he was friendly and wholesome and all-American. The kind of man she could've brought home, back when she had one, without sending her father through the roof.

Maybe she was being foolish—letting a few rumors get the best of her. He was offering more money than she could make in a week, and the night would only be half over. Judging by the wad he was carrying, he must be rich. Who knew? It was just possible, if he really liked her ...

"All right," she said. "You sweet talker, you." She slid into the passenger seat, sweeping the bills off the dash and tucking them inside her spandex pants.

"I'm glad." He fastened his seat belt, adjusted the rearview mirror, and turned the ignition. "This is going to be the greatest adventure of your life."

"Swell." She stroked the side of his face. "I'm excited already." It wasn't entirely untrue. She wasn't sure if it was the man or the money or both, but she was definitely feeling charged up.

The black van pulled away from the corner and zoomed down the street. In the darkness, she did not see his smile flatten and fade and become something else altogether, just as she did not see the black garbage bag in the back of the van, or the white silken cord, or the golden half-heart necklace.

PART ONE

* *

Tennessee Gold

* 1 *

Ben gnawed on the end of his pencil. Things were worse already.

The lawyer representing the defendant, Topeka Natural Gas Limited, had just completed the direct examination of his expert witness, and the expert was magnificent. Authoritative yet relaxed, confident yet not overbearing—everything an expert witness should be. Ben hadn't a chance of convincing the jury that the proposed gas processing plant would cause permanent damage to endangered animal habitats unless he came up with some way to take this expert apart on cross. And so far he hadn't come up with any.

Ben had prepared cross-examination questions in advance, but the expert had anticipated his every feint and effectively cut Ben off at the pass. To compound matters, Christina still hadn't shown up. It was hardly unusual for her to be late, but this morning he needed her more than ever, not just for her services as a legal assistant but for her intuitive leaps of insight and perception. To make matters even worse, his investigator, Loving, hadn't put in an appearance yet either. Times like these made Ben wish he could afford to hire an associate, but as a solo practitioner barely scraping by, such luxuries were out of his reach. Once again, Ben was on his own.

He grabbed his briefcase and popped it open. A black plastic object flew out and dropped onto the floor.

Judge Hart peered down from the bench. "Mr. Kincaid, what is that on the floor?"

"That . . . appears to be a plastic spider, your honor." He was going to have to stop letting his cat Giselle play in his briefcase.

"And I assume that is going to play some pivotal role in your cross-examination of this witness?"

"Well . . . you never know, your honor. On cross, one has to be prepared for anything."

"I see." Ben was glad he was in Hart's court this morning; at least she had a sense of humor. "Getting to the point of the matter, Mr. Kincaid, have you any cross-examination for this witness?"

"Uh . . . yes. Definitely. Pages and pages."

The judge seemed surprised. Apparently she found the expert's testimony as flawless as Ben did. "Do you anticipate that your cross-examination will be time-consuming?"

"That's entirely possible, your honor. Could we please have a short recess?" So I can dream up some more questions? Please?

"I suppose. Ten minutes, counsel."

Thank goodness. A reprieve.

The courtroom attendants stood and stretched as Judge Hart retreated to her chambers. Ben scanned the courtroom high and low—and it was low that he spotted a familiar pair of yellow leotards. Help was on its way.

"Christina! Glad you could make it."

"I hurried as fast as I could." She seemed out of breath, as did Ben's secretary, Jones, who was standing beside her. "Have you crossed the expert yet?"

"No, but I'll start in about ten minutes. What have you been doing?"

"Working, of course." She was carrying a huge posterboard. Even folded down the middle, the board was shoulder-high on Christina, who was just over five feet tall. "Am I not your faithful aide-de-camp?"

"Spare me your French." Ben focused on the poster. "What's that?"

"Your Exhibit A. Let's go somewhere private and talk *entre nous*."

Ben followed her to a relatively unpopulated corner of the courtroom. She was wearing a brown leather skirt, not quite knee length, a noisy chain belt, and a silky blouse. And she wondered why he didn't let her sit at counsel table!

"Did Loving discover anything?"

"No," Jones answered. His eyebrows bobbed up and down. "That's why I got into the action."

"Jones, when are you going to get it through your head that you're a secretary? You're not supposed to be skulking around dark alleys. That's Loving's job. You're supposed to answer the phone."

"Aw, Boss, no one ever calls except your creditors. That guy you stiffed for the photocopier is driving me crazy."

"I told him I'd pay as soon as some money came in."

"Yeah, but that was four months ago. Anyway, Loving was upset because you wouldn't let him talk to the expert witness directly."

"The Rules of Professional Conduct don't permit me or my staff to contact opposing witnesses."

"Loving felt stymied."

"There are methods of gaining information other than beating the witness into submission!"

"Perhaps," Jones said, "but that's sort of Loving's specialty. . . ."

"Okay," Ben said, "I know I'll regret asking, but what did you do?"

"I followed Mr. Expert Witness when he left Anglin's offices last night." Anglin was the attorney representing Topeka Natural Gas Limited.

"And where did he go?"

"To a classroom at Tulsa Junior College."

"Pick up the pace, Jones. I don't have a lot of time. Did you find out what the class was?"

"I didn't have to. The classroom was being used as a public meeting room. I knew because I've been there before with Christina."

This did not bode well. "And what undoubtedly auspicious group meets there?"

"The Tulsa Past Lives Society."

Ben slapped his forehead. Surely this was a mistake.

"See, Ben," Christina interjected. "I've been saying for months that you should attend some of those meetings with me. But you always refuse."

"I can't get too excited about spending the evening with a bunch of people who think Shirley MacLaine is on the inside track." He glanced at his watch. "I suppose you checked this out?"

"Of course." She tossed her long strawberry blond hair behind her shoulders. "Where do you think I've been? I wasn't at the meeting last night, but my girlfriend Sally Zacharias was, and she says that the expert was just the cutest man, very polite and a vegetarian—"

"Cut to the chase, Christina." He saw the judge's clerk reentering the courtroom. "What did you find out?"

She smiled. "Perhaps it would be simpler if you just looked at the exhibit."

Ben laid his hand on the oversize posterboard. He had a definite suspicion he was going to regret this.

"Mr. Kincaid, are you ready to proceed with your cross-examination?" Judge Hart asked when she returned to the courtroom.

"Yes, your honor."

"And you still believe it may be lengthy?"

"It's . . . possible I'll finish sooner than I anticipated, your honor."

The judge's eyes brightened. "Now that's encouraging. Remember, Mr. Kincaid, brevity is the soul of wit."

"I will, your honor." He approached the witness stand. "Dr. Lindstrom, you are a Ph.D., are you not?"

In fact, Dr. Lindstrom was the stereotypical picture of a Ph.D.—tortoiseshell eyeglasses, tweed jacket, salt-and-pepper beard. "I am. I received my degree in Environmental Sciences, with an emphasis on toxic gases."

"And you belong to a myriad of professional organizations."

He seemed pleased at the opportunity to flaunt his awesome credentials. "Yes, and I'm also a delegate to the National Environmental Congress for North America."

"I'm sure we don't want to bore the jury with a litany of your countless awards and commendations."

He sniffed. "Well ... if you say so."

"You also hold an endowed chair at the University of Oklahoma, correct?"

"I have been fortunate to receive the John Taylor Ross chair, yes."

"But the vast majority of your current income does not come from the University, does it?"

He paused. "I'm ... not sure what—"

"You make far more money these days as a professional expert witness, right?"

"I have been called on occasion to offer my expertise—"

"And always by right-wing groups or businesses that want to destroy something natural so they can erect something artificial."

Anglin rose to his feet. "Objection."

Judge Hart nodded. "Sustained."

"Your honor," Ben said, "I'm endeavoring to make the point that this witness has been paid to testify twelve times in the past three years, and in each instance he has testified that the project in question would not harm the endangered species whose habitat was being destroyed."

"Then perhaps you should establish that through cross-examination testimony," Judge Hart said, "rather than by making long-winded speeches."

"That's all right, your honor. I'm ready to move on." Especially since the point was already made. If Ben had learned anything in the time he'd been practicing, it was when to leave well enough alone. "Dr. Lindstrom, I'd like you to look at an exhibit."

Dr. Lindstrom reached for the stack of previously admitted documents.

"No, no, Doctor," Ben said. "I want you to examine a new exhibit." He lifted the posterboard off plaintiff's table, unfolded it, and propped it up against the courtroom easel. The poster was an enlargement of a full-length photo of an attractive platinum blonde in a white party dress.

Anglin was back on his feet the instant the blow-up was displayed. "Objection, your honor. What relevance can this possibly have to the question of whether the proposed gas treatment plant will cause environmental harm?"

The judge fingered her glasses. "I admit I'm a bit mystified myself. . . ."

"I will make the relevance clear very quickly," Ben assured her.

Anglin continued to protest. "Your honor, I have no idea what he's planning to do!"

"Well, life is an adventure," the judge said. "Let's just kick back and see what happens."

Obviously unhappy, Anglin returned to his seat.

Ben confronted the expert witness. "Dr. Lindstrom, do you know who the woman in this photograph is?"

"Uh . . . I believe that would be Jean Harlow."

"I believe you're right. And you're familiar with Miss Harlow, correct?"

He tugged at his collar. "I ... am familiar with her, yes ..."

"And can you tell the jury why you're familiar with Miss Harlow?"

"I ... uh ... was Jean Harlow."

"I'm sorry." Ben pivoted toward the jury box. "I'm not certain the jury got that. What did you say?"

"I said I *was* Jean Harlow. In a past life."

In the corner of his eye, Ben saw Anglin slump down into his chair.

"A past life. You know, Doctor, some members of the jury may not be familiar with that concept. Could you please explain exactly how that works?"

The doctor turned to face the jury. "In 1937," he explained, "Jean Harlow developed a painful inflamed gallbladder, probably exacerbated by kidney damage she sustained during a beating her ex-husband gave her years before on their honeymoon. Unfortunately, my—er, her mother was a devout Christian Scientist who refused to permit Jean to seek medical treatment. Jean lay helplessly in her bedroom, in great pain, becoming sicker by the hour. Eventually, her fiancé, William Powell, broke into the house with some friends, scooped Jean into his arms, and carried her to the hospital." He sighed. "William Powell. What a man he was."

After a long moment, Lindstrom broke out of his reverie. "Bill did the best he could, but he was too late. Jean Harlow died."

Ben nodded. "And then what happened?"

Lindstrom leaned forward in the witness box. "You see, it wasn't her time to die. She was only twenty-six. She was just getting started. She was engaged to be married. She hadn't had a chance to live, to *love*—" He made a choking noise, then covered his face with his hand. "She was so young."

Lindstrom didn't continue until he had fully recovered. "So she was reincarnated. As me."

Ben allowed a respectful silence. "And how do you know all this?"

"I recalled it under hypnosis."

"Do you have yourself hypnotized often?"

His left eye twitched. "From time to time."

"Before you testify in court?"

"It ... does help calm my nerves ... sharpen my memory—"

"Are you testifying today under hypnotic influence?"

"I'm fully awake and able to—"

"Please answer my question."

He pursed his lips. "Yes."

Bingo. "Now Doctor, getting back to your story—as the jury can see from the poster, you were quite a sexy gal."

"It was Hollywood. They insisted on photographing me in that objectified manner."

"No doubt. I understand you were often seen in the company of Clark Gable."

"Ugh. Horrid man. Had false teeth—was a dreadful kisser."

"I'm sorry to hear that. Let me ask you about your relationship with William Powell—"

"Your honor, I object!" It was Anglin again, giving it the old college try. "Mr. Kincaid is turning this trial into a circus!"

"Perhaps so," Judge Hart said. "But he's not the one who put the clown in the center ring. Proceed."

Ben eyed the jury. They were eating it up—barely suppressing their laughter. It wouldn't matter now if this guy had a degree from God. His credibility was shot.

"Dr. Lindstrom," he continued. "Isn't it true that Jean Harlow loved little furry animals?"

After the jury retired, Ben and Christina began packing their files and exhibits.

"Well, congratulations, Ace," Christina said. "Your

performance was *sans pareil*. You saved a lot of endangered prairie dogs today."

"The jury is still deliberating," Ben replied. "Let's not jinx it."

"Aw, the gas company hasn't got a chance. You were sensational on cross."

"Well, thanks for the show-and-tell. I would've been up a creek without you."

She batted her eyelashes. "My pleasure. I always enjoy pulling your fat out of the fire."

"How sweet." Ben closed his briefcase, leaving the plastic spider on top. He grabbed a document box and headed for the door.

"Excuse me. Mr. Kincaid?"

Ben saw an unfamiliar man in a gray business suit standing in the doorway.

"Look," Ben said, "if it's about the photocopier, I promise I'll pay you as soon as I can—"

"Oh, no. You misunderstand." He waved his hands rapidly in the air. "I'm not here to hit you up for money. On the contrary, Mr. Kincaid, I'm here to make you a wealthy man."

* 2 *

"You're here to do what?"

The man smiled pleasantly. "I want to set you up for life, Mr. Kincaid. If you'll let me."

"I'm afraid I don't understand."

The man gestured toward the front row of the courtroom. "Let's sit, shall we? You can come too, Ms. McCall. This offer involves you as well."

Ben and Christina exchanged puzzled looks. "Offer?"

"Perhaps I should start at the beginning." He reached into his suit pocket and withdrew a business card. "My name is Howard Hamel." A confident demeanor accented Hamel's clean-cut, well-scrubbed features. "I'm a member of the legal staff for the Apollo Consortium, an amalgamation of interrelated corporate entities. Have you heard of us?"

Ben nodded. Of course he had. The Apollo parent corporation was probably the largest business entity in Tulsa, possibly in the entire state of Oklahoma. It had started as a small oil exploration company, but during the boom years of the Seventies expanded into natural gas, manufacturing, transportation, and even entertainment. The diversification helped them survive the bust years of the Eighties—survive them quite well, in fact. Apollo was a Fortune 500 corporation—one of the few in the Southwest.

"Then you probably also know," Hamel continued, "that we have an in-house legal staff of over fifty lawyers. Heck, if we were a law firm, we'd be one of the largest in the state. And we'd like you to join our team. We can discuss the details at your leisure—salary, bonuses, pension plan, benefits—but I think you'll be pleased with the offer. If you don't mind my saying so, it'll be a step up for you."

And how. But then, Ben thought, almost anything would. "What kind of legal work would this involve?"

"That's one of the advantages to working at a place like Apollo," Hamel answered. "We have so much going on, you can do almost anything you want. Your background is in litigation, and rightfully so, I might add. You were magnificent in the courtroom today."

"Well ... thanks ..."

"I see you joining the litigation team and taking charge of some of the multimillion dollar cases that pass through our office on a daily basis. We like to keep these cases in-house whenever possible; outside counsel fees are exorbitant, as I'm sure you know. There's a new product liability case recently filed against Apollo that you would be perfect for."

The words rang in Ben's ears. In-house counsel. Products liability. Multimillion dollar cases. That would certainly be a step up from the Three Ds: divorce, deeds, and dog bites. "It's an interesting offer. How long will the position be open?"

"Perhaps I haven't made myself clear. There is no position. This isn't some slot we need to fill with a body. We want *you*—Ben Kincaid—on our legal staff."

Ben was flabbergasted. "But—why me?"

"We believe you have a real future in the law, and we want it to be with us."

Ben shook his head, trying to verify that he was hearing clearly. Kudos like this didn't come that often to the solo practitioner. "I'm not sure I'd be happy working for the same client day in, day out."

"Really? Most people prefer it—the satisfaction of being a team player trying to accomplish a worthwhile, common goal, rather than being a prostitute for whoever walks into the office that day."

"Well . . . I'm used to setting my own hours, taking lots of vacation time—"

"So am I. Apollo is a worker-friendly corporation. Myself, I love deep-sea fishing. If I could, I'd spend my entire life doing just that. Apollo gives me far more opportunities than anywhere else would. In fact, I'm leaving for Miami for a fishing trip day after tomorrow."

Ben eyed Christina. She was saying nothing, but something was definitely going through her mind. "Look, I want to be totally up-front with you. I worked for a large law firm once, and it was a complete bust."

Hamel brushed Ben's concerns away with a flip of his hand. "We know all about that, Ben, and we couldn't care less. Frankly, a sizable portion of our staff, myself included, came from Raven, Tucker & Tubb or other large law factories. They seem to suck up the new talent like a black hole. A few years later, though, the lawyers all start asking 'Is this what my life is about? Sixteen-hour days, constant billing pressure, invisible and interchangeable clients?' They start looking for something more—a client they can care about, a job that leaves time for family, friends, and personal interests. That's when they come to Apollo."

"I don't doubt that I'd make more money at Apollo," Ben said, "and probably with less trouble. But money isn't my paramount interest. I became a lawyer because I wanted to do some good in the world."

"Then by all means," Hamel replied, "come to Apollo. We take our role as a corporate citizen seriously. We're active participants in charity drives and several community service programs. We believe we have an obligation to use the Consortium's resources for the common good. And we don't merely hang back and do the politically expedient. We take an active leadership role."

Hamel gazed into Ben's eyes. "You can be part of that leadership, Ben. You can chart the course."

Ben didn't know what to say. He could barely contemplate the offer, much less its ramifications. "I have some outstanding obligations," he finally managed. "I have a solo office on the North Side."

"I know," Hamel said. "And don't feel obligated to wrap it all up overnight. Give us a trial run, see what develops. You can always go back to your private practice if that's what you decide. Frankly, with the salary we'll be paying you, you'll easily be able to pay the rent to maintain that office."

"I have a legal assistant on my payroll," Ben said, tilting his head toward Christina. "I would want her to come with me."

"Done," Hamel said flatly. "We'll make her part of our in-house staff of legal assistants and assign her to

you. We'll start her at ten percent above our usual starting salary, which, I might add, will be a significant increase from her current, ah, irregular salary. Will that
about cover your responsibilities, Ben?"

"No. There's more than just that. I have unpaid debts
. . . office supplies . . ."

Hamel grinned. "Ah—the photocopier company. I
know about that, too."

"Well, then you know how difficult it would be—"

"How much do you owe, Ben?"

Ben suddenly felt rather hot under the collar. "I don't
know exactly . . . Two thousand, something like that?"

Christina nodded in agreement.

Hamel withdrew a checkbook from his suit jacket,
filled out a check, and handed it to Ben. "Would that
about cover it, Ben? Consider it a signing bonus."

Ben stared at the check made out for five thousand
dollars. "That would definitely cover it. And my other
outstanding debts as well."

Christina pressed in between them. "How do you
know so much about Ben and his business, anyway?"

"Don't get the wrong idea, Ms. McCall—we're not
the FBI. Still, you must realize that a corporation the
size of Apollo would hardly make an offer of this magnitude without investigating the offeree."

"Sounds Big Brotherish to me."

"Not at all. It's just smart business. You don't buy a
used car without trying to find out where it's been. Ben,
we're acquainted with your past employment at the
D.A.'s office, and your current relationship with Clayton Langdell and his animal rights organization. We're
aware of your successful representation of Ms. McCall
a few months ago. In short, we're familiar with the total
package and we are very favorably impressed."

"Really," Ben said. "How impressed?"

Hamel flipped over one of his business cards, wrote
a number on the back, and passed it to Ben.

Ben took the card. He tried to mask his reaction, but

it was impossible. The number after the dollar sign had six digits. *Before* the decimal.

"Not bad, eh?" Hamel said. "And no, to answer your next question, we don't make offers like this to anyone. Just to you."

Ben coughed. "I . . . I don't know what to say. I'll have to think about it."

Hamel slapped his thighs, then stood. "I understand. Take all the time you want. And when you decide to accept, call me at the number on that card. I'll send some boys over immediately to collect your files and anything else you'll require."

"So soon?"

"Why wait?" He nudged Ben in the ribs. "Might as well start bringing home those big bucks as soon as possible." He hoisted his briefcase. "Enjoyed meeting you both. I'll be waiting for your call, Ben."

* 3 *

"You're not seriously considering his offer, are you?"

Ben and Christina sat at opposite ends of a table in the back of Louie D's, beside the grill and beneath the Renoir prints and Native American art. Ben was in the process of finishing his cheeseburger—the best in downtown Tulsa as far as he was concerned.

"How can I not seriously consider it? It's a very serious offer."

"Yeah—six digits serious."

"That's not the only advantage, but it's a definite selling point."

"I thought money wasn't so all-fired important to you."

"It isn't, but I've got to live. Think about it—I'll make more money in two months than I made all last year."

Christina frowned. "Do you know anything about this job you're so eager for us to latch on to?"

Ben hedged. There was no point in trying to bluff Christina. She always had the inside skivvy.

"No, of course you don't. Well, before you bid adieu to private life, let me provide a few hard facts. First, if you imagine you won't have to keep time records, you're wrong. They say it's for internal management, but really it's the same old same-old. The big bosses are checking up on you, ensuring that you're sufficiently profitable. It'll be just like the late unlamented days at Raven, Tucker & Tubb."

"I doubt it, unless my old boss steps down from the bench and goes corporate. And I can live with filling out time sheets."

"Do you realize who your boss at Apollo will be?"

Ben shook his head.

"Robert Crichton, one of the biggest, most sexist SOBs who ever lived. From what my friends tell me, he's the five-hundred-pound gorilla of Apollo Legal. Rules the department like a tinhorn demagogue. Total creepola."

"I've dealt with second-rate bosses before."

"You remember Emily Gozonka, don't you? She was a lawyer at Apollo—till they dumped her. She told me sexual harassment was everywhere—practically *de rigueur*. She had to put up with all kinds of crap—nicknames like 'Legs,' indiscreet fondling, comments about her bra size, being accused of having PMS every time she dared to disagree. You get the picture. She didn't play along, so they canned her. How, you ask? They gave her an assignment to work with the legal department's hatchet man, Harry Carter, another creep who's at least fifty—but acts fifteen. Drives a Camaro, dates teenage girls—the whole works. That's how they fire people like Emily; they give them an impossible assignment from Harry, and Harry rants and raves about what a horrible job they've done, thereby creating a record for the file to justify the firing. If the woman decides to file a lawsuit later on, they've got a perfect paper trail to back them up."

"Christina, Emily Gozonka is a world-class exaggerator."

"Granted. But this time I believe her."

"Well, I can't believe that systematic sexual harassment of that magnitude goes on in this day and age."

"You're living in a dream world, Ben."

"Then how do you explain yourself? You're a woman who's succeeded in a man's world."

"Because I'm a legal assistant, Ben—a subservient, clearly nonthreatening role. I could be at Apollo twenty years, but I'd still have to take orders from the greenest male attorney in the department. It's different for women trying to make it as attorneys. When they start invading the old boys' club, the old boys get nervous."

"Christina, I'm not going to judge an entire corporation based on one isolated rumor."

"Why not? That's your biggest problem. Don't you know that?"

"I didn't even know I had a biggest problem. What the hell are you talking about?"

"You won't trust your feelings. That was your problem in the courtroom today—you were planning to battle the expert on his own turf, challenging his empirical data. As a result, you missed what should've been apparent—that he was several irons short of a golf bag. Same here: all you see are the career advantages, the high-profile cases, the chance to be a corporate do-gooder."

"And what am I missing?"

"You're missing my gut feeling which says, in bold-

face letters: *don't do this!* I can't explain why. I just
know it's a mistake."

"But what if you're wrong?"

"What if I am? Your life is perfectly fine as it is.
Why risk screwing it up? The key to success is to find
something you enjoy doing and to do it. You already
have that."

Ben finished his cheeseburger and washed it down
with the last of his chocolate milk. "I don't know,
Christina."

She laid her head heavily on the table. "You've already decided, haven't you?"

Ben didn't reply.

The waitress came by and left the check. Christina
scooped it up. "You're thinking about your mother,
aren't you? How excited she'll be that you finally have
a respectable job."

Ben looked away. "The thought did cross my mind."

"Jeez. How old do we have to be before we stop or-
dering our lives to please our parents?" She examined
the tab. "What about Jones? And Loving?"

"Loving's private investigations are practically more
than he can handle. We'll let Jones secretary for him for
awhile, just to hold down the office. If this new job be-
comes permanent for us, we'll see about bringing Jones
over."

"I can't believe I'm going along with this. Kincaid,
sometimes you are almost more trouble than you're
worth."

"Thank goodness for the almost."

"Yeah." She tossed him the check. "Here, pal, you
can pay. After all, you're about to be rich."

* 4 *

Sergeant Tomlinson entered the briefing room and took his assigned seat on the end of the first row. All the other officers were already there, but Morelli wasn't, thank God. The last thing he needed was for Morelli to have another excuse to chew him out in public.

Tomlinson didn't understand why, but ever since he requested a transfer to the Homicide Division, Lieutenant Morelli had been riding him, humiliating him in public, and taking every opportunity to make him look like an idiot. Maybe he wasn't the brightest guy on the Tulsa police force. Maybe he hadn't gone to college like Morelli and couldn't quote Shakespeare at the drop of a pin. But he worked hard—harder than any of the other candidates. He did his homework and he never turned down an assignment. And once he took an assignment, he didn't give up. So why was Morelli always ragging on him?

Tomlinson supposed it was because he was married. Very married. And he and Karen had a six-year-old daughter, Kathleen, to boot. For some reason, that really seemed to jerk Morelli's chain. Once, in a booming voice in front of all the other officers, Morelli asked if Tomlinson had been playing paper dolls during the briefing. On another occasion he suggested that Tomlinson join a stakeout—*if* he could get his wife's permission to stay up late. Tomlinson had heard that Morelli himself was married a while back, but that it dissolved into a bitter divorce. Now he was apparently down on any police officers with families.

Tomlinson thumbed through the briefing book that had been left on his chair. As he suspected, this meeting was about the mutilation-murders of the teenage girls. After three dismembered corpses, there seemed little doubt—they had a serial killer on their hands.

Tomlinson pored over the materials, all of which he had seen before. He wanted badly to be assigned to this case, so he'd made a point of reviewing everything that came through the office on it. If he could track down this serial killer, he'd be transferred to Homicide for sure. Chief Blackwell would sign the transfer, even if Morelli wouldn't. And who knows? Maybe Morelli would back off. At least for a day or two.

As if on cue, Lieutenant Morelli came stomping into the room in that ridiculous tan overcoat he always wore. What a pretense. It wasn't even cold outside. Morelli gripped the podium and began talking, without any introduction or greeting.

"As you've probably figured out," Morelli growled, "you've been selected to be part of a special task force to investigate—and solve—this recent chain of murders."

Tomlinson grinned. A special task force. That sounded cool, very elite. The boys down at the bowling alley would be impressed.

"Don't get excited," Morelli said. He seemed to be looking directly at Tomlinson. "This is no great honor. You were chosen because ... frankly, you're all that's available. We've got every able-bodied person on the force working this case, and that's going to continue until it's solved. Everyone's in on this one—Homicide, Sex Crimes, the Special Investigations Unit—and just about anyone else we could round up. This could be the most grotesque crime spree Tulsa has seen since the race riot of the 1920s. I don't have to tell you how we've been crucified in the press since the killings began. This bastard has killed three teenage girls—and I want him caught. Because if we don't, he'll kill again.

"There's something else," Morelli added, "and this will really curdle your blood. If we don't solve these crimes soon, the FBI will be butting in. So far we've been lucky; all three murders have occurred within Tulsa County. Unfortunately, it looks like we've got a serial killer, so it's just a matter of time before those federal bozos descend with their profiles and high-tech geegaws. I don't care for that a damn bit. I want this case solved before it happens.

"Now open your books and follow along."

Tomlinson opened his briefing notebook to the front page.

"You'll find all the police reports, the medical examiner reports, and the forensic lab reports. Everything we've got is right in here."

Morelli's subordinates flipped to the next page, a photo taken at one of the crime scenes.

"As you probably remember, the first body was found on the morning of May second, the next was found on the fourth, and the third was found last night. In each case, the victims were teenage girls, found nude, with no identification"—he took a deep breath and stared down at his notes—"and with their heads and hands cut off."

Tomlinson saw several officers flipping ahead in their notebooks to the morgue photos. They must have stronger stomachs than he.

"The bodies have been impossible to identify. No face, no fingerprints. We have yet to figure out who any of the victims are. If there is a connecting link among the three, we don't know what it is."

Tomlinson raised his hand. "Sir, may I suggest that we make the identification of the victims our number one priority—even over identifying the killer? After all, if we can figure out the pattern, we may be able to save future lives."

"What a brilliant plan," Morelli replied. "Are you sure you aren't a lieutenant? Or maybe even a captain?" A mild tittering filtered through the room. "Or did you steal that idea from your wife?"

Tomlinson ground his teeth together. When would he ever learn?

Morelli resumed his briefing. "All the bodies have been found within a twenty-mile radius in an unpopulated area in the western part of Tulsa County. Everything has been neat and tidy; the killer hasn't left us a clue to work with. Even the amputations have been effected with almost surgical precision."

He looked up from his notebook and stared out into the sea of uniforms. "The bottom line is this: we're in the dark. We have a major crime, no leads, and no likelihood of preventing repeat offenses. We're looking for ideas, people. Any suggestions will be considered, and anyone who suggests something that helps will find some extra change in his or her pay envelope—and maybe another stripe on his or her shoulder. Even you, Tomlinson."

Another mild chuckle from the crowd. Tomlinson realized the insidious reason he must've been invited to this briefing: so he could be the butt of Morelli's jokes.

"On the next page of the notebook," Morelli continued, "you'll find an action plan I've devised in coordination with Chief Blackwell. Item one, as you can see, is to identify the victims. We'll call that the Tomlinson Plan."

Laughter again, even more unrestrained than before. What did the man want—his resignation?

"Other action items involve creating a useful profile of the killer, defining his working environment, and setting a trap. But we'll talk about those when the time comes." He flipped to the back of his notebook. "On the last page, you'll find orders informing you of your work assignment on the task force. A lot of thought has gone into these assignments, so I don't want to hear any bitching about them. We've tried to distribute the work so as to make maximum use of our available talent. We expect each of you to perform your assigned tasks to the best of your abilities."

Tomlinson turned to the back of his notebook and read the order sheet. Under his name, the assignment line read: SWITCHBOARD/RADIO DUTY.

Switchboard/radio? Tulsa was facing the most heinous crime wave in its history—and he was going to be the frigging telephone operator? Tomlinson slammed the notebook shut.

Morelli heard the noise, but didn't comment. He told everyone to "get their butts in gear" and dismissed the meeting.

Tomlinson followed the crowd out of the room, then started down the hallway to—he could barely even think about it—the switchboard room. He wasn't going to take this lying down. If Morelli didn't have any faith in him—*fine*. He'd prove himself without Morelli's help, and with any luck, he'd make Morelli look like a fool in the process.

He checked the duty roster. He would be off the switchboard by midnight. No problem—he'd start then.

Someone was going to have to make the first breakthrough. This time, it was going to be him.

* 5 *

Ben scanned the outer offices of the Apollo Consortium headquarters. The architecture was elegant and expensive—the general design was of spiraling glass columns and gold-plated panels. The glass glistened; the gold panels were polished and gleaming. The building was less than a year old; Apollo was probably the only business entity in all of Oklahoma that was ostentatiously spending money during the recession that had paralyzed so much of the Southwest.

Howard Hamel stepped out of the elevator after Ben had waited less than a minute. I don't get service this prompt when I visit my mother, Ben thought.

"Ben! Great to see you again," Hamel said, his hand extended. "I can't tell you how pleased I am that you accepted our offer."

"Well, it was a difficult offer to refuse."

"Good. It was intended that way. In case you haven't gotten the message yet, the Apollo Consortium wants you bad."

"I suppose I'll need to fill out some forms. Insurance, direct deposit . . ."

"Sure, sure, but later. Let me take you on a tour of the complex. Our first stop is at the top—Robert Crichton's office."

"He's the head of the legal department, right?"

"Right. In fact, he's general counsel for the entire Apollo Consortium."

"And he wants to see me?"

"Damn straight. He told me to show you in the moment you arrived."

Hamel ushered Ben into a glass elevator that rose up the south side of the office building. Ben watched south Tulsa recede as the elevator rose toward the penthouse floor.

"Great view, huh?" Hamel said. "Strictly speaking, these exposed elevators are illegal here, but we managed to pull a few strings with the city counsel and get a variance." He winked. "Called in a few vouchers."

"I'll bet." Ben gazed out through the elevator glass. He could spot Southern Hills, the Sheraton Kensington, and the Oral Roberts campus, with its shimmering towers like something out of a Fifties science fiction movie. He felt a sudden clutching in his chest; Ben was not handy with heights. He turned away. "The view must be terrific at night."

"It is. But don't take my word for it. Come up some night and see for yourself."

The elevator bell dinged, and they stepped off. They passed through an elegant private dining room staffed with waiters in formal attire, and a large health spa.

"Is this open to the public?" Ben asked.

"You must be kidding. We have over three thousand employees in this building. If the spa and restaurant were open to everyone, no one would be able to get a toe in edgewise. No, this whole floor is strictly for the top executives."

"Oh. Pity."

"Fret not, Ben. If you want in, we'll get you in."

They approached two huge wooden doors with ornate burnished paneling. A secretary sat at a desk outside.

"Janice, I have Mr. Kincaid."

She pointed toward the doors. "Mr. Crichton said you were to bring him in immediately."

"Right-o." Hamel pushed the heavy doors open. Ben followed. The outer office was large and luxurious. No surprise. The glass and gold design of the front lobby was repeated, although one wall was white stucco. A painted mural stretched from one end to the other. It was an N. C. Wyeth mural, if Ben wasn't mistaken. Could it possibly be an original?

They stepped quietly into the inner office. A man in his mid-forties was seated behind a desk, while a much younger woman slumped down in the chair opposite him.

"Look," the man said, "I'm not saying you should put your job ahead of your baby, but—" Mid-sentence, he noticed his two visitors. "Hamel, what's the meaning of this?"

Hamel stiffened ever so slightly. "I've brought Ben Kincaid to see you, Mr. Crichton."

Crichton's expression and manner changed the instant he heard the name. He rose to his feet. "Ben Kincaid. A pleasure." Ben stepped forward, and they shook hands. After a moment, Crichton looked back, almost regretfully, at the woman in the chair. "Shelly . . . why don't we continue this later?"

The woman in the chair was small, with a thin face and dishwater blond hair. She seemed to be pressed back as far as possible in the chair. Her eyes were red, as if she had been crying or was likely to start at any moment. After Crichton dismissed her, she turned and rushed out without saying a word.

"Thanks, Hamel," Crichton said. "I'll take it from here."

"Okay. Catch you later, Ben." Hamel left the office.

Ben took the chair the woman had vacated.

"Sorry about that business with Shelly," Crichton said. "Embarrassing to walk in on something like that, I know." Crichton was an attractive man who wore his age well; the flecks of gray at his temples only accented his full black hair. He tossed himself into a chair and propped his feet up on the desk. "I hate it when a member of my staff isn't performing up to snuff, but at the same time, I don't believe in mollycoddling anybody. And it always seems to be the women."

"Excuse me?" Ben said.

"Forget I spoke. I sometimes forget that I'm supposed to pretend that everyone is exactly the same these days. You don't have a wife or kids, do you?"

Ben shifted his weight uncomfortably. "No."

"Pity. I'm a big believer in families. My Emma is a saint; I don't know how I'd get along without her. And my four kids are the most important parts of my life. Sure, I work hard and I'm not home a lot of the time, but everything I do, I do for them. They wouldn't have it any other way."

Ben wondered if they had been consulted for their opinion on this issue.

"Has Hamel taken you through the paperwork yet?"

"No. He said we'd do that later."

"Take my advice, Ben. Let your secretary do it."

"I wouldn't want to take her away from important work for other lawyers."

"Other lawyers? What kind of fleabag outfit do you think this is? You've got a secretary of your own."

"My own? *All* my own?"

"Of course. Some of the worker bees at the bottom of the hive share secretaries—but a lawyer of your caliber? No way."

"You know . . ." Ben said cautiously, "I don't want to kill the goose that lays the golden eggs, but I can't fathom why you're so . . . interested in me."

Crichton spread his arms across his desk. "I can answer that question in three words, Ben. You're a maverick."

"I am?"

"You're a maverick, and that's just what this maverick corporation needs. I've been following your career for some time. I consider it part of my job—constantly scouting for talent that can serve the Apollo Consortium. I wanted a real honest-to-God litigator. Not just some flunky to make an occasional phone call while outside counsel does all the real work. Someone to take the bull by the horns! A maverick, goddamn it!"

Ben was overwhelmed. "My preference would be to work in the litigation department. At least at first."

"Done. And I have the perfect case for you to start on immediately. Hamel may have mentioned it—a products liability problem turned into a wrongful death suit. Rob Fielder has been working it, but he won't mind backing off in favor of someone with your experience."

"You know, sir, I've actually only been practicing for a few years—"

"The hell with that, Ben. It's not the number of years

that matter. It's what you've learned during those years. You've got the right stuff. I can feel it in my gut." He picked up a file on his desk and tossed it into Ben's lap. "Here's the case. We're barely into preliminary discovery. Documents are being produced tomorrow; plaintiffs' depositions are being taken the day after. I want us to get out there and win it." He laughed. "Hell, I'd like to see the look on those poor plaintiffs' faces when Ben Kincaid comes in to depose them! They'll wet their pants!"

Ben listened in stunned disbelief. Had he fallen down a rabbit hole, or what? "What's the case about?"

"Our transportation and automotive department designed a suspension system that our manufacturing department constructs and sells. They call it the XKL-1. Anyway, a local high school held a tractor pull after a football game—you know, sort of a hayride without the hay. Teenage boy fell off, got caught in the machinery, and was mangled to death. Horrible accident—but they want to blame it on us because we designed and supplied the suspension system used on the flatbed. It's preposterous. How much do you know about cars?"

"Not much."

"Well, here's all you need to know. The axle is attached by U-bolts to the leaf spring, which in turn is attached to the frame of the flatbed. Subsequent examination revealed that the leaf spring—a half-moon-shaped contraption that runs the length of the flatbed—was broken. That caused the flatbed to dip to one side. The kid's parents say our design was defective. We say they drove too fast on an uneven, bumpy dirt field."

"We deny any responsibility for what happened?"

"Believe me, no one sympathizes with that poor kid's parents more than me—I've got a boy about that age myself—but it's just not Apollo's fault. The parents' lawyer went looking for a deep pocket to pick up the medical expenses, and Apollo was the only one he could find."

"If we're really not culpable," Ben said, "we should be able to get summary judgment granted after we've taken the parents' depositions."

"That's great! Brilliant!" Crichton rose to his feet. "My God, you're winning cases for us already. I knew you were a champ."

Ben felt his face flushing bright red. He hadn't heard such effusive praise since he memorized "A Visit from St. Nicholas" in the second grade. "Of course, the validity of the summary judgment motion will depend on what we learn during the depositions. If the parents have a valid claim, it would be wrong to try to cheat them out of it with legal maneuvering. I believe that as officers of the court we have an obligation to see justice done."

"Admirable sentiment, Ben, although I think you'll find that in the corporate world most cases are somewhat less noble. Most of these lawsuits are just one asshole suing another asshole. Over money. It's not about ethics; it's not about right or wrong. It's about bucks."

Ben cleared his throat. "I'm sure that's true in some instances, but—"

Crichton slammed his hand down on a button on his phone console. After a short buzz, Janice answered. "Yes, sir?"

"Get Fielder in here," Crichton barked. "I want him to meet his new partner."

"Right away, sir." She clicked off.

"By the way," Crichton added, "this weekend I'm taking my legal staff on a DARE retreat. I want you to be there. You don't already have plans, do you?"

"Not that I recall. What's a DARE retreat?"

Crichton grinned from ear to ear. "Just wait and see. And we'll expect to see you turn out for our softball

game next week, too. We're taking on the Memorex
Telex team. We're going to clean their clocks."

"Is Christina also invited?"

Crichton was puzzled for a moment. "Christina? Oh,
she's the legal assistant you brought on board, right? I
saw a picture. What a babe—great ears on that cob. I
can see why you wanted to bring her along." He
grinned again. "Hell, Ben, as far as I'm concerned,
you've already made a significant contribution to the
office! Sure, she's legal staff, so she's invited. I can't
wait to see her in an exercise suit."

"Do we do a lot of these extracurricular activities?"

"Oh, yeah. I require it. Work hard, play hard—that's
what I always say. And I want you to be involved in all
of it."

Before Ben could reply, a young, athletic man in a
pinstriped suit inched into the office. "You called, Mr.
Crichton?"

"Yeah. Rob Fielder, meet Ben Kincaid. He's taking
over the Nelson case."

Ben closed his eyes. Oh, thanks. This will undoubtedly be the start of a beautiful friendship. "Pleasure to
meet you."

"The pleasure is mine," Rob replied. To his credit,
Rob showed no trace of resentment over the loss of his
case.

"As I said," Crichton continued, "tomorrow we're
producing documents. It's a paper blizzard, but you'll
have to endure it so you can be prepared for the depositions. Rob will tell you everything you need to know."

"Gladly," Rob said amiably. "I'll come by your office
around ten-thirty."

"That'll be fine," Ben said.

"Great, great, great," Crichton said. "I can tell already you two are going to hit it off. Ben, I'll let you
get on with your business. We'll have a staff meeting
later so you can meet the other lawyers. But don't work
too hard, okay?" He winked. "It's your first day, for

Pete's sake. No one's going to notice if you disappear around noon."

Hearing his cue, Ben started to leave.

"And Ben," Crichton added, "one last thing. If you need anything, and I mean *anything*, just come to me. Don't feel like you have to mess around with the toadies and middlemen. Just come to me. Understand?"

Ben nodded, then followed Rob out of the office. The truth was, his nod was a lie. He didn't understand. He didn't understand at all.

* 6 *

Ben sat behind his desk avoiding the view outside the window of his new office. Twenty floors up was nineteen too many for him. He focused on his deep-grain oak desk, his plush overstuffed chairs, and best of all, his desktop computer. He passed his hand over the smooth plastic finish. He felt breathless.

Christina appeared in the doorway. "What's up, Doc?"

Ben continued to gaze at the computer. "I'm . . . uh . . . working with my new computer."

"This isn't Star Trek, Ben. You have to turn it on first." She flipped the red switch on the side. The computer hummed and buzzed and, after a few seconds, a blue-and-white menu screen appeared.

"Look," Christina said. "You have e-mail."

"I have what?"

She sighed, then punched the Enter button. A new screen appeared, this one in the shape of a letter. It said:

WELCOME TO APOLLO. LOOKING FORWARD TO WORKING
WITH YOU. BEST OF LUCK. CHUCK CONRAD.

"Who's Chuck Conrad?" Ben asked.

"The biggest lickspittle in the legal department, from
what I hear." She plopped down in one of Ben's chairs.
"Not bad office ambience, Ben. Very cushy. Heck of a
lot better than what you had back at Raven, Tucker &
Tubb."

"No kidding."

"So how was your first day as *homme d'affaires* for
Apollo?"

"Incredible. I can't believe the treatment I've been
getting. They've really rolled out the red carpet."

"Enjoy it while it lasts, chum."

"What's that supposed to mean?"

"Nothing in particular. I just know megacorporations
don't do anything expensive without a reason. There
must be a catch. You just haven't spotted it yet." She
punched an overstuffed cushion. "You've been too busy
enjoying the empirical evidence."

"What a cynic. What's your office like?"

"Perfectly ordinary. Space dividers split it down the
middle. I share with three other legal assistants."

"That stinks."

"I'm used to it. Legal assistants always get treated
like dirt, especially by gigantic people processors like
Apollo."

"Well, since they're gaga for me, at least for the moment, maybe I can use my vast influence to get you a
more spacious office."

"Don't sweat it." She leaned forward conspiratorially.
"Say, what did you think of Crichton?"

"He had some good points and some bad points."

"What are the bad points?"

"Well, I suspect he's every bit as sexist as you said he
was."

"What are the good points?"

"He loves me."

"Ah. Don't let him get past second base on the first date."

"Ha, ha."

"Did he tell you about this humongous document production tomorrow?"

"Yeah. He's putting me in charge of the case. I get to depose the plaintiffs day after tomorrow."

"Great. You're in line for the glory. To me, it's just sludge. By the way, I stopped by your former office this morning."

"How is Jones doing?"

"Not bad, considering that his Number One Boss Man has dumped him for greener pastures."

"We could probably get him a job here."

"Just give him time to adjust. I'm sure he'll—"

"Excuse me. Am I interrupting?" Rob Fielder was standing in the doorway.

"Not at all, Rob," Ben said. "We were just comparing notes. Have you met Christina?" He introduced them. "You need something?"

"Just you. We're about to start our staff meeting. Normally we meet first thing in the morning, but we delayed it so you could participate."

"Great. Come on, Christina." Christina fell in behind him.

Fielder twitched. "I'm . . . sorry. I'm afraid the meeting is just for attorneys."

Ben stopped in his tracks. "Oh."

"It's nothing personal. It's just that we, uh, discuss many confidential matters, and if any nonattorneys were present, it might destroy the privilege."

Ben frowned. "Christina, I'm sorry—"

She patted Ben on the shoulder. "No problem. Like I said, I'm used to it. I'll just crawl back to my quarter of my office and try not to get in anybody's way."

She stopped on her way out and added, "But I may

sneak back while you're gone, Ben. Just to sit in your chair."

* 7 *

The conference room was perfect for a staff meeting; it must have been designed for just that purpose. The room was long and rectangular, as was the mahogany table that occupied its center.

Fielder steered Ben toward an empty seat a few chairs down from one end of the table. "Crichton sits at the head," he explained.

"Who sits beside him?"

"Depends. It's a battle of the ass-kissers. Chuck is generally considered Apollo's king of suck-up, but Herb is a close second." He glanced at the doorway. "There's Herb now. Uh-oh—Chuck is right behind him. Let's see what happens."

Ben saw a thin man with a Bugs Bunny mouth enter the room, followed by a burly, somewhat older man with thinning hair and a waistline that lapped over his belt. Herb and Chuck, apparently.

They both saw the empty chair beside the head of the table at the same time. Herb darted around the north end; Chuck sprinted south. The race was on. Halfway through, Herb saw Chuck approaching and accelerated. Chuck matched his speed and they both ended up on opposite ends of the chair almost simultaneously.

"Back off," Chuck growled. "This chair's taken."

"Is not," Herb replied. "I was here first."

"You sat here last time."

"And I'm going to sit here again, chump."

"Oh yeah?"

"Yeah."

"Says who?"

"Says—"

"Children, children," Rob interjected. "Let's not bicker. You can both sit in the chair. Chuck, you first. And Herb, you can sit in his lap."

Ben covered his smile as best he could.

Chuck grumbled something inaudibly, shoved the chair aside, and stomped to the other end of the table.

"Sore loser," Ben commented.

"Very." Rob glanced at the door again. "Now this is Candice, or, as we call her just to irritate her, Candy. Watch what happens now."

Ben saw a slender woman in her early thirties enter the conference room. She wore her business suit well; she was extremely attractive, if a bit on the anorexic side. She scanned the available seats at the table, then made a beeline for the empty seat between Herb and Ben.

"Oh, God," she moaned, loud enough to be heard throughout the room. "Looks like I'm stuck with Herb again."

"Christ," Herb said, wiping his forehead. "What happened to the bitch alert? Someone needs to get that thing fixed."

"What's with these two?" Ben whispered to Rob.

"They're lovers."

"Lovers?"

"You heard me. Can't you tell?"

Ben eavesdropped for another moment. "There must be some mistake."

"No mistake. They've been boffing one another for at least six months. But the complication, you see, is that he's married. To someone else. The affair is supposed to be a big secret. So they've been maintaining this hate-your-guts routine in public, trying to throw everyone off the track."

"Unsuccessfully, I take it."

"You take it right. The only ones being fooled are Herb and Candy."

"Does the Consortium condone relations between employees?"

"Well, the general attitude is that boys will be boys. This isn't Herb's first interoffice dalliance by a long shot. Herbert the Pervert, we call him."

A sharp increase in volume diverted Ben's attention.

"Just fuck off, you bastard," Candice said sharply.

"Don't you wish?"

"Not even remotely."

"That's because you're a frigid bitch."

"No, that's because you're disgusting."

"Probably a lesbian, too."

"You'll never know, you impotent toad."

"Why don't you shove a space heater between your legs and thaw yourself out?" Herb said.

"Why don't you shove a cucumber in your pants and pretend you're a man?" Candice sallied back.

Ben searched the room for a quieter haven, but alas, all the other seats except Crichton's were taken.

"Hey," Chuck said suddenly. "Where are the doughnuts?"

"Forget it." The words came from a large man perched behind a small laptop computer. "In the words of Robert Frost, the doughnuts came down a road not traveled. Today was Shelly's turn." He took a drag on his cigarillo, then released a puff of smoke.

Ben saw Shelly, the woman who had been in Crichton's office earlier, sitting three seats down the table, almost invisible. She didn't reply.

"Aww," Chuck said. "Don't tell me she forgot again."

"Worse," the cigarillo man said. "She brought those bulgur wheat muffins."

"Man! I hate those."

A stricken look crossed Shelly's face. She slumped down even lower, till her face was lost in the shadows.

"I think they look perfectly tasty," Ben ventured. He picked up one of the offending pastries. "What's wrong with wheat muffins? They're much better for you."

"I don't want health food," Chuck grunted. "I want doughnuts." He released a rumbling sound that might have been a sigh. "I love doughnuts."

Ben leaned into Rob's ear. "Who's the guy with the cigarillo?"

"Doug Gleason. Third-year employee. Fancies himself to be Ernest Hemingway. F. Scott Fitzgerald, at the least. Does nothing but write. Carries that damn computer everywhere. Doesn't go to court, doesn't negotiate, doesn't do research. He just writes. Appeals, briefs, contracts, whatever."

"Kind of a narrow specialty. He must be talented."

"The jury's still out. Personally, I'm not sure if he's talented or if it's all they trust him to do."

"Well, at least he's got a job he enjoys."

"Maybe. I don't know if he really likes writing or he just likes fancying himself a writer."

At that moment, Crichton walked briskly into the conference room. Ben checked his watch; Crichton was a fashionable fourteen minutes late. He took the chair at the head of the table and rolled up his sleeves. "Let's get to work, people. No more screwing around. I want to hear that projects are being completed, and that everyone is busting their butts to help the Apollo Consortium find the perfect proactive solutions."

Ben winced. *Proactive?*

Chuck withdrew a stack of stapled papers from his briefcase and handed Crichton the top document. "I've taken the liberty of preparing an agenda, Mr. Crichton. Just to help you keep us in line."

Crichton glanced at the top sheet for a millisecond, then turned it face down. "Any emergencies?"

No one volunteered any.

"First item, then: I want to formally introduce you to the newest member of the team, Benjamin Kincaid. Let me tell you—I have nothing but admiration for this guy. Ben is a hell of a litigator, and we're damn lucky to have him. I want all of you to spend as much time with Ben as possible, whenever you have a chance. You could learn a lot from a lawyer of his mettle. I want you to watch him closely."

Ben felt the rest of the room scrutinizing him, but sensed that their feelings were something other than admiration.

"You'll have the opportunity to see Ben in action right off the bat," Crichton added. "He's taking over the Nelson case."

"The Nelson case!" Candice said, far louder than necessary. "I thought Rob . . ." Her voice trailed off. "Oh, gosh. I'm sorry."

"I'll just bet," Rob mumbled.

"Where's the coffee?" Crichton barked suddenly, staring at the empty mug on the coaster before him. "Damn that Janice." He whirled around in his chair, lifted the phone receiver on the credenza behind him, and dialed the four-digit number that connected him to his secretary.

Ben noticed a full coffeepot on a burner on the credenza. "Doesn't he see—"

"Shhh," Rob replied. "Just wait."

A few seconds after Crichton hung up the phone, Janice hurried into the conference room, a fretful expression on her face. For the first time, Ben saw her standing up, and noticed the low-cut, high-hemmed dress that was not so much worn as affixed to her hips.

"Hurry it up," Crichton grumbled. "You're delaying the staff meeting."

"I'm sorry, Mr. Crichton." She walked to the credenza, picked up the same coffeepot that had been inches from Crichton's hand, and filled his mug.

Ben watched, marveling. "What, he doesn't know how to pour his own coffee?" he whispered.

"Men at Crichton's level don't pour their own coffee," Rob whispered back. "And he enjoys any excuse to drag Janice in here."

"Why?"

"Just watch."

Janice circumnavigated the table with the coffeepot, swinging her ample hips from side to side. She had a bounce like a well-tuned metronome, full and rhythmic. Ben noticed that Crichton's eyes followed her back and forth, back and forth.

"Anyone else want coffee?" Janice asked, practically pleading for customers. Unfortunately, everyone else appeared to be capable of pouring for themselves.

"Thanks, Janice," Crichton said dismissively. "I'll call if I need a refill."

Janice sashayed out of the office.

Crichton blew the steam off the top, then inhaled a steep swig of java. "All right, Chuck, give me a status report on your contract negotiations."

Chuck jumped to attention. "Yes, sir." He removed a thick notebook from his briefcase. "The contracts for the license agreement with Amoco have been drafted and approved. I've brought copies—"

"I don't want to hear about Amoco," Crichton said abruptly. He downed another load of caffeine. "Tell me how the Ameritech joint venture negotiations are proceeding."

"Ameritech? Joint venture?" Chuck appeared to be stalling.

"That's right. I gave you that assignment over a month ago. Surely you haven't forgotten."

"Oh . . . uh, no. No, of course not, sir." He scanned the room, desperately seeking salvation. "Shelly!"

She practically jumped out of her seat. "What?"

"I asked Shelly to research the possible antitrust ramifications of a joint venture, Mr. Crichton." Chuck swiveled his chair toward hers. "What about it, Shelly? Where's my memo?"

Shelly's face slowly emerged from the chair. Red blotches were creeping up her neck. "But you just gave me the assignment Friday afternoon—"

"Don't make excuses," Chuck snapped. "You knew we had staff meeting today."

"But it was already four-thirty."

"Then you should've stayed late."

"But I had to pick up Angie—"

"No one else expects special treatment just because they have children, Shelly."

"No one else—" She paused, then let it die, apparently realizing it was useless.

"Typical," Rob whispered to Ben. "Chuck screws up, dumps the project on someone else at the last moment, and lets them take all the blame."

Chuck swiveled back to Crichton. "I'm sorry about this, sir. I'll take care of it immediately." He glared again at Shelly, then tossed his notebook angrily into his briefcase.

Ben could feel himself perspiring—and he wasn't even the one in the hot seat. At least, not yet.

Crichton drained the last of his coffee. "Damn," he said. "Herb, call Janice. I need more coffee." He peered across the table as if he were selecting candidates for a firing squad. "All right. Who's next?"

* 8 *

Sergeant Tomlinson leaned back in the metal folding chair and stretched. He was so exhausted that he hurt. And with good reason. He saw by the clock on the wall that it was almost four in the morning. He'd been in the library since midnight—and that was after completing a full eight-hour shift on the switchboard.

The library was in the basement of the central head-quarters building. It still looked like a basement, too—it was dank, poorly ventilated, and lit by a single phos-phorescent lamp dangling from the ceiling. Not exactly ideal working conditions.

But his diligence was paying off. He was slowly as-sembling a profile of the serial killer and how he oper-ated. The perpetrator was obviously highly organized. Clever—and what's more, smart. Every action—the murders, the dismemberment, the disposal of the bodies—had been meticulously planned and executed. The killer was in charge at all times. As a result, he was very difficult to catch.

Tomlinson had spent the wee hours of the morning poring over comprehensive data accumulated by the FBI. The Behavioral Sciences Unit at the Training Academy in Quantico had been investigating the serial killer phenomenon for decades, but in 1978 they began the Crime Analysis and Criminal Personality Profiling Program. FBI agents systematically interviewed im-prisoned serial killers (who were almost always anx-ious to talk) about their backgrounds, their motivations, and their methods of operation. Startling similarities emerged.

Broadly speaking, the FBI divided serial killers into two categories: the organized personality and the disorganized personality. Tulsa's killer fell into the first category. According to the FBI profiles, this conclusion provided Tomlinson with considerable information that was more than likely true about the killer.

He was (a) a man, (b) between the ages of twenty and forty-five, and (c) almost certainly white. He was probably a first-born son. Parental discipline from his father had been inconsistent or nonexistent; his mother may have been abusive. During his childhood, he engaged in what the FBI called the *homicidal triangle*: the torture or abuse of animals, followed by bedwetting in his early teens, followed by a period of firestarting. He learned early in life that he obtained sexual gratification from inflicting pain.

He had a better than average I.Q., but his grades in school were mediocre. Not because he was stupid, but because he was apathetic. For similar reasons, he probably had a low-profile job and a spotty work history. He was living with someone—parents or maybe a girlfriend. He was an abuser of alcohol, or drugs, or both.

The list of probabilities went on and on. He loved nothing more than to drive. Serial killers were almost always trollers; they often put eighty thousand miles on their cars in a single year. He was friendly and socially adept. (All his friends said no one was smoother than Ted Bundy.) He captured his victims without using force. He would kill them in an efficient manner; he would always clean up afterward. He would probably keep a souvenir of each kill and he would be certain to follow the press coverage of his murders. Scrapbooks were not uncommon.

That was the portrait of the man they were hunting,

as Tomlinson saw it. And unlike the rest of the force, he had an idea of where to look.

Before Tomlinson became a plainclothes officer, he'd walked the beat and driven a patrol car in downtown and north Tulsa—the best and the worst districts in Tulsa. In central downtown, it was all suits and ties—not much for a beat cop to do. Occasionally he even got to ride the Mounted Patrol horse. If you traveled a bit in the wrong direction, though, you ended up in the oldest and worst part of the city. Street crime was everywhere; it was just a question of where to begin. Tomlinson saw the full array: drunks, con men, prostitutes, pimps, drug addicts, drug pushers. After a few weeks, he came to know them well. And he was there for three years.

During that seemingly endless time, Tomlinson learned more about the people of the streets than he had ever wanted to know. He saw runaways jump off the bus and fall into the arms of their future pimps. He saw desperate druggies risking AIDS just to get that hot white magic shooting through their veins. But most importantly, he knew the significance of a certain twenty-acre tract in west Tulsa County—the area in which all three victims' bodies had been found.

It was The Playground—the street people's amusement park, the druggie's Disney World. Every now and then, a bunch of heads, or maybe some ladies of the evening, would leave Eleventh Street (The Stroll, as its denizens called it) and throw a party. Usually the party was a large-scale sex and drugs group event. Sometimes the host would be a pusher who'd scored big; sometimes it would be an outsider—say a wealthy john trying to set a new personal record. The Playground was easily accessible, but safe, secluded, and absolutely unpoliced. The revelers could do anything they wanted out there.

And now it appeared that someone was.

Anybody in the Eleventh Street in-crowd would

know about The Playground and might well consider it a fail-safe place to dump a body.

Tomlinson closed his books and threw down his pen. Just thinking about this was making him sick. He'd been learning all about the grisly activities and tragic backgrounds of America's worst. He felt as if he knew this nameless killer, maybe even better than he knew himself. And he was repulsed. For the first time, he felt the horrible inefficiency of the criminal justice system. Due process? Probable cause? Someone just needed to grab a gun and put a bullet through this man's forehead.

Tomlinson rubbed his aching eyes. There was so much more he needed to do. He wanted to access the FBI archives at the National Crime Information Center. He wanted to visit the morgue and see what Dr. Koregai could tell him about the victims. And he wanted to stake out Eleventh Street, to keep a watchful eye and an alert ear for possible clues. That was his edge, as far as solving this crime went—his link to the Eleventh Street criminal subculture.

But a stakeout would have to wait; now he had to get home. Karen would be furious. She wasn't too keen on his staying up till he was blurry-eyed and frazzled. She'd much rather he stayed home with her and Kathleen.

For that matter, he'd rather be at home, too. But this was something he had to do; Karen and Kathleen would have to understand. He had to prove himself to Morelli. He had to prove that he belonged on the Homicide team. And most of all, he had to keep this maniac from striking again.

* 9 *

Ben and Rob climbed the stairs to the twentieth floor of the Apollo building. The elevators were out of order—some kind of electrical short.

They'd spent almost the entire day in the document retention offices in the basement. Ben was punch-drunk from staring at endless reams of internal memoranda that Apollo was producing in the Nelson case. His fingers felt as if the friction ridges had been rubbed smooth; his body had acquired the musty smell of warehoused files.

"What's the time?" Rob asked.

Ben checked his watch. "Almost eleven. Man, I can't believe we spent the day—and night—reviewing documents."

"Yeah," Rob concurred. "And we only covered about a hundred thousand pieces of paper. We must be slow or something."

"Is this fascinating activity par for the course?"

"I'm afraid so. Litigators are obsessed with documents, especially when corporations are involved. Everyone hopes that if enough documents are produced, somewhere in the bowels of the corporate file cabinets they'll find an incriminating memo written by some wayward employee in a bad mood. And if it takes hundreds of hours of document-sifting to find that one memo, well, so much the better for the private law firm billing its client by the hour. For in-house guys like you and me, though, it's hell on wheels."

"Everyone has to pay his dues."

"Yeah, everyone just starting out. Don't worry, though—my impression is that you've entered the department much too high on the totem pole to get stuck with a lot of document productions. Soon you'll be making legal assistants suffer through all this. Then *they* prepare a summary and you just read it. In fact, if you weren't taking those depositions tomorrow, before a summary could be prepared, I bet Crichton wouldn't have sent you along today."

"That's so strange," Ben said. "I don't understand why Crichton's treating me like some kind of superstar. Everyone in the department must hate me."

"Nonsense," Rob replied. A slow grin crept across his face. "Well . . . perhaps. Present company excepted, of course."

They shared a brief chuckle and headed toward their offices. About halfway down the corridor, Ben heard loud banging and shuffling noises coming from the LEXIS room, a small alcove that housed computer terminals used to access online legal research databases. The LEXIS room was an interior office, separated from the main corridor by the central computer room, where accounting, litigation support, and other computerized records were kept.

Ben heard another bang, followed by a low moan. "What's going on in there?"

Rob shrugged his shoulders. "Can't imagine. Mice, maybe?"

"I don't think so." Ben walked through the computer room and stopped at the entrance to the LEXIS alcove. He could still hear some kind of disturbance inside, but he couldn't identify it. Cautiously, he turned the doorknob and pushed the door open.

It was hard to tell who they were at first, since the man was facing away from him and the woman's face was obscured by his bare-bottomed body. She was lying on the main table between two computer terminals, and he was hunched over her, his pants dangling around his knees.

The thin figure finally tipped Ben off. It was Herb, busily doing what he did best—which in turn suggested that the shapely object beneath him must be Candice.

Ben quietly tiptoed back, but bumped into Rob, who was standing just behind him. Rob emitted an *oof!* and fell against the door, slamming it loudly against the wall.

Herb, intent on his business, didn't even notice, but Candice did. She looked over Herb's shoulder and screamed. She shoved Herb away and rolled over on the table, grabbing a computer manual to cover her breasts. Herb groaned, a pathetic expression of *lustus interruptus* on his face. He swirled around and saw Ben and Rob standing in the doorway.

"What the hell are you two doing here?" Herb shouted, as he grabbed his pants.

"Shouldn't that be our question?" Rob said.

Herb buckled his britches and shoved his shirttail inside. "You didn't see this, Kincaid."

"I didn't?"

"No, you didn't. Let me spell it out for you." He walked right up into Ben's face and stood so close they could slow dance. "You don't want me for an enemy. Bob Crichton and I are tight, got it? I can make life miserable for you. So you'd better learn to keep your trap zipped."

"The way I see it," Rob said, "you'd better learn to keep your zipper zipped."

Herb snarled. "Look, jerkface, this is serious. I'm not just screwing around here."

"I beg to differ."

Herb slapped his hand against Rob's chest and pushed him back against the wall. "Last warning, punk. If word of this gets out, you'll be chin-deep in document productions for the rest of your life. That goes for you, too, Kincaid."

Herb glanced back at Candice, who was by now fully dressed. "C'mon, babe. Let's get out of here." He scooped his suit jacket off the floor and threw it over his shoulders, then put his arm around Candice and marched defiantly out of the alcove.

"Jeez," Ben said, "I can't believe him. Herbert the Pervert—you weren't kidding."

"Let me give you some advice, Ben. Herb isn't nearly as tight with Crichton as he thinks, but he's tight enough. If I were you, I'd keep a low profile around Herb for a while. If you have to be near him, be all smiles. Laugh at his jokes. Don't mention what you just saw. Given the way Crichton's been larding it over on you, Herb probably hated you already. But if he didn't before, he certainly does now."

"Message received and understood." They walked back through the main computer room. "Let's dump these files in my office. It's just across the hall."

As they approached his office, Ben noticed that the door was closed. "That's odd. I'm sure I left my door open. Do the cleaning people do that?" He reached for the doorknob.

"On the contrary; they're supposed to leave the doors open all night. Fire codes or something."

Ben froze in his tracks. "Did you hear that?"

"Hear what?"

"A noise. Inside my office."

"No."

"Well, I did. You don't suppose Herb and Candy reconvened their lascivious rendezvous, do you?" He grabbed the doorknob and pushed the door open. "Look, you horny lustbuckets, I want you out—"

Ben stopped in mid-sentence. Herb and Candy were not there. Everything appeared to be just as he had left it, except his desk chair was facing the back window.

Ben approached slowly, crouched down, and swiveled the chair around. Something heavy was in it. Just as the chair pivoted to face Ben, the body of Howard

Hamel fell forward. Ben reflexively caught him, then screamed and stumbled backward. The body continued to fall. It hit the carpet with a horrifying thunk. Ben saw a flat, square object bounce out of Hamel's hand.

"Oh, my God," Ben murmured. "Oh, my God, what's wrong with him?"

Rob crouched down beside the body. "I have Red Cross certification in emergency aid. Let me see what I can do." He pressed two fingers against the side of Hamel's neck. "Well, you can forget about the emergency aid. He's dead."

"Oh, my God." Ben felt a creeping chill race through his body. "How long?"

"I'm not a coroner, Ben. But I can tell if a body has a pulse or not. And this one doesn't."

Ben pulled Rob back out in the corridor. "First Herb, now this. What are we going to do?"

"Get on the phone and call the police. We have to report this."

"I'm not calling from my office where he ... was."

"Then go into the conference room at the end of the hall. The sooner the better. I'll go to my office and call for someone from building security to come up and take over. Hurry!"

Rob bolted down the corridor and turned the corner toward his office. Ben ran the other direction into the conference room and dialed a number he knew by heart.

The party answered on the sixth ring. "Yeah?"

"Mike, this is Ben."

"Hey, Ben." Ben heard him stifle a yawn. "Say, it's kind of late ..."

"Sorry about that. I didn't have much choice."

"You sound strung out, Ben. What's happening?"

"In a nutshell: I just walked into my office and a corpse fell on top of me."

There was a short pause on the other end of the line. "Have you reported this to the police yet?"

"That's what I'm doing now, ditz."

"I'm at home, Ben. This is not exactly the standard procedure."

"Are there rules for reporting dead bodies found in your office? I'm sorry, I didn't get my copy of the Caring for Corpses handbook!"

"Ben, you're becoming hysterical. Look—"

"Mike, I need help." Ben took a deep breath. "The stiff was in my office. On my second day at a new job. I'm in trouble here."

Mike groaned. "All right, kemo sabe. Give me the address."

After his conversation with Mike, Ben met Rob back in the corridor. "Did you contact security?"

"I accessed their answering machine," Rob replied. "Gives you a real feeling of comfort, doesn't it?"

"Yeah." He tugged at Rob's arm. "C'mon."

"What? Why are we going back ... you know ... where he is?"

"We need to block off the area, make sure Herb and Candy don't stumble in inadvertently and spray sperm all over the crime scene. It'll be at least fifteen minutes before Homicide arrives."

Grudgingly, Rob trailed down the corridor after Ben. They turned the corner into Ben's office—and froze.

"Oh, my God," Ben whispered, not for the first time that night.

Rob's eyes were wide as saucers. "How can this be? How is this possible?"

Ben checked his watch. "We've only been gone about three or four minutes. Five minutes, tops."

"Ben, this is freaking me out."

Ben tried to respond, but found that he could only stare at the carpet as he murmured, "Oh, my God. Oh, my God. Oh, my God."

The body was gone.

* 10 *

An hour later, Lieutenant Mike Morelli trudged up the stairs to the twentieth floor.

"I can't believe these elevators are out of order!" he bellowed. "Every goddamn one of them!"

"Sorry," Ben said.

"Do you have any idea how long it takes to climb twenty flights of stairs?"

"It's good for you. Gets you back in shape. I've been noticing your expanding midriff."

"We can't all maintain your Ichabod Crane-like physique."

"If you're really hot, why don't you take off that silly overcoat?"

"Can't. It's part of the image." Mike gasped for air, then leaned against the wall for support. "Ben, my men have scoured this building. Every floor, the stairwell, the basement, every conceivable nook and cranny. They've found no corpse."

"Then they need to start all over again."

"They will. Nonetheless, it's unlikely they overlooked something the size of a corpse. You can't exactly tuck that away in a desk drawer."

"I didn't imagine this, Mike. Neither did Rob."

"Okay. Then you tell me. Where could the body be?"

"I have no idea."

"Who could have taken it?"

"I'm similarly clueless."

"How could anyone move a heavy corpse off the

twentieth floor in just a few minutes when the elevators are out of order?"

"Beats me."

"You're a hell of a lot of help, Ben. Who else was in the building when you found the body?"

Ben thought for a moment. "To my knowledge, only myself, Rob Fielder, Herb, and Candice."

"The last two say they left immediately after your . . . encounter with them. What about your buddy Rob?"

"Rob has been with me all day long, and we only came upstairs about an hour ago. We were together until we found Howard, and we were only separated for about three or four minutes after we found his body. I called you, and Rob called security. At least, that's what he told me."

Mike nodded. "I checked. He did call the security desk downstairs. Left a message on their answering machine."

"Anybody who works in this building could've stayed late. Just because I didn't see them doesn't mean they weren't here. Have you got a list of all persons who signed out after eleven P.M.?"

"We're working on it. I saw those overweight babysitters you call security guards though. Someone could've slipped by them without signing, particularly if it was someone the guards recognized."

"I've seen them wave people through myself," Ben said.

"Even assuming someone could've relocated the body in the few minutes you were gone, which is difficult to believe in and of itself, where could they have gone with it? Especially with the elevators out of whack. I don't think they could've moved the stiff off this floor, much less out of the building."

"Have you checked for other exits? Maybe some secret, executives-only passageways. Or maybe the windows?"

"I'll ask people tomorrow about secret passageways,

but it strikes me as rather unlikely. The windows are all, without exception, hermetically sealed. Any other suggestions?"

Ben pressed his fingers against his temples and tried to remember every second of the past hour. In his mind's eye, he saw himself with Rob, walking toward his office, opening the door, seeing the body fall. . . .

He snapped his fingers. "There was something in Hamel's hand. It fell out when he hit the floor. I couldn't tell what it was."

"Whatever it was, it's not there now. What did it look like?"

Ben tried to recall. "It was square and flat. Not large. About the size of the palm of his hand."

"And you didn't look at it more closely?"

"I was a bit stressed out at the time, Mike. I apologize for not performing the Sherlock Holmes routine to perfection."

Mike grunted. "Well, if you think of something more, let me know."

"Of course. What's your plan of attack?"

Mike twisted his shoulders, sending ripples through his overcoat. "I'm not sure I have a plan, Ben."

"Isn't that what they teach in crime school?"

"Ben, you have no idea what my schedule is like right now. . . ."

"You're not going to let this drop!"

"Ben, I'm a homicide investigator. There's no proof so far that there's been a homicide! Or even a death!"

"You have my testimony."

"I need more. To be specific, I need a body."

"That's just a technicality. You don't absolutely have to have a body to initiate a murder investigation."

"But it sure facilitates matters. The D.A. would appreciate it, too." He shoved his hands deeply into his coat pockets. "Have you been keeping up with the murders of the teenage girls?"

Ben nodded grimly. "Three murders in less than two weeks."

"Yeah. Grisly, too—heads and hands cut off. Apparently a serial killer with a serious grudge against teenage girls. First bona fide serial killer we've ever had."

"What's your point, Mike?"

"My point is that every available resource in the department, including me, has been diverted to these murders, and given the magnitude of the crimes, rightfully so. How much interest do you think I'm going to be able to stir up for your alleged murder with no corpse?"

Ben didn't like what he was hearing, but he knew Mike was right. "Any recommendations?"

"You could look into this matter yourself. Do some checking on your own. You've done it before, and not altogether unsuccessfully. If you can uncover more information, or better yet a corpse, maybe I can pull some men off the serial killer case and put them on this one."

"Where would I start?"

"You need to find out everything you can about the victim. When he doesn't show up for work tomorrow, people are going to start talking. Listen to what they say. Find out whatever you can about your new colleagues. Given where the body was found, the guilty party may be an Apollo employee."

Ben hated to become the company mole. It seemed like a betrayal—only two days on the job, and already he was going to be investigating his co-workers, possibly trying to incriminate them. "I'll see what I can do. Mike—thanks for coming out."

"No problem. If you see your sister any time soon, put in a good word for me."

"I could try, but she wouldn't listen."

"Alas, 'tis only too true. Before I go, Ben—mind if I ask a question?"

"Ask away."

"What the hell are you doing working for this big corporation?"

"I don't under—"

"I thought you got this money-grubbing routine out of your system during the Raven, Tucker & Tubb fiasco."

"I hardly think that was typical—"

"Have you read much Samuel Clemens—Mark Twain?"

"You're the English major, not me."

"Do you know the story of Tennessee gold?"

"I don't think so."

"It's something Twain's father talked about when Twain was young. He was always dreaming of easy wealth. Some of his get-rich-quick schemes involved land speculation—Tennessee gold. He never found any gold, but that desire for instant security infected Twain for the rest of his life. Even after he became a successful writer and was relatively secure financially, he continued to pursue the dream. He invested in an unperfected typesetting machine. It was supposed to revolutionize the publishing industry and make him rich beyond his wildest imagining.

"But there were development problems, complications, demands for additional start-up cash. To make a long story short, the machine drained Twain dry. And it bombed, never made a cent. Instead of being reasonably well-off, suddenly Twain was penniless. To pay off his debts, he went on the road, taking on a nightmarish schedule of speaking engagements—and this was late in his life and during a time when travel was not easy. He wrote a flurry of books of dubious quality. He did almost anything he could for money. He eventually got back on his feet financially, but it embittered him, cost him his health, estranged him from his family, and possibly contributed to the death of his wife and two daughters." Mike's eyebrows bounced up and down. "Get the message?"

Ben pursed his lips. "I suppose in your subtle lit-crit

way, you're suggesting that I'm chasing after Tennessee gold."

"Yup. And I think you got it the same place Twain did. From your father."

"Really? Christina attributed this career decision to my mother."

"That's possible, too."

"Better stick with the detective work, pal. As a shrink, you stink."

"Says you. Anyway, try to get some sleep tonight. Snuggle with your cat. Forget about the nasty world of serial killers and corpses that tumble into your arms."

"Thanks." Ben felt another chill creeping down his spine. "But I doubt it."

* 11 *

The brunette duty officer at the front desk gave Sergeant Tomlinson directions to the X-ray room. She was good-looking and, by all indications, interested. But he wasn't. Not that she didn't appeal. He just had a hunch Karen wouldn't approve, and he wasn't about to put his relationship with his wife and daughter at risk for a quick romp with the duty officer.

He pressed the button outside the X-ray room, and a moment later the automatic lock released and the door popped open. Good—Koregai must have received his message. Tomlinson had called ahead and learned that Koregai was doing a rework on the second of the three corpses. Sounded like a golden opportunity to Tomlinson;

he crossed town in less than fifteen minutes. Of course, the blaring siren on his car helped somewhat.

Koregai had been the downtown coroner for years, far longer than Tomlinson had been on the force. In that time, Koregai had become the stuff of legends. Notoriously difficult to work with, he seemed to think that the entire law enforcement division existed solely for his benefit and pleasure. He chafed at commands and resisted all direct orders; pushy demands had a mysterious habit of causing autopsy reports to be delayed or lost. He probably would've been dumped long ago, if not for the fact that he was the best in the state at his job, and he was even better in the courtroom.

Tomlinson approached the table in the center of the dark room. An icy blue female corpse atop the table gave off an eerie glow under the dim fluorescent lighting. Tomlinson didn't have to ask who she was; the absence of her head and her hands explained everything.

"I'm Sergeant Tomlinson. I'd like to observe if possible."

There was no response from Koregai, not even a grunt.

Tomlinson decided to take his silence as approval. He read the clipboard at the end of the table. The preliminary autopsy report was on top. Tomlinson scanned the form; the phrase *within normal limits* jumped out at him time after time. The only deviation from the norm appeared at the bottom of the page. In the space labelled ABNORMALITIES, Koregai had scrawled: *No head, no hands*.

Very informative.

Koregai extinguished the overhead light. He was a short, dark man of Asian-American descent. Hardly friendly, but that was all right with Tomlinson; he couldn't imagine anything worse than a chummy coroner. Koregai flipped the power switch on a gray box about the size of a toaster oven. A row of green lights danced across the front of the device. He picked up a small metal wand connected to the box by a spiraling cord.

The coroner activated a small tape recorder, then pressed a button on the wand. A blue beam of light emerged.

"What's that?" Tomlinson asked.

To his surprise, Koregai answered. "Laser," he muttered.

"What does it do?"

Koregai pressed the wand against the top left clavicle of the corpse. Slowly, methodically, he scanned her entire body, an inch at a time. "Theoretically, the synchronized laser light stimulates atoms so as to cause them to emit light in phase."

"Oh really," Tomlinson said. If the police academy covered this, he must've been absent that day. "And that's desirable?"

"So I am told. It is supposed to make visible what would not otherwise be so."

"I get it. Fibers. Trace evidence."

"Exactly. Or fingerprints."

"Wow." Tomlinson stepped forward into the blue glow. "What a great gadget. It must be a tremendous help to you."

"Hmmph." Koregai's gloved fingers moved the wand down the torso. "High-tech vacuum cleaner."

Tomlinson observed the subtle note of disapproval and changed subjects. "I'm surprised this hasn't been done already."

Koregai paused for the barest of seconds, then proceeded with his examination. "I have already examined the corpse. Thoroughly."

Tomlinson was beginning to catch on. "Then this rework wasn't your idea?"

"No. Decidedly not." Koregai's fingers pressed against the flesh surrounding her pelvis, letting the light refract at a variety of angles. "They have become desperate, because they want this killer so badly. Unfortunately, they have no clues, no evidence. The killer is too careful. He has cleaned his victim, removed all trace evidence. That is why I found nothing before. That is why I find nothing now."

This unwanted assignment might be a hassle to Koregai, but it was a blessing for Tomlinson. Angry, Koregai was uncharacteristically talkative. "You haven't found anything of interest?"

"Why do you ask?"

"I just thought maybe if I knew what you knew, maybe I could find something in the field that would"—he struggled for words; obsequiousness was not his strong suit—"that would assist you in preparing your report."

"Are you working on this investigation?"

"Uh . . . yes. Unofficially."

"Unofficially?" Koregai's forehead wrinkled, then he resumed his work. "Might as well. The official investigators need all the assistance they can get."

Tomlinson suddenly shot forward, jarring the table. "What's that?"

Koregai lost his balance and fell to one side. "By all that's—" He muttered some words in a language Tomlinson didn't understand. "I want you to leave im*med*—"

"I thought I saw something!" Tomlinson said hurriedly. "Something in the blue light."

Frowning, Koregai returned the wand to the body. He was scanning the center pelvis, just above the pubic hair.

"A little higher."

Koregai obediently elevated the wand. He moved it back and forth, then rotated it, letting the light sparkle and radiate. After a few more moments, he saw what had caught Tomlinson's attention. With a small pair of tweezers, he removed a stray hair. He dropped the hair into a glass vial.

"What do you think it means?" Tomlinson asked.

"I . . . don't know. Will have to run tests . . ."

Tomlinson could see that Koregai was disturbed. He was accustomed to being flawless. Now some stupid police sergeant had seen him make a mistake.

"Look, Dr. Koregai, I'm sorry I startled you like that. I'm sure you would've seen that hair in a second. In fact, you probably noticed it when you did your preliminary report. It just didn't seem important enough to write down."

Koregai stopped his work, shut off his tape recorder, and peered at Tomlinson. Gradually, his face relaxed; he realized a peace offering was being extended. "Is there . . . some way I can help . . . *you*?"

Tomlinson smiled. "I don't know, Doc. Have you come across anything during your examinations of the three corpses that might give me a leg up? Something everyone else has overlooked, or didn't think was important. It might be the most trivial detail in the world to you, but it might break the case wide open for me."

Koregai stood for a moment, poised in thought. Without speaking, he turned back to the corpse and gently lifted her left breast with the wand. On the underside of the breast, in the blue glow, Tomlinson saw a small tattoo. It was a butterfly, with a garland of flowers across its wings.

Tomlinson knew that the coroner could determine how long ago the ink had stained the skin. "How old?"

"The tattoo is of recent origin."

"Has anyone else seen this?"

Koregai nodded. "It's in my report. But they don't know what to do with it. They attempted to trace it. Without success."

Tomlinson beamed. "Thanks, Doctor. I really appreciate it. And if you get anything on that hair, please let me know."

Koregai bowed politely, then returned to his work.

Tomlinson raced out of the X-ray room. He wished he could follow up on this lead right away, but unfortunately there was a switchboard waiting for him and he was already late. That was all right; he'd probably have more luck after midnight anyway.

He could understand why no one else knew what to do with the tattoo. They probably classified it as a detail that could confirm a suspected identity, but was of no value in identifying an unknown.

And that's where they were wrong. Maybe the tattoo didn't mean anything to the hotshot detectives, but it meant a lot to Tomlinson. Especially combined with what he had figured out already.

Tonight he was going to get lucky.

* 12 *

Ben was sleeping, or attempting to, when he felt something cold and wet brush against his face.

"What the . . . !" His eyes opened. It was Giselle, the huge black cat Christina had gifted him with last year. She was standing on his chest, two paws around his neck, rubbing her wet nose against his cheek.

"Maybe you don't understand, Giselle. I already have an alarm clock. And it's not set to go off for another hour and a half."

Giselle wedged her furry head into the crook of his neck and purred.

"What's the urgency? I just fed you last night." He sighed. "Oh, very well. I might as well have a baby."

He hauled himself out of bed, threw on a robe, and walked into the kitchenette of his small apartment. Giselle followed along, close at his heels. Reaching into the topmost cupboard, Ben withdrew a can of Feline's Fancy and opened it.

The distinctively fishy aroma filled the room. Giselle raised her head and looked up at Ben expectantly.

"All right, Giselle, let's try Stunt A again." He patted his shoulder with his free hand. "Jump."

He waited. Nothing happened. "Jump, Giselle. Jump." He waited. Still nothing happened.

"Giselle, the idea is for you to leap into my arms. Then, as a reward, I give you some food. There's no reason why you can't master these simple tricks. Now *jump!*"

Giselle padded over to her cat-food bowl, plopped her considerable weight down, and waited.

"C'mon, don't be so lazy. Work for your dinner. Jump!"

Giselle lifted her head ever so slightly and stared at him with wide, hungry eyes. A small, pathetic mewling emerged.

"Oh, all right then." He bent down and scraped the cat food into her bowl. As soon as he was done, Giselle dipped her head in and began to eat. The mewling converted to a soft purr.

"Yeah, well," Ben said, straightening his robe, "we'll work on the jumping tonight. Next time, no exceptions." He put a Christine Lavin CD on, then, from a cabinet beside his refrigerator, pulled down a cereal bowl and a box of Cap'n Crunch. On second thought, he dispensed with the bowl and ate it right out of the box. He plucked a mildly dirty glass from the sink and poured himself a glass of chocolate milk. In one satisfying swallow, he downed half the glass, then licked the brown chocolaty mustache from his upper lip.

There was a gentle knock on his front door. Ben checked the oven clock: barely six-thirty.

He opened the door and found his landlady outside.

"Good morning, Mrs. Marmelstein."

"I understand you have a new job, Ben."

"True. With the legal department of the Apollo Consortium. Looks like I finally made the big time."

She sniffed. "I guess that explains why you didn't come by to check my books last night."

"Ohmigosh." Ben tried to assist Mrs. Marmelstein whenever he could by managing her business affairs, such as they were. Mrs. Marmelstein had lived comfortably off her late husband's oil holdings—till they gave out. Her wealth had long since been depleted, but she hadn't quite figured that out yet.

"I'm sorry, Mrs. Marmelstein. I had to work late at the office last night and—"

"And I was left on my own to deal with Mr. Perry."

Mr. Perry was the downstairs roomer, a man Ben had never met. "What's his complaint this time?"

"He says the air-conditioning in his room doesn't work and he's in a twist about it. Can you imagine?"

The ingrate, Ben thought. After all, it was only ninety-five degrees yesterday. "Did you call Jack Abel?" Abel was a local handyman Ben used whenever possible to keep Mrs. Marmelstein's repair costs down.

"No. Mr. Perry was so aggravating I decided to call a professional."

Ben groaned. "Who'd you call?"

"Air Professionals. They're professionals, you know."

Yeah, and they bill like professionals, too. Oh, well, Ben thought, what's done is done. I'll find some money to pay them somewhere.

"I suppose this is the shape of things to come," she said sadly. "Now that you have this big important corporate job, you won't have time to look after my unimportant little problems."

"That's not true. It's just that I had to stay at the office so late—"

"Save your excuses. I'm sure I seem very insignificant next to those cigar-chomping fat cats at Apollo. From now on you'll spend your days whizzing around in corporate jets and cavorting with well-endowed floozies."

"Well," Ben said, "I don't want anything to do with corporate jets."

"If I see you at all in the future, it'll probably be in the company of your police buddy—"

Ben's ears pricked up. "Police buddy?"

"He'll be tramping through my garden, dragging the nasty element into this nice neighborhood."

Ben was certain Mrs. Marmelstein was the only person in town who would describe this low-rent district on the North Side as *nice*. "What brings my police buddy to mind?"

She shrugged her shoulders lightly. "He's outside."

"Mike? Mike is here?" He rushed past her and started down the stairs.

She sniffed again. "Soon you won't be able to tell the people who belong here from the pimps and the pushers."

Ben bounded down the stairs and opened the torn screen door. Mike glared at him, looking very impatient.

"About time, Kincaid. I thought I was going to have to get a search warrant."

Over Mike's shoulder, Ben saw four other men, two in plain clothes, two in uniform. There were two police cars parked on the street; a red beacon swirled around, casting an eerie glow on the faces of the police officers.

"I take it you aren't all here to escort me to work," Ben said.

Mike shook his head. "We found your corpse."

"Hamel?"

"That's the one."

"And he's dead?"

"Very."

"Boy, that was fast. You guys must be great detectives."

"I wish we could take credit for this, but we can't.

Someone else discovered the body. We received an anonymous phone tip."

"Well, however it happened, that's great news."

"Don't be so sure."

Ben's enthusiasm clotted in his throat. Why did Mike have such a grim expression on his face?

"Where did you find the body?" Ben asked slowly.

"In the alley behind this boardinghouse," Mike replied. He pointed toward the back. "You know. Where you park your car."

"Behind this house?" Ben found himself repeating the words, but not assimilating their meaning. "How did it get *there*?"

Mike exchanged a look with the police officers on either side of him, then turned back to Ben. "Well, the popular opinion is that he arrived in your car, given the copious quantities of his blood and hair we found there."

Ben felt a sudden tightening in his stomach.

The large man standing to Mike's left stepped forward. "Mr. Kincaid, I'm Chief Blackwell, Chief of Police here in Tulsa. I'd like to ask you a few questions."

∗ 13 ∗

Ben gazed at the imposing figure of Chief Blackwell. He was a thick, strong man. The muscles in his neck and shoulders tensed as he spoke.

"A—a few questions—?" Ben stuttered.

"Just a few harmless inquiries," Blackwell said non-

chalantly. "You can imagine how we might be somewhat curious."

"I want to see the body first," Ben said, trying to
remain calm.

Blackwell flipped open his notepad. "All in good
time. I want to ask—"

"I don't see any harm in letting him see the body,"
Mike said. "Sir. After all, it's just around the corner.
Maybe a quick look-see will illuminate his answers."

Mike grabbed the sleeve of Ben's robe and pulled
him through the door before Blackwell had a chance to
protest. Blackwell grunted, obviously annoyed to have
his authority usurped.

The alley behind the house was usually just a rough
patch of gravel and weeds where Ben parked his aging
Honda Accord. Today, it was a hotbed of activity such
as Ben had never seen before. At least ten different officers, some uniformed, some not, swirled around the
crime scene with tweezers, cameras, and magnifying
glasses. Three interns had lifted Hamel's body onto a
stretcher, which they were now loading into an ambulance.

Ben stifled his natural revulsion and looked at the
body. It was just as it had been when he had last seen
it. There was no visible mark anywhere on Hamel or his
clothes. He was just dead, that's all. There was a certain
peacefulness about him—perhaps even a suggestion of
contentment. If Ben hadn't known better, he might've
suspected Hamel was just sleeping.

"What killed him?" Ben asked.

"Koregai hasn't even done a preliminary examination
yet," Mike answered.

"I don't see any bloodstains. Where'd the blood you
claim you found in my car come from?"

"Don't know. We're going to let the coroner explain
that to us, too."

Blackwell approached another officer and barked out
some instructions. Ben tried to stay out of his line of

sight. He saw another man with a camcorder packing up his equipment; the scene had no doubt been photographed and videotaped from every conceivable angle. Two more men were crawling back and forth across the alleyway, crouched on their hands and knees, their eyes close to the pavement.

"Hair and fiber boys?" Ben asked.

Mike nodded. "We've already searched for prints, both in the alley and in your car. Didn't find any. Except, of course, yours."

"You realize you had no right to search my car without a warrant."

"I disagree. The driver's side door was wide open when we arrived. Under those circumstances, we don't believe you had any reasonable expectation of privacy."

"How convenient."

Mike stepped toward Ben and lowered his voice. "Look, Ben, I can't hold off Blackwell much longer. If you have anything you want to tell me privately—"

"I didn't kill him, Mike."

"I know, I know," Mike said, although he appeared relieved to hear the words spoken aloud. "But do you have any idea who did?"

"Not a clue."

"What about your boss, Crichton? Was Hamel having any problems with him?"

"Could be. I don't know."

"What about that guy who was with you last night? We know he was in the office building."

"I already told you. Rob was with me all day, right up until we found the body. We weren't apart for ten seconds. So unless this stiff has been dead for over twenty-four hours, Rob is out."

"I don't need a coroner's report to confirm that he hasn't been dead that long."

"Ditto."

Mike shoved his hands into the pockets of his overcoat. "What about some of those other goons at your office? For one, the clown you caught *in flagrante delicto* last night. Maybe he didn't like being caught with his pants down. Literally. Maybe this is a revenge frame."

"Maybe. Then again, maybe not. I have no idea. I don't know enough about these people." He paused. "Yet."

"Good attitude. Your involvement could be key, Ben. I'll have my men search the area thoroughly, and I'll send some boys around to question your neighbors—but as I told you, we're up to our eyeballs in this serial killer mess. That's why Blackwell is here. He's coming to every homicide site until that case is solved."

"Taking a personal interest in the murders?"

Mike smiled thinly. "Taking a personal interest in his public image. The press has not been kind to the Tulsa P.D. since this wave of murders started. The heat has been on Blackwell, even to the point of the city council calling for his resignation. I think Blackwell decided it might help if he put on a show of aggressively investigating these murders. Healthy fodder for the six o'clock news."

"Yeah, but does his involvement mean a speedier solution to the murders?"

Mike bent over and lit his pipe. "Rather the opposite, I'd say." He took a few swift puffs, then removed the pipe stem from his lips. "Blackwell doesn't have many resources available to assign to this unrelated murder. It would be much simpler for him if this minor distraction were solved quickly. And the best way to bring an investigation to a hasty close is to bear down on the most obvious suspect. And that suspect, Ben, is you."

"Can you define *bearing down*?"

"Taking you in for questioning, locking you up on suspicion, maybe even planting leaks of dubious veracity to convict you in the press. And, of course, pounding on you till you crack. That's the gist of it."

"Oh." Ben tried to smile. "Thanks for the colorful details."

"My pleasure."

Ben saw Joni and Jami Singleton, the teenage twins who lived with their family in one of the upstairs rooms of his boardinghouse. They were both peeking around the corner of the building.

"Hiya, Joni," Ben said, wiggling his fingers.

Joni cautiously stepped out of the shadows, with Jami close behind.

"Don't worry, I'm unarmed. Hi there, Jami."

"It's not you I was worried about, Benjamin," Jami said, eyeing Mike and the other police officers. "What's happening? You helping the cops solve another case?"

Mike arched an eyebrow.

"Well," Ben replied, "this time it seems I'm Suspect Number One."

"Oh?" Jami fluffed her long black hair with the palm of her hand. "What's the charge?"

"Murder."

Her eyes widened. "Really?"

"In the first degree," Mike added. "Maybe."

"Wow!" Joni said, echoing her sister. This development obviously increased their estimation of Ben many times over. "Was it, like, a crime of passion?"

"I don't know," Ben said. "I didn't do it."

She folded her hands across her chest, clearly disappointed. Then she noticed the police officers swarming around. "Oh, I get it. Of course—you're innocent." She winked. "That's your story and you're sticking to it. You were probably framed."

"As a matter of fact—"

Chief Blackwell swaggered back to Ben, interrupting their conversation. "Are you ready to be grilled, Kincaid?"

"Well, since you put it like that . . ."

"Good. Let's get started."

"Don't you want to wait till the Action News team arrives?"

Blackwell straightened and patted down his hair. "You think TV people are com—" He stopped. "Oh, I see. You're a wiseass."

"Guilty as charged."

"Morelli already gave me the line you fed him about what happened at the Apollo offices."

"The *line*? I told him the truth."

"Yeah? Then maybe you can explain how someone got that stiff out of that high rise?"

"Sorry. I can't."

"I lifted that body, and let me tell you—it wasn't light. According to you, you were only gone three or four minutes."

"True."

"So where did he go?"

"I don't know."

"What was he doing in your office?"

"I don't know."

"How did he get in your car?"

"I don't know."

"How did he get in the alley behind your apartment?"

"I don't know."

Blackwell made a loud growling noise. "Goddamn it. You lawyers are all alike. Always got a slick answer for everything."

Ben and Mike exchanged a glance.

"Maybe you think you can bullshit your old college roomie, but I'm not buying it, kid."

"I'm not asking you to buy anything, Chief. Just don't lock me up because I'm the most convenient suspect. I'm more valuable to you on the outside."

Blackwell cocked his head to one side. "How so?"

"Since Hamel was killed in the office building, the key suspects are his colleagues in the legal department at Apollo. Where I work." He leaned in close to

Blackwell. "Leave me free, and I can check out these people, see if I can turn up any leads."

"You?"

"I've investigated crimes before. Ask Mike. I used to work at the D.A.'s office. It's clear you don't have enough free men to staff this case. Let me take up the slack. And if I don't come up with anything, you can still lock me away and throw away the key. You haven't lost anything."

Blackwell appeared to be considering. "You've got access to the office where Hamel worked?"

"Yes."

"And access to all his co-workers?"

"Yes again."

"Hmm. It *is* better having someone on the inside than having some cop march through taking statements. No one ever wants to tell us anything. And this would be a lot simpler than trying to plant someone undercover. All right, I'll give you a try. You have one week to see what you can find out. I expect you to report in with Morelli every day. *Every day*. Understand?"

"Perfectly."

He laid a finger on Ben's chest. "If you don't have another suspect for us, with solid evidence, by this time next week, my boys'll be hauling you into the station for questioning. Very lengthy questioning. Could go on for days. And if we don't hear what we want, we could become very grumpy."

"Got it," Ben said.

"Good," Blackwell said gruffly. "Remember, one week. Period. No extensions." He spun on his heel and almost slammed into Mrs. Marmelstein.

"Mrs. Marmelstein," Ben said. "What are you doing out here so early in the morning?"

"I brought you a fruitcake," she said. She held the comestible chest-high. "I thought that if you men are going to stand out in the chill all morning long, you should at least have something to eat."

Ben saw a pained expression cross Blackwell's face, then a similar expression on Mike's, then on those of the other officers, all of whom appeared to be subtly inching away.

Didn't anybody like fruitcake?

* 14 *

Ben tossed his files into his briefcase and hurried toward the conference room where the depositions were to be taken. Fortunately he had prepared yesterday; he had certainly had no time to prepare this morning. After finding a corpse in his backyard and narrowly escaping a trip to the big house, he was lucky to make it to the office at all.

Ben mentally reviewed his plans and goals. A deposition allows an attorney to ask the opposing party questions while a court reporter takes down everything the witness says. Objections can be made, but since there is no judge present to rule on them, the objections are made *for the record*, to be ruled upon later if necessary. The witness answers the question regardless of any objections made, unless specifically instructed not to answer by his or her attorney.

It was supposed to be a simple, unemotional fact-finding exercise. Ben hoped that proved true.

He certainly didn't plan to protract matters any longer than necessary. He would ask the essential questions to elicit the plaintiffs' version of what happened and gather any other information that might help defend Apollo against the design defect claim. Then he would close the deposition as gracefully and painlessly as possible. At least, that was the plan.

"Morning, Ben," Rob said, as Ben entered the conference room. "You're late."

"Don't start with me, Rob. I'm not having an Up-With-People kind of day."

"Sure, no problem," he said, backing away. "Let me introduce you to everyone." He pointed toward a pleasant-looking woman in a blue skirt. "Trudy here is going to be our court reporter this morning." Ben shook her hand. Then Rob directed his attention to an extraordinarily obese man perched on the edge of a chair in the corner of the room. Rolls of flesh cascaded from his chin; he had no neck at all. "This is the attorney for the plaintiffs, George Abernathy."

Ben stepped forward and shook the immense man's hand. "George Abernathy. Seems like I've heard that name before."

Abernathy beamed. "Perhaps you've seen my commercials on TV."

"Your . . . commercials?"

Abernathy adopted a deep anchorman voice. " 'Have you got a bone to pick with your boss? Have you been fired for no reason? Have you been injured, and no one wants to pay the bill? If so, then you need a fighter in your corner.' Then you hear the sound of the bell, and we show some footage from one of the Tyson prize-fights." He resumed the anchorman delivery. " 'George Abernathy will go the distance for you. And you don't pay a penny unless he collects. Call—' And then we give our phone number. It's been a big hit."

"Sorry," Ben said. "I guess I watch the wrong programs."

"Then maybe you saw my ad in *TV Guide*. The headline reads PERSONAL INJURY PROFESSIONAL in great big letters."

"I don't watch that much TV anymore."

"Oh, well," Abernathy said jovially, "you big shots

don't have to worry about small-timers like me." He reached into his wallet. "Here, let me give you my card. Who knows? You might get some personal injury situation too messy for you to deal with and consider tossing it my way."

Ben took his business card. It was a mélange of phosphorescent colors; it glowed as it caught the light. Embossed in the center was GEORGE ABERNATHY— PERSONAL INJURY PROFESSIONAL.

"Thanks for the card," Ben said, immediately hiding it in his coat pocket. "Does all that advertising pay off?"

"Like you wouldn't believe. It's hard as nails for a small practitioner like me to keep going."

"Tell me about it."

"But since I started placing those ads, business has been booming. I get your regular, salt-of-the-earth, hard-working blue-collar man—he gets hurt and he doesn't know what to do about it. He doesn't know anything about lawyers and lawsuits. He's lost. That's where I try to help out. It's a public service, really."

"Most public servants don't work on a contingency fee," Ben observed.

"True," Abernathy agreed. "But that's the only way my clients could ever pay. It's the poor man's ticket to the courthouse. Surely you don't think courts are just for corporations?"

"No, I don't."

"In my experience, clients are happy to pay any contingency fee, even up to fifty percent. Tell you what, Ben, after we finish this depo, let's you and me have a squat and try to polish off this mess. An early settlement would be in everyone's best interest."

The conference room door opened. "Have you met the Nelsons yet?" Abernathy asked.

As if on cue, a middle-aged couple entered the room and approached Abernathy, who wrapped his ample arms around them. The man was stocky, square-faced.

His white undershirt bore detectible underarm stains. The woman was a petite shadow in a plain sea-blue dress. "This is Carl and June Nelson," Abernathy said.

Ben saw the recognition light in their eyes just as it did in his. "We've met before," Ben said. "I thought your names seemed familiar, but I couldn't quite place them."

Now he did. Ben had represented Carl and June Nelson in a dog bite case shortly after he left Raven, Tucker & Tubb and started his own practice. They were kind, unassuming people—but they had a neighbor who kept a Doberman. The Doberman got out one day, and Carl was unfortunate enough to cross its path. His injuries were not life-threatening, but he did incur some steep medical bills and was expected to have both physical and mental trauma for some time. The nerves in his left leg were weakened, and he showed signs of severe stress, even paranoia. Ben managed to arrange a friendly judgment by which the Nelsons took home forty thousand dollars for their injuries and pain and suffering.

"I've represented the Nelsons on a previous matter," Ben said.

"Really?" Abernathy's eyebrows danced. "Hey, I wonder if we have a conflict of interest here?"

Yeah, you'd like that, wouldn't you? Ben addressed the Nelsons. "Do you understand that in this lawsuit, I represent the Apollo Consortium—not you?"

They nodded their heads.

"To your knowledge, does this lawsuit relate in any way to the action I handled for you?"

Carl shook his head. "No connection that I can see, Ben."

"Do you believe any client confidences I obtained during the previous lawsuit could be used to your disadvantage in the present lawsuit?"

Carl and June looked at one another, then back at

Ben. "I don't see that they have anything to do with one another," Carl opined.

"Would you be willing to execute a waiver allowing me to continue working on this case?"

"We thought you were a fine young man," June interjected. "In fact, we called you first when this incident arose, but your secretary told us you were tied up."

"Hate to see you workin' for the other side," Carl said good-naturedly. "But we'll sign whatever you want us to sign."

"Thank you. Mr. Abernathy, it looks to me as if we have no conflict here." The disappointment on Abernathy's face was apparent. "Shall we get started?"

After the court reporter swore in June, Ben asked his preliminary background questions about her education and occupational history (none). She had not been deposed before and she had not reviewed any documents in preparation for her deposition.

"Mrs. Nelson, if at any time during this proceeding you want to take a break, for any reason at all, just tell me and we'll do it, all right?"

She laid her hands flat on her lap. She was obviously nervous—every deponent was—but she was doing her best to contain it. "All right."

"I'll try to make my questions as clear as possible. If at any time you don't fully understand my question, just tell me, and I'll rephrase it, okay?"

"Okay."

"And if you do respond, I'll assume you understood the question."

"That's fine."

Standard deposition babble. Try to cozy up to the witness, make her feel relaxed enough to say something she shouldn't. It also made a useful record if, at trial, the witness tried to squirm out of an answer by claiming she didn't understand the question.

Ben realized June might not be able to maintain her

brave front for an extended period. He decided to proceed directly to the night of the accident. "Can you tell me what the occasion was that caused everyone to be riding on the flatbed behind the tractor?"

June licked her lips and thought carefully before answering. "It was Homecoming night, just after we won the football game. Our son, Jason, was the star quarterback, you know." Ben saw a twitch in the corner of her eye, but she fought it back and proceeded. "The tractor pull was intended to be a celebration."

"Realizing that you're not an engineer, Mrs. Nelson, can you describe the physical layout of the mechanism for me?" Ben glanced at Abernathy. To his surprise, there was no objection. Abernathy was doodling on his legal pad, only barely paying attention.

"The tractor was nothing out of the ordinary—one of those big John Deere machines. The flatbed behind it was large, wooden, and flat. Enough room for thirty or forty of us without much crowding. Plus an ice chest filled with Cokes."

"And what did you do on this flatbed?"

"We just rode around on the dirt north of the football field. I don't know why. They're teenagers, for God's sake. What they do for fun . . ." Her voice trailed off.

"And parents were involved in this? As well as the kids?"

"Oh, yes. We try to do everything we can with our children. Especially . . . Jason." Another twitch, quickly stifled.

"And then what happened?"

She released a stream of air through parted lips. "At first, nothing. Everyone was having a great time. Laughing, shouting, passing around the Cokes. Jason was swinging his legs off the edge of the flatbed, flirting with Terri, his girlfriend. Everything was wonderful."

Ben bit down on his lower lip. He hated this. What

could possibly be worse than forcing a woman to relive the night her oldest son ...

"And then?" he said, nudging her along as gently as possible.

"And then ..." She shook her head. "I don't know what happened. I still don't understand. There was a sudden ... lurching. We heard an awful sound—metal grating against metal—then the flatbed pitched violently to one side. I immediately thought of Jason, dangling off the edge." Her face twisted, tightened. "I saw him waving his arms, trying to regain his balance. He was always such a coordinated boy, so strong, so light on his feet. ..."

Her eyes began to water. "I reached out to him." She extended her hands, as if reliving the entire horrific incident. "I shouted, 'Jason! Someone grab Jason!' But no one did. He fell." Tears were streaming down her face.

Ben paused while June tried to regain her composure. The tension was affecting everyone in the room.

"Did you see anything after that?"

"Oh, yes," she cried. "Oh ... yes." She wiped the tears from her face, but more streamed down to replace them. She was full out crying now, no turning back.

"What did you see?"

She breathed deep and raspily. "Jason held onto the flatbed as long as he could. Too long. As he fell, he pulled himself back under the flatbed. He got caught— between the tires and axles and—" Her eyes widened. "I ran toward him, but I was too late. He was caught in the metal workings under the flatbed. He screamed out in pain. Blood splattered into my face. It was hideous. He was ... *mangled* in the machinery. *Jason!*—"

She collapsed into the arms of her husband, crying and gasping for air. She would never have agreed to bring this lawsuit, Ben thought, if she had realized she would have to relive that nightmare.

Ben wiped the perspiration from his brow. Everyone

else in the room seemed equally edgy. Even the court reporter appeared near tears.

"Let's take a five-minute break," Ben said. There was no dissent.

The five-minute break became a fifteen-minute break; Ben made certain everyone had all the time they needed to recover from the stress of June's testimony.

When the deposition resumed, Ben departed from the night of the accident for less emotional grounds— matters that could only interest an attorney.

"Do you have any idea what caused the *lurching* of the flatbed you described?"

June glanced at Abernathy. "The defective leaf spring made by your company." It was more a question than an answer.

"Is that something your attorney told you to say?"

"Objection." Abernathy proved he was awake for the first time in the deposition. "That's protected by the attorney-client privilege. I instruct the witness not to answer."

"Do you personally have any knowledge regarding the design of the Apollo suspension system?" Ben continued.

"Well, no," June answered.

"Do you know what is referred to as the XKL-1?"

"I'm . . . not sure."

"That's the trade name of the suspension system Apollo designed and manufactured that was used in the flatbed. Have you seen any documents suggesting there is a design defect in the XKL-1?"

"Not that I recall."

"Do you have any reason to believe there are any documents suggesting the existence of a design defect in the XKL-1?"

She looked again at Abernathy, but he was no help. "I . . . don't know of any, no."

"Did you personally observe any machinery you believed to be defective?"

"I'm not very mechanically inclined. I can't even start the lawn mower—"

"Please answer my question, ma'am. Did you see any machinery you believed to be defective?"

"No. Not that I was aware of."

"How fast was the driver of the tractor going?"

"I'm . . . not certain . . ."

"Mrs. Nelson . . . isn't it possible the flatbed just hit a bump?"

She seemed to be focusing on a point in the center of the table. "I don't think so . . ."

"But you don't know for sure?"

"The dirt field had been recently graded . . ."

"Do you have personal knowledge of that fact?"

She placed her hands under her arms. "No."

"Can you say with absolute certainty that the flatbed didn't just hit a bump?"

Abernathy hoisted himself up again. "To which we object."

"On what grounds?"

"On . . . ummm . . . I object to the form of the question."

Ben rolled his eyes. "Mrs. Nelson, that's what we call an objection for the record. Your counsel will renew it at trial, if he's not too embarrassed. For now, however, you must answer my question."

"I don't think it was a bump."

"But you can't rule it out?"

"No. I suppose I can't."

"And it isn't Apollo's fault that the driver took that flatbed over a bumpy field, is it?"

"No. Of course not."

"Thank you," Ben said, relieved to be done with it. "I appreciate your honesty."

* 15 *

Ben stared hopelessly at the map.

"I'm sorry, Christina. I'm lost."

Christina clicked her right turn signal and pulled onto the side of the road. "I knew I shouldn't let you navigate. You have no sense of direction whatsoever."

"I offered to drive."

"Yeah, but then we'd have to take that beat-up Honda of yours, and I don't carry enough life insurance for that. Your Honda is seriously déclassé. When are you going to get a new car, anyway?"

"After Apollo makes me wealthy beyond my dreams of avarice."

"Any day now." She tugged at the map. "Here, let me."

He resisted the tug. "I'm perfectly capable of reading a map."

"I know," Christina said. "Unfortunately, you're reading it upside down." She took the map from him and turned it right side up. "Now this could solve a lot of your navigational problems."

"Is it my fault the orientation wasn't clearly marked?"

Christina declined to comment. "I've been turning left off this dirt road when I should've been turning right. Which more than likely explains why I keep missing Camp Sequoyah."

"Well, speed it up. We're late."

"Aye, aye, commandant." She started the car and returned to the road. "Personally, I'm suspicious of anything that takes place this far from civilization as we know it. What is this DARE retreat, anyway?"

"All I know is that DARE stands for Daunting Athletic Ropes Encounter, and frankly, that's more than I want to know. The schedule says we have Training Exercises at noon, Crackerbarrel at eight, and tomorrow, at six A.M., something called the High Course."

"I don't much care for the sound of that."

"Ditto. But Crichton seems to think this is important. Fosters team bonding and leadership skills and all that rot. And something called the Universal Yo!"

"I hope he's right. Personally, I haven't bonded too much in my short time at Apollo."

"Well, maybe Crackerbarrel will do the trick. I'm sure Herb will be there. Mark my words, you're going to love Herb."

Christina spotted the overhead arch that announced they had arrived at Camp Sequoyah. "You're too late. I've already met Herb. Great guy. Real savoir faire. The whole time we talked, his eyes never rose above breast-level."

"Well, maybe Candy will keep him in line."

Christina drove down the narrow country road that led to the main campsite. "I don't see a parking lot."

"Nor do I think you're likely to. Just watch for a lot of other cars. I'm sure Herb and Chuck have been here for hours buttering up Crichton."

"Ben, do you really think you should be doing this? So soon after the murder, I mean?"

"Christina, I've got one week to find out who killed Hamel. And my best modus operandi is to find out whatever I can about these legal eagles. And what better way to do that than here, at this corporate pressure cooker, where all my chief suspects are conveniently gathered?"

She tapped her fingers pensively on the steering wheel. "I suppose you're right. . . ."

"So what's your problem?"

She pulled her car beside a row of BMWs and Land Rovers. "My problem is, it's entirely possible that one of these legal eagles has committed murder, and we're now about a million miles from any kind of help. If the killer finds out you're after him, he or she may be tempted to give a repeat performance. With you in the starring role. Capeesh?"

Ben fumbled with his overnight bag. "Well . . . when you put it like that . . ."

Ben trailed in from the training exercises about eight-thirty, a portrait of complete exhaustion. He and his colleagues had been training since noon; it seemed like forever.

He stumbled through the door of the stone bunkhouse and found to his dismay that everyone else in the group was standing at the bar, fully showered and changed, staring at him.

"Have a bit of trouble with the last group of exercises?" Chuck chuckled. "Everyone else has been back for half an hour."

"I have a problem with heights," Ben muttered. "Ever since I was a kid."

"I can see where that would make it hard to finish the course," Chuck replied. "After all, you were almost six inches off the ground."

"Hey!" Crichton interceded. "We're here to bond, not to denigrate. This is Ben's first time on the course. Cut him some slack."

Thanks, Dad. "I'm going to take a shower."

"Please do," Candice tittered.

Ben mounted the stairs, threw his clothes on his bunk, and crawled into the shower. The day had been filled with a variety of exercises designed to teach noble workplace skills such as teamwork, mutual trust, assertiveness, and leadership, via sixth-grade problem-solving scenarios. Transporting five people across a ravine with three two-by-fours. Lifting one another through the spider's web (a vertical lattice of latex webbing). Moving "toxic waste" (a glass of water) to safety on a rope swing—while blindfolded. All peppered with inspirational lectures about the Universal Yo!

The worst was the Trust Fall. Victims—er, participants—were supposed to climb to a platform about seven feet up a tree, turn around, fold their hands across their chests (very symbolic), and fall. Backwards. The idea was that your bosom buddies on the ground would catch you in their outstretched but unlinked arms. That was the idea, anyway. You were supposed to trust that they would be there, even though you couldn't see them as you fell. Unfortunately, Ben didn't trust any of them, except Christina, and he knew she couldn't catch him by herself.

He'd been up there a full fifteen minutes before he fell, and even then it was just because he got dizzy and lost his balance.

On the last leg of the course, everyone was supposed to complete a lightweight obstacle course on a slightly raised platform. The course involved jumping, swinging on ropes, and balancing on telephone poles and thick metal cables. Ben started near the front; he ended dead last. Worst of all, he had to smile and pretend to be good-humored about it as colleague after colleague passed him. Even Christina overtook him, after he refused her offer to haul him through the tough spots.

After he finished drying off, Ben dressed, shaved, and descended to the ground floor of the bunkhouse for Crackerbarrel.

Crackerbarrel?

Chuck saw him first. "Hail, Ben Kincaid, mighty warrior!" he shouted, then snorted into a fistful of potato chips.

Ben made a mental note that if he ever became uncommonly wealthy, he would devote all his resources to making Chuck's life miserable. Ignoring Chuck, he found a spread of chips, veggies, and other snack foods laid out on the kitchen counter.

Ben felt a sudden swat on the back. "Glad you made it in before midnight," Herb said, grinning. "We were afraid we would have to release the dogs."

"Ha, ha," Ben said, without much enthusiasm. "Very funny."

"Just a little humor, Kincaid. I'm sure a luminary of your stature can take it. Say, here's a tip. Stay clear of Crichton tonight. He's on the warpath. He's been yelling at everyone in sight since we got back to the bunkhouse. No one can figure out why."

"Surely he didn't yell at *you*, Herb."

Herb's lips pursed. "He did. Threatened me within an inch of my job, the SOB. I know he's your biggest fan, Kincaid, but I'd stay away from him just the same."

Herb passed through the food line and gravitated to the other side of the room, where Candice coincidentally happened to be standing.

"Need help carrying your plate, mighty warrior?" Christina asked Ben.

"Now I understand," Ben said. "Crackerbarrel must mean gathering place for the great wits of the twentieth century."

"Oooh. Not the usual *homme d'esprit*, tonight, huh? Didn't mean to offend. I'm just glad you're here."

"So I can serve as the butt of your jokes?"

"No, so you can protect me from Herbert the Pervert. What a lech that man is. Can't keep his eyes—or his hands—to himself. Practically pawed me up in the chow line. And with Candice, the object of his *amour fou*, standing right beside me."

"Maybe he was using you as a diversion. You know, to throw everyone off the track."

Christina shivered. "More likely he's just an insufferable toad."

Ben exited the snack line and took a seat at the table

beside Doug, who was sitting with a plate full of tortilla chips and queso and, of course, his laptop computer.

"I hear Crichton's in a lousy mood tonight," Ben said.

"You are a master of understatement."

"He got to you, too?"

Doug drew heavily on his cigarillo, then set it on the corner of his paper plate. "Oh, yes. Took my American Airlines litigation plan and threw it in my face. Told me to get back behind the typewriter where I belong." He shoved a few chips in his mouth. "Stupid ass. Doesn't know the difference between a PC and a typewriter."

"Who else incurred the wrath—" Ben's sentence was cut off by a sudden outburst from the back of the room.

"Good God, they're at it again," Doug said. "Like characters from a Noël Coward play."

"Who?"

Doug pointed. Herb and Candice had finally managed to connect, so to speak.

"You were pathetic today," Candice said. "You run like a girl."

"Oh, yeah?" Herb retorted. "Well, you run like a man, not that that's any big surprise."

"Dickhead."

"Bitch."

"Prick."

"Double bitch."

Ben turned back toward Doug. "Looks like they didn't do much bonding today."

"I rather suspect that will come later tonight," Doug replied.

Ben suddenly became aware that Shelly was sitting opposite him. Had she been there all along, invisible as ever, or had she just mysteriously appeared? He couldn't be sure.

"Hi, Shelly. How's everything?"

She didn't reply, but Ben did think he saw the corner

of her upper lip twitch, which he took as a sign of encouragement.

"Where's your baby girl this weekend?"

She looked at him strangely, as if startled to find someone actually noticing she was present. "Angie is at a twenty-four-hour day-care center," Shelly said quietly. Her voice was almost as fragile as she was. "Costs a fortune, but Crichton insists we attend these retreats."

"Did Crichton yell at you, too?"

"Of course not. He only yells at the ones he likes."

Ben thought about that for a moment. "Any chance of Dad looking after Angie? It'd be cheaper."

He immediately wished he could take it back. Her face flattened; her eyes became watery. "Not likely."

Ben tried to smooth over his unconscionable gaffe. "Must be tough, working full time and raising a baby on your own. How do you manage?"

Before she had a chance to answer, Chuck plopped down at the table beside Ben. "Shelly, have you got that memo on the antitrust ramifications of the Ameritech deal?"

"I-I thought this was supposed to be a no-work-allowed weekend."

"No excuses. Your memo is overdue."

"But you just gave me the assignment. And I've been buried in—"

"I'm tired of your failure to deliver, Shelly. You're skating on thin ice."

"Look, Chuck, I'll get you the memo by Monday morning. I don't know how, but—"

Chuck snarled, picked up his plate, and walked away without saying another word.

"What a charmer," Ben murmured. "Look, Shelly, if I can help—" But she was already gone. She ran to the back of the room and raced up the stairs to the women's bunks.

Well, Ben thought sadly, at least Chuck left. But before he could derive any pleasure from the situation, Herb took the now empty seat beside him.

"Ben," Herb said, "I need your help."

"Why? D'you run out of synonyms for *bitch*?"

"Huh?"

"Never mind. What's the problem?"

"Well, you've known that Christina McCall babe for some time, right?"

"Ye-es. . . ."

"So I thought you'd know best what to do."

"About what?"

Herb leaned in closer. "Did you see her coming on to me?"

"No, I missed that."

"Oh, man, she was practically panting. Not that that's unusual, but I thought she was going to rip my clothes off and do me right then and there!"

"Did you really?"

"Not that I would mind, under the right circumstances. She's a real looker, as I guess you know. Cute legs, boffo boobies. She really turns me on."

"Herb, I don't want to hear about—"

"I just wanted to make sure I wasn't treading on your toes. You know, first come, first served, I always say. Is there anything going on between you two?"

"Well, nothing like that."

"Then the field is clear. Great! You know her better than I do. What do you recommend? So I can get close to her."

In a flash, Ben realized that a supremely humanitarian opportunity had arisen, if he could only suppress his nausea long enough to continue conversing with Herb. "If I were you, I'd play hard to get."

"Really?"

"Oh, yeah. She despises easy men. Be distant. Don't speak to her. Have as little to do with her as possible. Before you know it, she'll be on your doorstep modeling skimpy lace from Victoria's Secret."

"Wow, that sounds great. You're a regular guy, Ben."

"Well, I try."

Herb pushed away from the table. Ben felt better than he had since he'd arrived; he had done his good deed for the day. He suddenly noticed his new boss at the end of the table. Crichton pulled Ben aside.

"Don't let the teasing bother you, Kincaid. It's only natural for the hoi polloi to feel threatened when a man of your stature joins the team."

"I'll try to ignore them." Ben changed the subject. "Shelly seems depressed tonight."

Crichton shrugged. "What else is new? Like most of her female colleagues, she's never satisfied. Women fought for years to break into the marketplace, and now that they're finally here, they realize, 'Holy shit! This is hard! And I thought it would all just be one blissful enriching experience after another!' "

Ben could feel his teeth tightening. "But surely you'll agree that women should have an equal position in the marketplace. . . ."

"If I'm being considered for the Supreme Court, yes. If I'm trying to take care of a major corporation, no. Female employees present all kinds of special difficulties, and the hell of it is, I'm not even allowed to ask about the concerns that affect my company most significantly."

"Such as?"

"Such as social life, marriage, pregnancy. If a woman comes looking for a job, I want to know if she's on the executive track or the mommy track. But I can't ask! The labor jocks tell me that if I ask that simple commonsense question about a matter that can have an enormous impact on her ability to perform her job and her likelihood of remaining here for any length of time, I could get slapped with a gender discrimination suit. Can you believe that? Hell, when we put *our* time and money on the line to train Shelly, we expected her to be in for the long haul. But damned if she doesn't turn up pregnant. And she isn't even married!"

"But . . . she still seems to be working."

"Sure, sure. But it isn't the same. She's strictly an eight-to-fiver now. Complains that she has to pick up the baby at day care. Can you believe that?"

"Well—"

Before Ben could comment, Chuck forced himself into their conversation.

"I was truly moved when you were explaining the Universal Yo!" Chuck told Crichton. "This has been a life-changing experience for me. It's not often a grown man cries, but when you got to the part about facing the future unafraid, I wept like a baby."

Ben tried not to gag.

Crichton smiled politely and tapped a spoon against a glass.

"May I have your attention please?" The room quieted in a heartbeat. "Thank you. I want you all to know I was proud of what I saw in the field today. I always say, work hard, play hard, and today I saw a lot of hard play. I think some long-term relationships were forged in the sweat and dirt of those obstacle courses, and I saw some genuine, heartfelt trust during the Trust Fall."

Ben couldn't see him, but he could definitely hear Chuck whisper: " 'Cept for Kincaid. He didn't trust. He just fell."

Crichton continued. "Tomorrow, each of you will confront the High Course. For many of you, this will be the greatest physical challenge you have ever faced. Even harder than today's obstacle course six inches off the ground."

Is he really looking at me, Ben wondered, or am I just imagining it?

"Nonetheless, I know each of you will meet the High Course head on, with the same spirit of trust, teamwork, and resourcefulness you bring to your work every day. Most importantly, I know you will bear in mind the critical elements of the Universal Yo!: an open mind, a willingness to be flexible, and the courage to step out of the comfort zone. And win."

Ben was missing most of the rhetoric. He couldn't seem to get past the part about the Greatest Physical Challenge You Have Ever Faced.

Crichton lowered his voice and adopted a sepulchral tone. "Our office has been visited with great sadness this week. One of our own, Howard Hamel, a trusted, faithful colleague, has been taken from us for reasons that remain unclear. And yet, there is always a balance in the universe. For every day, a night. For every birth, a death. For every yin, a yang. And just as we are grieved to lose Howard Hamel, we are blessed to gain Benjamin Kincaid. Ben, stand up for a moment."

Ben's throat went dry. Mortified, he pushed himself to his feet. A rather tepid round of applause followed.

"Now hit the sack tonight, as early as possible. You'll need your strength tomorrow, and your wits, so don't stay up all night telling dirty jokes. Tomorrow morning, at six A.M. sharp, you will have your chance to be all that you can be, as you make your proactive assault on the High Course. God, I envy you. Good luck."

* 16 *

Ben leaned against a tree trunk, strips of thin neon webbing wrapped every which way around his pelvis and backside.

"How do I look?" Ben asked.

"Like a chic mountain climber," Christina answered.

"Very macho. But I think you got the Swiss seat wrong."

The Swiss seat was the name given to the particular manner in which the webbing was wound around a belayer so he could be linked relatively painlessly to the belay line. "I wouldn't be surprised," Ben said. "It's very complicated."

"True," Christina replied. "And Crichton only went over it about fifteen times. Here, let me." She bent down in front of Ben and started retying his seat.

"Thanks. By the way, you look sharp in those cutoffs. But I know at least one gentleman who will be crushed that you're not wearing skintight spandex."

"I wonder who that would be," Christina muttered. "So what do you think of DARE so far?"

"Well, as macho outdoor get-in-touch-with-yourself retreats go, I suppose it's better than a bunch of naked men beating drums in the forest."

She relooped the main cord around Ben's waist. "There, you're fixed."

"And just in time." Ben pointed at Crichton, who was crossing the top of the hill with some belaying equipment. He and Chuck were engaged in a serious-looking conversation. Probably another violation of the no-work-weekend rule, Ben thought.

"All right, DARErs," Crichton said, stepping into their midst, "assemble front and center."

Doug, Herb, and Candice disassembled their conversational huddle and looked raptly his way. Shelly, predictably enough, had been given lunch duty. She was spreading mayonnaise on sandwich bread, but when Crichton gave out the call to arms, she wrapped everything up and joined the rest of the group.

"It's time to confront the High Course," Crichton announced. "Follow me." Ben, Christina, and the rest of the Apollo legal crew followed Crichton across the top of the hill and down toward a nearby valley surrounded by tall oak trees.

"Boy, just look at him," Herb whispered to Ben. "He says march and just assumes everyone will march. Doesn't even look behind to see if we're following. How arrogant."

"Still stinging from last night, Herb?"

"I don't like my career being threatened."

Ben nodded. He saw Rob marching alongside. "Have you ever done this before?" Ben asked.

"Oh, sure," Rob replied.

"And?"

"Not to worry. Piece of cake. You'll do fine. Unless, of course, you have a problem with heights."

"A problem with heights?" Ben whispered. "I'm *terrified* of heights. I can't ride an escalator without getting sick. I had a panic attack once in a stairwell!"

"In that case, I predict you're in big trouble."

They descended into the valley. The trees formed an almost perfect circle, closing off the central meadow. Ben saw various wires and poles stretching between trees about sixty feet up in the air, and something that looked like a gigantic ladder hanging almost to the ground.

"Surely we're not going up where all those wires and other gizmos are?" Ben asked nervously.

Rob smiled, but didn't answer.

"This is the High Course," Crichton announced, for the benefit of those who hadn't managed to figure it out for themselves. "The general principles of belaying should be clear to you from yesterday's exercises. Remember, you must overcome that me-against-them mentality. Teamwork is critical. One partner, the captain, remains on the ground, holding tight to your belay line. The line reaches up to the high wire, cycles through the wheel lock for support, then descends to the carabiner on your Swiss seat. It's like a gigantic pulley system. As long as you're harnessed to the line, and your captain doesn't let go, you're perfectly safe, whether you're sixty feet in the air or six hundred feet in the air."

"But what if you're afraid of heights?" Ben asked quietly.

"Get over it." Crichton walked to the large wood-and-wire ladder and pointed like a game show model. "This is the giant's ladder. It is the initial means of assault. Standing on this tree stump, you grab the bottom rung of the ladder." Crichton demonstrated, looping his hands around the four-by-four wooden plank he called the bottom rung. Then, leaping into the air, he swung his legs around the plank and pulled himself on top. Balancing himself by one of the two wires connecting the planks, he pulled himself upright. "Easy, isn't it? And all you have to do is repeat that nine more times, and you'll be sixty feet in the air."

"Nine more times?" Ben felt a gnawing sensation in the pit of his stomach. "I don't think I could do that once."

"If you simply can't pull yourself up by your arms," Crichton said, narrating as he climbed, "you can brace one foot against the connecting bolts on the wires. But that's strictly for wimps and over-seventies."

Ben grimaced. "Seventy months, I hope he means."

Christina smiled. "I don't think so."

"I'm never gonna make it up that thing."

"I'm inclined to agree. By the way, Ben, have I mentioned recently what a brilliant idea this new job was?"

"Cheap, Christina. Very cheap."

At the top of the giant's ladder, Crichton pulled himself upright between two taut wires and sidestepped to a nearby tree. Crawling sideways down the tree, he lowered himself onto a small wooden ledge. "From here you can attack the Burma bridge. Three ropes stretched between two trees—the simplest bridge known to man—yet perfectly effective. If you have the strength to make the crossing. Remember, push out with your arms against the two higher ropes, and step toe-to-toe on the low rope."

"I'll remember," Ben murmured. "I'll remember."

"After you cross the Burma bridge, the next step is to walk across a telephone pole connecting one tree to another. A simple balancing trick. If it were on the ground, it would be easy. Sixty feet in the air, less so." He smiled at his own witticism.

"The final step is the easiest of all—two wires, one high, one low. Hold one with your hands, keep your feet on the other. Sidestep from tree to tree. If you don't lose your balance, you'll do fine. If you do lose your balance, well, we'll get to see if your captain is paying attention."

"What a humorist. Regular Mark Twain." Ben looked grimly at Christina. "I think I'm sick already."

"Finally," Crichton announced, "you descend on the zip line, a pulley and wire slingshot, if you will. Detach your carabiner from the support wire and attach it to the zip line. Crawl onto the seat and push. You'll be on the ground in a heartbeat. Better than a roller coaster."

"Assuming your heart doesn't stop," Ben said.

Christina jabbed him in the side.

"All right, then. Pair off into teams of two and let's begin your assault. I'll take volunteers."

"Well, Ben," Christina said, "wanna be my proactive partner?"

"Sorry, no. I'm taking Rob."

"You like him better than me?"

"No, but he's a hell of a lot stronger, and that's the principal quality I'm looking for in the person who's going to be holding onto the end of my belay line."

Four hours later, most of the Apollo legal staff had confronted the High Course. Christina had finished in a fearless forty minutes, putting her in third place for speed, behind Rob and Chuck. Some were graceful;

some were graceless. Some had struggled, strained, wobbled, and weaved. But all of them had finished.

Except Ben. He hadn't even started.

"C'mon Kincaid," Crichton growled. He hunched over Ben's shoulder and whispered insistently into his ear. "Look, kid, you know you're my favorite, but I can't go on making excuses for you. Candice is almost finished, and she's the last one. You're going to have to try to get through this thing."

"Couldn't I just not—and say I did?"

"No way, Kincaid. I can't make exceptions. Especially not for my favorites. It wouldn't look right."

"What if we build another high course, just like this one, only connected to the ground?"

"I'm afraid not. C'mon—that legal assistant of yours finished in nothing flat."

"Christina can do a lot of things I can't, including all things that take place sixty feet off the ground."

"Damn it, Kincaid, you're being a pussy!"

"Sticks and stones . . ."

"There are no wimps on the Apollo legal team."

"Probably because they've all been killed off by the High Course."

"Look, Kincaid, I'm going up again. You can follow right behind me. I'll be with you the whole time, just a few steps ahead. Okay?"

Before Ben could reply, a bloodcurdling scream pierced through the air.

Ben turned toward the sound. "Whaa—?"

"It's Candice," someone yelled. The group ran en masse toward the point of descent from the High Course.

By the time they arrived, Candice was unstrapping herself from the zip line.

"What happened?" Ben asked. "We heard you scream."

"It was exhilarating," Candice said. "Shooting down the zip line, I mean. The wind whipping through your hair, bracing your face." She shimmied from head to toe. "What a turn-on."

"Probably the closest you've come to orgasm in months," Herb commented, just loud enough that everyone could hear.

"Probably closer than you've come in your entire life," Candice retorted, "unless you count the nights you've spent alone."

Ben was content to stay and enjoy the repartee, but unfortunately Crichton's hands clamped down on his shoulders. "It's time, Kincaid."

"No last-minute reprieve from the governor?"

Crichton shook his head no.

Rob fell in behind them and they returned to the entry stump for the giant's ladder.

"Just keep your eyes on me, Kincaid. Don't look down at the ground. Watch me."

"Got it." Ben watched as Crichton leapt onto the first rung of the giant's ladder, this time without even standing on the stump. Less than five minutes later, Crichton was standing between the two wires at the top.

"Now it's your turn, Kincaid."

"Swell." Ben stood on the stump and closed his eyes. "Are you holding tight to that line, Rob?"

"Of course I am."

"Just checking." Ben threw his arms back and jumped up as high as he could. Too high. His arms wrapped around the bottom rung, and a second after, his chin banged down on it, but hard.

"Oww!"

"Don't let go," Crichton shouted down. "Never turn back. Never lose ground."

Right. Twisting with all his strength, Ben brought himself right side up. Slowly, he stood upright on the narrow beam. To his dismay, he found it wasn't solid footing at all. The entire ladder swayed back and forth in the wind.

"Don't stop," Crichton shouted. "Don't lose your momentum. And don't look down."

Cut me some slack, Ben thought. I'm only six feet in the air. He opened his eyes and looked down.

Big mistake. The bottom seemed to drop out of his stomach. Worse, he looked up at Crichton and saw how far he had yet to go. He felt himself dizzying. What a great time to be sick, he thought. When your entire office is watching and you're dangling in the middle of the air.

"I'm going to start on the Burma bridge," Crichton yelled. "Keep going."

Thanks, I will. Ben threw his arms up . . . and missed the next rung entirely. He clutched the side wire desperately, swinging the entire ladder back and forth like a pendulum. He could feel the tug of the belay line at his back; Rob was pulling the rope super-taut, trying to keep him from falling. Thanks for the assist, pal.

The hell with it. Let Crichton call him a wimp—he was cheating. Ben placed his foot on the connecting bolt on the wire closest to him and boosted himself up. From that point, he was able to grab the next rung.

"Holy—!"

What was that? Ben became aware of a great commotion on the ground; everyone was staring at the Burma bridge and pointing. Ben peered up into the sun. Shielding his eyes with his hand, he saw a silhouetted Crichton waving his arms, flailing in midair about forty feet above him and four or five feet to one side.

Ben squinted. Crichton appeared to have lost his balance and slipped off the wooden ledge that led to the Burma bridge. Crichton tried to grab the tree, but it was out of his reach. Fortunately, this was the difference between belayers and tightrope walkers; his belay line held him tight. So what was everyone screaming about?

Ben traced Crichton's belay line from his carabiner through the wheel lock and back down toward—*My God!* That's what everyone was screaming about. There was a split in Crichton's belay line. The sun glinted off a ragged tear. It looked as if it would rip clean through at any moment. And when it did, Crichton would be severed from his belay captain and all means of support.

Crichton had seen the tear, too. He was desperately trying to swing himself back to the tree, but making no progress. He was too far away. He was dangling in the air, helpless. And fully aware that he was about to plunge sixty feet to the hard earth.

Ben saw the rope split even further. He knew that in a matter of seconds it would be too late; Crichton's weight was tearing the line apart. If someone didn't secure his line fast, Crichton was a dead man.

Ben tensed his muscles, threw his arms back, and leaped off the giant's ladder. He flew through open space, arms extended, and grabbed Crichton's belay line just above the tear. A second later, the rope ripped in two. Once severed, the rope ricocheted upward like a rock from a slingshot. Ben held tight, and the rope rocketed him into the sky.

Ben shot toward the apex of the belay pulley. The rope burned in his hands. It hurt like hell, but he held fast. *Come on, Rob!*

Suddenly, he felt a wrenching jerk on his back. Rob had tightened Ben's belay line to keep him from flying over the top, and since Ben was holding tight to Crichton's line, that stopped Crichton's descent before he splatted into the dirt.

Ben gritted his teeth and clenched the rope tightly. The strain on his arms was incredible; Crichton felt as though he weighed a thousand pounds. Now that Ben had a moment to think about what he was doing, a rush of panic spread through his body. His pulse was out of control; he was dripping with sweat. He was dangling in the air, for God's sake! With nothing solid under his feet whatsoever. Sixty feet off the—

Ben slowly opened his eyes, one eye at a time. Rob

was shouting at him, telling him to hold tight while he lowered them both to the ground. Thanks, Rob—as if I was considering just letting go. Ben only hoped he could delay being sick until his feet were planted on terra firma once again.

Earthward, he saw Rob fighting with all his strength to hold onto the line. Chuck and Christina were clutching Rob's feet, anchoring him to the ground. Ben's eyes followed the line burning in his hands, through the wheel lock, then down to Crichton, who was hovering just above the ground.

Another three feet and he would have been dead.

PART TWO

* *

Pennies and Butterflies

* 17 *

The man tossed his van keys on the dresser beside the room key. It was one of those modern hotel keys, a flat card with punched holes like Swiss cheese. All the best places used them now. He hated them; he could never make them work without cramming them into the door scanner twenty or thirty times. Why did the world have to change? Why were people always looking for something better, tossing away the old, embracing the new? Why couldn't everything remain simple, tidy, constant?

He saw the girl's reflection in the mirror over the dresser. She was in the bathroom. The water in the tub was running, and she was sliding out of her skintight fluorescent green pants. It must be winter, he mused; the snake was shedding her skin.

The girl pulled off her halter top and removed a blue butterfly clip from her hair. She saw him watching her. "What are you doing?"

He smiled—a brilliant, friendly smile. "Watching you."

"Oh yeah?" She crossed her arms over her breasts in mock modesty. "What do you think?"

"I think you're beautiful." He walked slowly into the bathroom. His black boots clickety-clacked against the tile floor. "You're making me hard."

"Hey now, don't start getting all excited. You have to wait."

His smile faded, just a touch. "I'm not very good at waiting. I want what I want—now."

109

"Look, Romeo, you promised I could have a bath."

"And you shall," he said, spreading his arms wide. "You may bathe all night. You may bathe forever."

"There you go again." Giggling, she dropped her underclothes and jumped into the steamy tub. "What are you, some kind of poet?"

"I like to think so."

"Wow. Way cool." She stretched out in the tub. "I never had a poet before. Most of my johns are suit-and-tie types. You know, bankers, accountants, architects, lawyers."

The man's head jerked. "You've had . . . lawyers?"

"Oh, man. Like you wouldn't believe. What a nightmare." She laid a hot washcloth across her forehead. "Believe me, everything people say about lawyers is true, only more so. But never mind—I don't want to talk about it. I don't even want to think about it."

"Have you . . . talked to anyone else about it?"

"Why do you ask?"

"Oh, no reason. It's just that—sometimes it helps to talk about what troubles you."

"Forget it, Romeo. You aren't paying me that much."

"How much would I . . ."

"Would you forget it already? Look, why don't you get in here with me?" She winked at him, fluttering her long false eyelashes. "It's a big tub."

The man thought for a moment. "Perhaps I will. Let me get something first." He walked out of the bathroom.

While he was out, she took a bar of soap from the dish and began lathering herself. "So what is it you do, anyhow? I figure it must be important, whatever it is. That van you drive looks customized, and I bet it wouldn't be cheap even without the extras. Then there's that wad of cash you flash around, and what you offered to pay me for a couple of hours' work—way over market value, I must admit. Not to mention the way you dress, the way you look. No, I figure you've got to be someone at the top, like maybe a car salesman or a politician. Something like that."

She heard him reenter the bathroom. Clickety-clack, clickety-clack. "So what is it? What do you do—"

Her sentence ended abruptly as his hands clutched her throat. He pulled the black garbage bag over her head, plunging her into darkness. He tied the silken cord around her neck, fastening the bag to her head and constricting her windpipe. She sputtered and gasped, desperately trying to catch her breath, finding none.

She began to struggle. She flailed in the tub, splashing water onto the tile floor. She reached back and grabbed at his arms. Raising himself up, he pressed down on her shoulders, pushing her head, bag and all, down under the water. She tried to fight back, but it was impossible. She couldn't get a grip on anything. She just kept slipping and sliding, down, down, down, beneath the water.

He had exactly what he wanted, what he needed. She was powerless, totally subject to his control. He pulled the ends of the cord, drawing it even tighter around her throat, causing blood to trickle out. *Sweet Jesus!*—she made him feel so good! He pulled even tighter, savoring the sweet constriction in his groin.

And then—it was over, in one final magnificent climax. He felt a sudden surge, then release. He dropped the silken cord; her body slid lifelessly into the water. The man fell back against the bathroom counter, utterly and deliciously drained.

He picked up her butterfly clip. A dainty thing; it would make a lovely souvenir.

After he had rested, after the afterglow faded and his strength returned, he began picking up the clothes she had carelessly thrown on the floor. He hated people who made a mess.

* 18 *

Mike threw his dirty overcoat onto one of Ben's over-stuffed office chairs. "Christ, Ben, you're turning into a goddamn homicide magnet!"

"Attempted homicide," Ben corrected. "Crichton survived the attempt."

"Just barely."

"Barely means his heart is beating. Ergo, no homicide."

"Only because you were in the right place at the right time and decided to play Superman off the giant's ladder. By the way, I'm impressed. What's next for you, bungee jumping?"

Ben waved his bandaged hands in the air. The rope burns on his hands were deep and slow to heal. "I just did the first thing that occurred to me. I didn't have time to think about it."

"Don't soft soap me, Ben. I think it was a damn gutsy move for a guy who used to get woozy sitting in his high chair."

"Who told you that?"

"My ex. Your sister. So don't bother denying it."

"Yeah, well, those high chairs are damn high when you're only two feet tall." He closed the thick evidence treatise he'd been reading to prepare for the discovery motion he was arguing that afternoon. "So how's the murder investigation coming?"

"Which one? The teenagers? Or Howard Hamel?"

"Let's start with the teenagers. I saw in the paper that the killer claimed another victim."

"Right. His fourth." Mike slammed his fist into his hand. "Goddamn it, I'd like to catch that bastard. Four victims now, and we're still virtually clueless."

"There must be some leads. Some pattern."

"Other than the obvious—all his victims are teenage girls—no. Or at least, none that we've detected."

"What about the mutilation?"

"Repeated on this victim as well. No head, no hands."

"I don't want to hear about it."

"I don't blame you."

"What've you got on the Hamel murder?"

"What've *I* got? You're the one who's supposed to be cracking that case wide open. What've *you* got?"

"Well, I think I flushed out the killer. From sixty feet in the air."

"Quite possible." Mike paced agitatedly across Ben's office. "The lab finished its microscopic analysis of Crichton's belay line. No doubt about it—it was cut. We searched the area, as you know, and searched everyone on the site. We didn't find anything. And unfortunately, you didn't see who did it."

"No, but I've got an office building full of suspects. Man, you wouldn't believe this Apollo crew. What a collection of back-stabbing, butt-licking—"

"Hey, don't complain to me. You're the one who thought this job would solve all your problems."

"I did not—oh, what's the use? Has Koregai finished his autopsy report on Hamel?"

Mike tossed himself into a chair and plopped his muddy boots on Ben's desk. "He says Hamel was strangled to death. Hamel was wearing a high-collar shirt, you'll recall—that's why you didn't see any marks on him. While the killer was relocating the body, Hamel cut his hand on something—that's the source of the blood in your car. The cut must've occurred fairly soon after the murder—otherwise there wouldn't have been so much bleeding."

"Did your men turn up any physical evidence?"

"Nothing that appears useful. We not only searched the Apollo building, we searched the alley behind your boardinghouse and scoured the entire neighborhood. And Jesus, what a neighborhood you live in. I could've found more people willing to talk to cops at the penitentiary. We didn't learn a damn thing."

"I saw Hamel's office roped off with yellow crime scene tape. Find anything there?"

"Nothing that held any significance to me. You're welcome to take a look yourself."

"Thanks, I will. What about Hamel's house?"

"The widow's been giving us some trouble there. Normally I'd be able to get a warrant in a heartbeat, but it turns out Judge Carter is a personal friend of the family and is making a lot of noise about us not intruding on her grief with an unnecessary search. He refused to sign the warrant and put out the word that he'd consider it a personal affront if any other judge did. And he is Chief Judge this term."

"And to think people blame lawyers for the slow wheels of justice."

"Yeah. And it's only true about ninety percent of the time. Don't worry, we'll get the warrant eventually."

"Great. Call me as soon as you do. I'd like to help."

"I think I can arrange that. Especially since Chief Blackwell has practically deputized you."

"Yeah, with a threat of life imprisonment. You think he's serious about hauling me in at the end of the week?"

"I'm afraid so. Deadly serious."

"Swell. My time is running out. So call me as soon as you get the warrant."

"Will do, kemo sabe. I'll be in touch. And Ben?"

"Yeah?"

"I picked up a brochure you might be interested in. Have a nice day."

Ben glanced at the brochure Mike had placed under a paperweight on his desk: SAM AND JERRY'S FLYING CIRCUS—SKYDIVING ON THE CHEAP.

* 19 *

Ben had hoped to spend the remaining hour until his hearing preparing. Unfortunately, only seconds after Mike left, Crichton sailed in.

"Mr. Crichton!" Ben said, jumping out of his chair. "I didn't expect to see you in the office today. How are you feeling?"

Crichton waved the attention away. "Don't make a fuss, Kincaid. I'm fine. The ER docs told me to take it easy for a few days. I was just shaken up, that's all."

"If I had fallen fifty feet only to be jerked back a few seconds before impact, I'd be more than just shaken up."

"Well, I've had close shaves before. I've known all along I wasn't going to live forever." He glanced back at the doorway. "Who was that man in the trenchcoat I saw leaving your office?"

"Oh, that was my brother-in-law, Mike," Ben hedged. "Er, ex-brother-in-law. He's a friend."

"He's the cop."

"Well, yes."

"Came to talk to you about Howard's murder."

"Right."

Crichton sat down in one of Ben's chairs and pressed

a finger to his lips. "Ben . . . I think your interest in Howard's unfortunate demise is admirable. I really do. But I'm concerned that it might distract you from your duties here at the office."

"I've been timely with all my assignments, Mr. Crichton."

"I need more than just timely compliance from you, Ben. I need your total concentration. An absolute, twenty-four-hour devotion to your client." His eyebrows knitted. "You know, I have a family, and I love them dearly, but my job comes first and they know it. They understand. I mean no disrespect to Howard's memory. But the Apollo Consortium is at a critical juncture now—the proposed acquisition of ConSteel, the Ameritech venture, and a dozen other equally important deals. We can't afford the distraction—or the negative publicity—of a damaging piece of litigation. I'm counting on you to nip the Nelson case in the bud."

"I'm doing everything I can, Mr. Crichton. As I told you, the Nelsons' testimony was convincing and consistent. The average Oklahoma jury will be sympathetic to them. If we're going to beat them, we're going to have to do it on a legal issue. Before trial."

"Then find me a legal issue, Kincaid."

"I'm working on it, sir, but discovery is still ongoing. Tomorrow, Abernathy, the Nelsons' attorney, is deposing one of our design team vice presidents. After that, if all goes well, I may know enough to put together a convincing summary judgment brief."

"See that you do."

"Even if I write the best brief in the world, though, there's no guarantee Judge Roemer will grant it."

Crichton gazed over his strategically placed hands. All Ben could see were his eyes burning across the room. "Ben, is it my imagination, or are you making excuses for your failure before the motion has even been filed?"

"Not at all, sir. But as you know, there are no guarantees in the world of litigation. Sometimes people assume that if their cause is just, that automatically means they will be successful in the courtroom. Of course, that isn't always the case."

Ben could feel Crichton's eyes burrowing into his forehead. "See that it *is* the case in this lawsuit, Kincaid. Understand?"

Ben shifted uncomfortably. "I understand."

"Good." Crichton removed his hands. "So tell me about this hearing this afternoon."

"Well, as you know, we produced an enormous quantity of documents to Abernathy last week."

Crichton grinned. "I know. We threw in stuff from twenty years back that didn't even relate to the XKL-1. I expected that small-time practitioner to be buried for months."

Without commenting on Crichton's tactics, Ben continued. "He hired emergency support staff from a temporary agency and completed the job in a few days. He's figured out our internal numbering system, and by tracking the numbers, he's deduced that ten pages are missing. He filed a motion to compel production of the missing pages, and asked the court for an emergency hearing before the documents are lost or destroyed."

"This entire hearing is about a lousy ten pages? Good grief, we must've given him a hundred thousand pages!"

"True. And now he wants the other ten."

"What makes him think those ten are so important?"

Ben ran his fingers across his desk. "Principally, the fact that they are missing, I would imagine. I've talked to Imogine, the supervisor in Document Retention, but she says she doesn't know where the documents are or what information they contained." He chose his words carefully. "I . . . don't suppose you do, by any chance?"

To Ben's surprise, Crichton leaned across his desk and smiled. "As a matter of fact, I do. I remember removing ten pages myself. They didn't have anything to do with the XKL-1. They contained a design for a new suspension system—frankly, one that would remedy some unrelated problems we'd experienced. It would have no bearing on the alleged leaf spring defect the Nelsons are complaining about. I didn't mean to create any problems—we just considered the new design top secret. Do we have to produce that?"

Ben thought for a moment. "Well, there is a legal doctrine protecting proprietary information. Companies are not required to disclose trade secrets, especially where, as here, they have no relevance to the lawsuit."

"Makes sense to me."

"There's also a rule excluding evidence of subsequent repairs. The theory is that, if evidence of repairs made after an incident were admissible at trial, no one would ever make repairs, for fear that the fact of the repair would make it appear at trial that they acknowledged the fault. As a result, more people would be harmed. So the courts have made a policy decision to exclude evidence of subsequent repairs."

"That's great!" He walked around the desk and slapped Ben on the back. "That sounds like exactly what we need. By God, I knew you were going to be a winner, Kincaid. What a proactive player. I wish I had ten more just like you."

"Thank you, sir. Oh, I'll have to see the missing documents, of course."

Crichton stiffened. "Why? I already told you what they say."

"I know. But if I'm going to make representations to the court about their contents—"

"Ben, I don't have them anymore."

"Who does?"

"I'm not sure. I think I gave them to Imogene."

"Imogene says she doesn't have them."

"Okay, I'll instigate a search."

"Sir, I don't have time for a search. The hearing starts in less than an hour."

"Just tell the judge you can't show them around because they contain trade secrets. I'm sure he'll understand."

Ben frowned. "Either that or he'll cite me for contempt."

"You'll handle it. You'll be great." Crichton started for the door, but stopped just before he passed through the threshold. "By the way, Kincaid . . ." He cleared his throat, then stared at the floor.

Ben watched this curious spectacle. Crichton, the boss of every room he entered, suddenly seemed . . . uncomfortable.

"What I'm trying to say is . . . well, I probably got out of line . . . calling you a pussy and all that. What you did on the giant's ladder, when you saved my butt from splatting on the dirt . . . that was amazing. Most men would've been too scared by half to try something like that. Hell, I'm not even sure I could have brought it off."

"Really, Mr. Crichton, it was no big deal."

"The hell it wasn't. And to think you did that just minutes after I was riding your ass." He shuffled his feet some more. "What I'm trying to say is I think I owe you an apology."

"That's not necessary."

"No. But I wanted to do it anyway. Now get in that courtroom and give 'em hell, tiger." And with that, Crichton faded down the hallway.

* 20 *

Ben and Rob sat at one of two counsel tables in Judge Roemer's courtroom and waited. Roemer's courtroom was one of the smaller ones tucked away on the seventh floor of the state courthouse at Fifth and Denver.

Ben checked the clock on the wall. "The judge is already fifteen minutes late. I hate waiting around like this, but it seems to happen every time."

"Is this sort of like being fashionably late to a party?" Rob asked.

"Well, this is more a power-of-the-judge pose. You know: you have to be on time; I don't."

"That must be irritating."

"True. On the other hand, state judges don't have clerks, much less magistrates. They have to do everything themselves. Roemer's probably back in chambers reading our brief."

Ben apparently was not the only person in the courtroom getting restless. Abernathy lumbered over and plopped another business card in front of Ben. "Wanted to make sure you gentlemen had my new card. It's got my 1-800 number."

"You have a 1-800 number? For your law practice?"

"Sure. Doesn't everyone?" He laughed. "It's the wave of the future, Ben. Mass marketing. Media referrals."

"So if I want to call you up and talk about the pending motions or something, I can just use this number?"

"Well ... er, no ... This is really for prospective clients ..."

"Ah."

"Have you seen my new commercial? It's running during reruns of *Laverne and Shirley* on Channel Six."

Ben glanced at Rob. "You know, I don't keep up with *Laverne and Shirley* like I used to. . . ."

"It's a great spot." Abernathy shifted his considerable weight into action, reenacting the commercial. "It starts with the camera tightly focused on me."

"What a surprise."

"Then the camera pulls back, and you see I'm wearing a black leather jacket and straddling a great big Harley. I lean into the camera lens and say, 'If a doctor makes a mistake, I believe he should be held accountable. If you're hurt on the job, I believe your boss should be accountable.' Then I rev up the Harley and say, 'And if you're injured by some pig on the highway, I believe he should be held accountable.' By this time, the music is swelling. Really exciting stuff—we looped it from *Top Gun*. It's very moving."

"No doubt."

"And I finish off with, 'Don't give up your claim prematurely. Don't accept a nuisance settlement from someone who owes you more. You need a hot rod in your corner. Call George Abernathy.' And then the 1-800 number flashes. It's beautiful. The first time I saw it, I got choked up."

"Better than *Casablanca*," Rob said.

"Oh, a hundred times over," Abernathy replied. "If you ever go back into private practice, you should try TV, Ben."

"I'll pass. Thanks."

"Hmmph. You guys who act like you're too classy to advertise are going to be left behind in the dust."

"Maybe so," Ben said, "but at least I won't be straddling a great big Harley, begging people to sue their friends and neighbors."

"Since you apparently loathe litigation so much, we could avoid this whole unpleasant hearing if you'd sit down and talk some settlement."

"Thanks, but no thanks, Abernathy. I'm not convinced you even have a case."

Judge Roemer chose that moment to enter the courtroom. Roemer was one of the more laid-back state judges; in fact, Ben reflected, some might call him comatose. He never took an active role, he let the lawyers do whatever they wanted, and he hated to make a decision. "Please be seated," he mumbled into the microphone.

He glanced at the papers on the bench, frowned, and then said, "I understand we have a discovery dispute today." His voice was thin and reedy. "I hate discovery disputes. Can't you boys work this out on your own?"

Abernathy waddled toward the podium and went into his *gosh*, *shucks* routine. "Darn it all, Judge, I've talked to Mr. Kincaid about this, but he refuses to produce those ten pieces of paper."

Roemer addressed Ben. "Is this true?"

"Yes, your honor. We're claiming privilege as to those documents because they contain proprietary information. Furthermore, they would not be admissible at trial as they contain evidence of subsequent remedial repairs."

"Any reply, Mr. Abernathy?"

Ben watched as Abernathy struggled for words. Ben expected that he would request the judge to examine the documents *in camera*, or would offer a confidentiality order restricting the dissemination of the trade secrets, or would argue that ultimate inadmissibility should not preclude production during discovery. But Abernathy did none of that. He just stood there, fumbling and foomferalling, obviously unprepared.

Beads of sweat poured down from Abernathy's hairline. "Well, gosh, your honor. I haven't even seen these documents. How can I know what's in them?"

Roemer's bored impatience was evident. "You've just heard an officer of the court make a representation as to their contents. Do you have any reason to dispute it?"

"Well, no, I'm sure Mr. Kincaid is an honest young man—"

"And you do agree that evidence of subsequent remedial repairs is inadmissible, don't you?"

Abernathy blinked, then wiped the sweat from his forehead. "Now, I don't see why that should be. If a company repairs something, that's a darn clear indication that there was something wrong with it in the first place."

"Mr. Abernathy has, of course, just pinpointed the entire reason for this evidentiary doctrine," Ben interjected. "If such evidence was admissible, companies would be disinclined to make repairs, even where lives are at stake."

"Anything further?" Roemer asked Abernathy, tapping a pencil.

Abernathy was steadying himself against the podium. "Gosh, your honor, I'm not sure what to say. This is a new one to me."

Ben's eyes crinkled. This was first year law school stuff. Abernathy apparently was so used to settling cases quickly—taking the money and running—that he never had to do any real legal work.

"Can you cite any cases in support of your position," Roemer asked, "assuming you have one?"

"Uh . . . Judge, I'm not really prepared to do that at the moment."

"Then I have no choice but to deny your motion." Typical Roemer—he didn't want to take any longer than necessary. And he didn't want to order anyone to do anything if he could avoid it. "In the future, Mr. Abernathy, don't waste this court's time if you can't defend your motions any better than this." He reached for the gavel. "This hearing is concluded."

Everyone rose as Roemer drifted out of the courtroom.

"All right!" Rob said, punching Ben on the shoulder. "You killed him! Crichton's going to be pumped."

"I suppose." Ben watched Abernathy lumber out of the courtroom. "I didn't win on the merits, though. I won because the Nelsons hired a walking *TV Guide* ad instead of a lawyer."

"What's the difference? Man, you've been on this case less than a week, and you've already turned it completely around. Crichton was right—you're the greatest!"

Ben smiled pleasantly, but said nothing.

"C'mon," Rob said enthusiastically. "Let me buy you a chocolate milk. You must be feeling great."

Ben followed Rob out of the courtroom, wishing Rob were right. But he wasn't. He wasn't right at all.

* 21 *

Sergeant Tomlinson sauntered down Eleventh Street, his hands shoved in his tight pants, his tattered jeans jacket hanging open. If there was anything he knew from the days when he walked this beat regularly, it was how to blend in. He was like a chameleon; he could walk the walk and talk the talk. He could come off as sleazy as anyone.

It had taken him far too long to get out here and follow up on the lead Koregai had provided. After the fourth corpse was discovered, all hell broke loose. Everyone on the force was in demand, even more so than before, even people with lowly switchboard duty. All efforts had been intensified; he'd even heard a rumor that Chief Blackwell was riding around in a squad car. Unfortunately, for all their efforts, they appeared to be no closer to figuring out who the victims were, much less the killer.

Now that he finally had a few hours off, Tomlinson planned to do some investigating on his own. He knew he had seen the tattoo on the second victim before—at the Rainbow Boutique, just off Eleventh near Cincinnati. Since he had already linked the body dump site to the Eleventh Street subculture, this connection seemed all the more likely.

The Rainbow Boutique catered to the varied professionals of the district: prostitutes, pimps, drug dealers, and assorted other hoodlums. It was a combination drug store, head shop, and tattoo parlor. Something for everyone.

Tomlinson maneuvered past a group of tattered winos hovering around a shared bottle of stoop booze and entered the boutique. He walked briskly through the shop, heading for a small room in the back. He pushed away the strings of beads hanging in the doorway and stepped inside.

A white-haired man sat behind a table cluttered with tattoo needles. The man was withered and drawn; he couldn't have weighed more than a hundred pounds. Around him, posted on all four walls, were countless multicolored tattoos. Hearts, anchors, cherubs, flags—a lifetime of illustration and design.

Tomlinson examined a series of tattoos on the wall just inside the door. There it was, just as he remembered it—a lovely blue butterfly with a garland of pink flowers around its wings.

The man's eyes darted around the room, then peered up at Tomlinson.

"How's business?" Tomlinson asked.

"Not bad." The man's eyes narrowed. "It'd be better if I could keep the police off my tail."

So much for the chameleon. Tomlinson had to hand it to him—the man was nothing if not quick. "Don't worry. This isn't my beat. I'm here . . . unofficially."

"I'll believe it when you leave."

"Police been giving you a bad time?"

"Constantly."

"I didn't realize tattooing was illegal among consenting adults."

"It isn't." He rubbed his tongue against yellow teeth. "Just disfavored."

"They confiscate your needles?"

"Of course. Want to make sure I'm not spreading diseases, like everyone else on The Stroll."

"I'm sure everyone else gets hassled, too."

"Everyone who can't afford not to."

Tomlinson decided it was best not to ask what he meant. "I've been thinking about getting a tattoo myself. I thought maybe one of these colorful butterfly jobs."

"You some kind of queer?"

"No. Why?"

"I never had no man ask for a butterfly before. It's the ladies that like them."

"Really? Is this a . . . popular design?"

"Some of the street girls like it."

"Anyone recently?"

The man looked at Tomlinson, a suspicious expression on his face. After a brief hesitation, he answered. "Did one not more than three weeks ago for a girl named Suzie. Pretty little Suzie."

"Does Suzie have a last name?"

The man reared back his head and laughed.

Point taken, Tomlinson thought. "Don't you need parental consent to tattoo a minor?"

"Suzie don't have no parents. Not around here, anyway."

Let it drop, Tomlinson told himself. This is not the time. "Is Suzie still working The Stroll?"

The man pondered a moment. "Can't say for sure. Haven't seen her for over two weeks."

"Really." That would tie in nicely with the murder of the second victim. "Do you normally see most of the street girls on a regular basis?"

"I live here, don't I? Sometimes they take off suddenly, though, and we never see them again. Never know why they were here, or why they left. Runaways are like that."

"Yeah." Tomlinson absently glanced over some of the other tattoo designs. "Do you know where she lived?"

"Lived?"

"Lives. Or lived before she blew town." What a stupid slip. Damn, damn, damn.

"No. But Trixie would."

"And who's Trixie?"

"Her best friend. On The Stroll, anyway. They worked together, if you know what I mean. Did a lot of joint jobs. Whenever the opportunity arose."

Great. An honest-to-God lead. "What does Trixie look like?"

"Are you going to get her in some kind of trouble?"

"Absolutely not. I give you my word. I'm trying to help her. She may be in great danger."

The man thought for a long, hard moment. Eventually, the words dripped out of his mouth. "She's young. Fifteen, sixteen, I'd guess. Blonde."

"Aren't they all?"

"She's different. You'll understand when you see her. It hasn't gotten to her yet. She can still smile."

"Got anything more tangible?"

"Look for a scar." He drew a line on his face. "Right across the bridge of her nose."

"Any idea where I could find her?"

The man made a sweeping gesture toward the street.

"On The Stroll. Where else?" His lips turned up slightly. "Look for the trail of pennies."

Pennies? He wanted to ask, but he was afraid he was already pushing his luck. "Thanks. You've been a big help." He dropped a twenty-dollar bill on the table.

"What?" the man said. "No tattoo?"

"Maybe next time." Tomlinson started back through the beads.

"If I find out you've hurt Trixie, or caused her to come to harm, I'll personally come after you. With my needles."

"I'll keep that in mind."

Tomlinson hustled out of the shop. He could barely restrain himself. He was close, closer than he'd ever been before, closer than anyone else working the case. Maybe he could pull this off; maybe he could shove that stupid switchboard down Morelli's throat.

But first he had to find a teenage girl named Trixie. Before the killer did.

* 22 *

"Let me tell you about depositions," Ben told Albert Consetti, Apollo's vice president in charge of transportation design.

"Fine," Consetti replied. "Just make it short."

"Mr. Consetti ... this is an important deposition. Millions of Apollo dollars are on the line."

"Kid, may I be blunt?" Consetti was a short man, balding, with a ruddy complexion. "I don't like lawyers. As far as I'm concerned, lawyers are a blight on mankind, a necessary evil. It's bad enough that I have to waste the better part of a day playing with you lawyers when I could be accomplishing something of importance. Don't compound the injury with a lot of unnecessary chitchat."

"Regardless of how busy you are, Mr. Consetti, the attorney on the other side will ask you tough questions, and a court reporter will take down every word you say in response. It's best to be prepared."

Consetti seemed unperturbed. "Don't knock yourself out, kid. I've been deposed twice before. We get sued all the time."

"Just the same," Ben insisted, "I'd like to review some of the basics. Once the deposition starts, there's not much I can do."

"That's not the way my last attorney handled it. What was his name? Herb something or another, I think. Man, he was constantly butting in, making objections, arguing, shouting rude remarks, getting the other attorney steamed up. He was great."

Ben smiled thinly. That was one of the biggest problems with litigation today—the most disreputable tactics were the ones clients enjoyed most. And lawyers like to please their clients.

"I won't be doing that," Ben said curtly. "If I make an objection, it will just be for the record. You will still be required to answer the question."

An angry tone crept into Consetti's voice. "What about instructing me not to answer? Herb used to do that all the time."

"I won't. Not unless the questions invade the attorney-client privilege or become unduly abusive."

"Are we going to let these chumps walk all over us?"

"No. But neither are we going to obstruct the discovery process with frivolous behavior designed to obtain a cheap tactical advantage. Understand?"

"Sounds like a wimpy approach to me."

"Well, Mr. Consetti, this wimp is going to win this

case, if you don't screw it up during this deposition. Okay?"

Consetti folded his arms unhappily across his chest. "I suppose."

"Excellent. Now let's review your testimony."

When Abernathy entered the deposition conference room, he passed Ben without saying a word and plopped himself into a chair opposite Consetti.

"Can this be?" Rob whispered. "No play-by-play of his latest commercial? I expected him to be using bill-boards and skywriters by now."

"I think he's still stinging from yesterday's defeat," Ben said. "We made him look seriously stupid in the courtroom."

"Don't bother with the royal *we*," Rob said. "It was all you, you old trial hound."

"Shall we begin?" the court reporter asked.

Ben nodded.

Abernathy began with the usual questions about Consetti's educational and occupational background. After spending almost an hour with that, Abernathy plunged into Consetti's work at Apollo—his duties, the members of his staff, the various projects they worked on during the past eleven years. Three hours and two bathroom breaks later, Abernathy had yet to mention the XKL-1 design project.

It was clear to Ben that Abernathy had not adequately prepared, if indeed he had prepared at all. He had no notes, no outline. His terminology was awkward; he had not personally reviewed the documents that had been produced. He couldn't focus; his questions roamed all around the issues without honing in on the critical de-tails.

Finally, about an hour after the lunch break, Abernathy began the line of inquiry that mattered.

"Were you personally involved in the XKL-1 de-sign?"

"No." Thus far, Consetti has been an ideal deposition witness; he just answered the question, without elaboration or explanation.

"You were the head of the department, weren't you?"

"Of course."

"Did you have any idea what your design team was doing?"

"Of course I did." Ben could see Consetti struggling to keep his lips zipped. Unfortunately, Abernathy had successfully baited him into expounding. "I am intimately involved in the day-to-day affairs of everyone who works under me. I believe in hands-on management, and I take full responsibility for the acts of all my employees."

"Indeed? Full responsibility?"

"You got it."

"We'll talk about that later," Abernathy replied. "Did you supervise the design of the XKL-1 suspension system?"

"Yes."

"The XKL-1 was a project of your department, then?"

"Right."

"Who were the principal designers involved?"

"That would be Al Austin and Bernie King."

"And where are they today?"

"Bernie is a vice president out at the Oklahoma City office. I have no idea what happened to Al."

"He's no longer in Apollo's employ?"

"Correct."

"Was he fired?"

"Not by me."

"Who would know where he is?"

Consetti shrugged his shoulders. "Beats me. Might ask Bernie, I suppose."

"Was a study ever made of the performance of the leaf spring under stress?"

Consetti drew himself up and put on his fighting face.

"Mr. Abernathy, every aspect of every design project that passes through the Apollo Consortium is thoroughly tested, retested, and tested again for safety. That's our motto, you know. *An Apollo product is as safe as a mother's hug.*"

"Very catchy."

"We were in total compliance with every applicable federal regulation."

"I'm sure. But I specifically asked whether you tested the leaf spring. Did you?"

Ben shot Consetti a pointed look. Don't prick this guy's curiosity by being evasive. Just answer the question.

"Yes, we did."

"Are there any documents reflecting or memorializing the testing that was performed?"

"I'm sure there are."

"Where would those documents be?"

Consetti glanced at Ben. "I produced all my files to counsel."

"They were produced to you last week," Ben added.

"Right," Abernathy said. "Along with approximately a hundred thousand other documents. It's just possible I overlooked those." He picked up a pencil and began fidgeting with it. "Do you recall whether you or anyone else at Apollo considered an alternate design that would strengthen the axle-to leaf spring-to frame connections?"

"I'm not sure what you mean."

"I mean did you consider design alternatives that would prevent the leaf spring from crumbling when subjected to sudden shocks?"

"I never said the leaf spring would crumble when subjected to sudden shocks."

"Well, it sure as hell did when my clients' son was riding that flatbed!"

"Objection," Ben said. "Move to strike."

"I'm tired of your client dillydallying with me, Kincaid."

"If you have another question," Ben replied calmly, "ask it. Otherwise, we're ready to leave."

Abernathy turned back toward Consetti and growled. "Answer my question."

"What question was that?"

"About suspension system design alternatives."

"No, I do not specifically recall any such study."

"Fine. Thank you for your courtesy." Abernathy stretched his arms and cracked his knuckles.

"Would this be a suitable time to take a break?" Ben asked.

"No!" Abernathy barked. "I have a few more questions for your witness. If he'll deign to answer them." He hunched down over the table. "Have you ever been convicted of a felony?"

Consetti's face was the picture of outrage. "How dare you ask me such an offensive question!"

"Just answer."

"I refuse."

"Pal, you have no choice."

Consetti turned toward Ben. "Do I have to answer that question?"

Ben nodded. "I'm afraid so."

Consetti glared back at him. Obviously, he wanted an attorney who would scream and shout, not one who would instruct him to obey the law. "No. I've never been convicted of a felony."

"Have you ever been arrested on a felony charge?"

"Of course not."

"Really?" Abernathy reached into his briefcase and withdrew a thin manila folder. "What about the time you were picked up on the Broken Arrow Expressway on a DUI after you crossed lanes and smashed into a car going in the opposite direction?"

Consetti's eyes flared. "This is outrageous!"

"Save the righteous indignation for the jury," Abernathy said. "Just answer the question."

"I'm going to object," Ben interjected. "I fail to see any relevance of this question to the subject matter at hand."

"You don't see any relevance in learning that the XKL-1 was designed by a drunk!" Abernathy yelled.

"Objection!" Ben repeated. "Move to strike."

"I think the people of America would like to know if every time they enter a motor vehicle with an Apollo component they're putting their lives in danger!"

"I renew my objection, counsel. This is grossly improper."

"Not as improper as letting teenage boys die because you're too cheap to change your design!"

"I've had enough!" Consetti shouted. He pushed himself out of his chair. "I don't have to sit here and listen to this. I'm leaving."

Ben grabbed Consetti's shoulder and shoved him back down in his chair. That was exactly what Abernathy wanted, of course; Consetti was playing into his hands. Abernathy had already asked all the questions he could think of—and he had come up with nothing. But if he could create a big scene and cause the witness to walk out before the deposition was officially terminated, Abernathy would have an excuse to recall Consetti later when he'd done more work and had more questions.

"Last chance, Abernathy," Ben said. "If you have any more legitimate questions, ask 'em. Otherwise, we walk."

Abernathy shuffled through his file, obviously disappointed that Ben had prevented his ploy from paying off. "You were arrested for DUI, were you not?"

"I was not. I was detained. I was never charged."

"Ah. Now that is an elegant distinction. I commend you on your cleverness. You were taken to police headquarters, Eastern Division, were you not?"

"That's true," he replied grudgingly.

"And you were placed in a holding cell?"

Consetti's teeth were tightly clenched. "Yes."

"But you were never charged?"

"I was completely exonerated."

Abernathy shook his head thoughtfully. "Funny. I didn't find that in the file. But I did find that you were allowed to make one phone call, and soon thereafter Chief of Police Blackwell arrived at headquarters. Shortly after his visit, you were released."

"Was that a question?" Consetti snarled.

"No, but this is. You and Blackwell are members of the same country club, aren't you?"

"What of it?"

"Nothing. Just comforting to know the good ol' boy network is still in fine shape. Were you aware that there were two teenage girls, ages sixteen and fourteen, in the backseat of the car you hit?"

Consetti hesitated before answering. "Yes."

"And those two girls died, didn't they?"

"That is . . . my understanding."

"And you got off scot-free, right? You didn't pay their families a cent. You didn't even offer to repair their car!"

"Again I object," Ben interjected. "This line of questioning is abusive and not remotely relevant to the case pending before the court."

"Not relevant!" Abernathy was practically screaming. "This man killed two girls and took no responsibility for his actions. How can we expect him to take any more responsibility for what he did to Jason Nelson?"

"Objection! Save your jury argument for the courtroom."

"And for that matter, how can we expect him to take any responsibility for what he may have done to untold other children who died because they had the mistaken belief that the Apollo suspension system was . . . as safe as a mother's hug?"

"Move to strike," Ben repeated. "If you continue in this abusive manner, I'm filing an emergency application for a protective order with Judge Roemer."

"Don't bother. I'm finished." Abernathy laid down his pencil and smiled. "Your witness, Kincaid."

* 23 *

"What the hell was that all about?"

Consetti was pacing back and forth in Ben's office, banging his head against the wall figuratively and literally.

"It was just a cheap intimidation tactic. His case is falling apart, so he's clutching at straws."

"He's clutching at my good name, that's what he's doing!" Consetti's face was flush red; spittle flew from his lips.

"Look, any fool can drop by the station and review the police records. He doesn't have anything factual to help him win this case. So he's going after our witnesses."

"What was that shit about me killing teenagers?"

"That jab was best ignored."

"The press won't ignore it! What if he calls the *World* with that crap and they print it? Think what that would do to my reputation! Not to mention the Apollo Consortium."

"He won't. He can say anything he wants in a deposition—he's got immunity. If he repeats it to a newspaper, though, it's actionable slander. Trust me, he won't take the risk."

Consetti continued pacing. "I just can't believe I let that swaggering mound of flesh treat me like that. I should've . . . I should've—"

"You should've ignored him."

"Ignore him!" Consetti took a swing at the air. "Goddamn it, I don't understand why you're being such a milquetoast about this. Herb would've shoved that man's words right down his throat."

"And then Abernathy would've gone to court complaining about how we obstructed discovery and asking for sanctions and extensions of time. Again, I would've been playing right into his hands."

"Goddamn . . . *lawyers*!" Consetti took another swing at the air, this time perilously close to Ben's face.

"Excusez moi," said a voice from behind them. Ben turned and saw Christina poised in the doorway. "I'm sorry to interrupt, Ben, but Lieutenant Morelli is here to speak with you."

Ben looked at Consetti apologetically. "I'm sorry, sir. Can we continue this conversation later?"

Consetti gritted his teeth and barreled through the door, pushing Christina to one side. "Goddamn . . . *lawyers*!"

Ben grinned sheepishly at Christina. "I don't suppose Mike is really here?"

"As a matter of fact, he is, although he's perfectly content to wait. I thought you needed a save."

"You were right."

"I take it Abernathy tried some cheap sleazemeister tricks at the deposition?"

"Like you wouldn't believe. He realizes he hasn't got any proof of design defects and he's getting desperate. Plus, he was unprepared for the deposition—didn't know anything about the suspension system or any of the important issues. All he had was a police report and a lot of experience with tawdry discovery tactics."

"Of course," Christina replied, "what he probably

hoped to do was scare Apollo's upper management into early settlement."

Ben knew better than to doubt Christina's instincts. "Probably right."

"And from the looks of Consetti's major over-reaction—"

"Exactly. Mission accomplished. If I don't win this case soon, Apollo's going to end up writing Abernathy a big check."

"Well, if anyone can do it, you can. I heard you creamed Abernathy at the hearing yesterday."

"True. But only because he was so pathetically un-prepared."

"Sure. It couldn't possibly be because you did any-thing right. By the by, you need to call Jones."

"Why? Is he in trouble?"

"No. He just misses the sound of his master's voice. Maybe you could phone him and ask him to draft some motions for you, just for old time's sake."

"I'll give it some thought."

"Well, I've got to get back to work. Crichton's got me feeding documents into a litigation support com-puter program. You should see him in the computer room. He loves to play with gadgets."

"The male prerogative."

"Yeah. I just wish he'd stop trying to look up my skirt."

"Perils of the workplace."

"This one, anyway. I'll send Mike in."

"Thanks."

A few seconds after Christina left, Mike strolled into the office.

"What's up?" Ben asked.

"You are. You're coming with me."

Ben blanched. "You're kidding. Blackwell is hauling me in? My time isn't up yet."

"No, no, no. We're going to search Hamel's home."

"Oh." Ben exhaled, relieved. "What about his widow?"

"She's consented. In fact, she called this morning and asked us to come."

"I thought she was mounting very serious opposition. What made her change her mind?"

"A very serious pair of fists. Impacting repeatedly on her face."

* 24 *

Ben and Mike drove to the Hamel residence in an unmarked silver Trans Am.

"How did you ever get the department to spring for a slick pair of wheels like this?"

Mike grinned. "Let's just say Chief Blackwell and I have an extremely close working relationship."

"What does that mean? You have photographs of him in drag?"

"That would be telling." Mike rolled down the driver's side window and barreled into the fast lane. "Snazzy car, though, don't you think?"

"Yup. It's every sixteen-year-old's dream."

"Every guy's dream, you mean." He glanced at his reflection in the rearview mirror. "I think I wear it well."

"Well, it looks better on you than that dirty overcoat. If you'd had this four years ago, you might have Julia sitting in the front seat instead of me."

"Not unless I filled the glove compartment with credit cards."

Just as Mike finished his sentence, a red Ferrari weaved around him and zoomed past.

"Did you see that?" Mike cried. He groped around in the compartment between the seats. "Where's my siren?"

"Forget it, Mike. We have other business. You're not a traffic cop."

"I will not forget it. I hate reckless drivers. Especially when I'm driving my Trans Am." He clamped the red bulb onto the roof of his car and pressed down on the accelerator. Ben felt his stomach fly out of his body as the Trans Am kicked in all eight cylinders.

"Mike, would you cool it, for God's sake! I do not want to die in a high-speed chase!"

"Show some nerve, Ben. We're catching bad guys."

"I don't want to catch bad guys. I want to live to a ripe old age." They whizzed by a black pickup so quickly that Ben ducked. "Look, I already know you're a hardboiled two-fisted male-machismo sumbitch. You don't have to prove it to me by nailing some moron in a Ferrari!"

"It's a matter of principle," Mike muttered. "He didn't even use his left turn indicator."

"Oh, well then—life imprisonment for him." Ben glanced fearfully at the speedometer. "Mike! You're doing a hundred miles an hour!"

"Is that all? No wonder I haven't caught up." He pressed harder on the accelerator.

"Mike, listen to me. I'm an innocent. A civilian. I don't want to perish in the line of duty. I want out!"

"Sorry, Ben, no time," he said, his hands tightly clenching the steering wheel. "Justice is on patrol."

Forty minutes and three tickets later, Ben and Mike arrived at the home of Gloria Hamel in the plush residential section surrounding the Philbrook Museum. They rang the door, and a few moments later she opened it.

Ben was horrified.

Mike's description, although gruesome enough, left him utterly unprepared for what he saw. Mrs. Hamel's face was a scarred and bloody nightmare. Her nose had been flattened; her eyes were so swollen she could barely see. She had two deep lacerations, one beneath each cheek, creating a macabre symmetry. Both appeared to have been sutured. A white bandage stretched down the middle of her face, covering the place where her nose used to be.

"I apologize for keeping you waiting," Gloria said. Her words were slurred and unenunciated; she was only barely able to move her mouth. "I'm having some trouble getting around this morning."

Ben was astonished she was even able to stand. "I'm Ben Kincaid."

"I know," she said, nodding. "Lieutenant Morelli told me you would be coming when he visited me at the hospital."

"Are you feeling any better?" Mike asked gently.

"It's hard to say." She looked at them as if she might find her answer in their eyes. "The doctors said I could go home, although I have to return to the hospital tomorrow for more sutures. They think my brain may be partially detached from my skull.

Having grown up with a doctor father, Ben had had an opportunity to see injuries of all sorts and degrees. Nonetheless, he could not recall ever seeing anyone so hideously damaged, so . . . ruined. "Forgive me for asking, but have you consulted a plastic surgeon?"

"Just long enough to find out they are very expensive. Too expensive for me. Especially now that Howard is gone."

"Surely your husband's medical insurance at Apollo—"

"Terminated the instant he died. I've already spoken to Robert Crichton about it. He said he was sorry, but there was nothing he could do."

Mike gave Ben a pointed look. "Some boss you got there, Ben."

Ben didn't reply.

"Please come in," Gloria said. "I don't like to stand out in the open."

They stepped into the foyer of the house. Now that he was inside, Ben realized that the house was even more palatial than it seemed from the outside. The furnishings were absolutely top-drawer—much better than he would have expected a mid-level member of the Apollo legal staff to be able to afford.

"How many rooms have you got here?" Ben asked.

"Twenty-two. Not counting the attic, garage, or basement."

Ben whistled. "Mike, we're going to need help."

"Agreed. Although I doubt we'll be able to divert many men from the serial killer investigation. Let me make a call."

Gloria pointed to a telephone in the den. Mike dialed headquarters, leaving Ben alone, and extremely uncomfortable, with Gloria.

"Do the police have any idea who did this to you?" Ben asked.

"Not that I've heard." Her diction was so slurred that Ben at first thought she had said "God how I hurt." A shiver shot down his spine. "Not that I've been any help."

"You didn't help the police?"

"I couldn't. I didn't see a thing. It was about one A.M. I wasn't sleeping well—I haven't since Howard was killed. I heard a noise downstairs. Like a fool, I got up and looked around. I startled the intruder, who proceeded to beat me into unconsciousness—I suppose so he could get away before I called the police."

Ben gazed sadly at the woman's tragic face. Whoever did this was seeking more than just a hasty retreat. Whoever did this was a deeply cruel human being.

"Do you have any idea what the intruder was doing here?"

She shook her head, then winced, as if the tiny movement pained her. "He seemed to be searching for something. What, I don't know."

"You said *he*. Are you certain it was a man?"

"Well, I just assumed—but no, I suppose I really don't know. It was too dark to see anything."

"That must be a horribly ... invasive feeling," Ben said. "To have someone break in, to learn that you're not safe in your own home."

"This is just one more ... incident," she murmured.

"There have been others?"

"I don't mean like this. I mean ... everything." She lowered herself slowly into a chair. "One more blow. One more incomprehensible slap in the face. When Howard was killed, I thought my life was over, thought I had no reason to live. And now ..." Her head bowed till she was staring at her hands. "... now, I wish I could die."

* 25 *

By five-thirty, Ben, Mike, and three uniforms from the Central Division had been through each of the twenty-two rooms in Gloria Hamel's house twice. Some more.

And come up with nothing.

"Maybe we're wasting our time," Ben said. He sat dejectedly beside the fireplace in the den. "Maybe Hamel's murder had nothing to do with his home life."

"Whether it did or didn't, he lived here," Mike replied. He was opening drawers, looking under rugs, and checking all the other places he had already checked twice before. "There must be something helpful here, something that would give us a hint of what happened to him."

"Well, I don't want to sound like a quitter, but I don't think there's anything here."

"That's where you're wrong."

"How can you be so sure?"

"Think about it, Ben. Last night someone took an enormous risk by breaking in here. A very desperate person, if what he did to the lady of the house is any indication. And why? Because he was looking for something. Gloria Hamel interrupted him before he found it, and he fled immediately after the beating. I don't know what he was searching for. But I know it's still here."

"Well, since you put it that way . . ."

Ben pushed himself away from the fireplace and resumed his search.

"I'm going to check with Sergeant Mattingly. He's searching the garage."

The garage? "Mike, there's also a basement and an attic. In addition to the twenty-two rooms we've already searched."

"Are you sure?"

"Positive. Gloria told me."

Mike slapped him on the back. "All right, Sherlock Kincaid. I'll take the basement, you take the attic." He poked Ben in the ribs. "Unless that's too high up for you. I don't want you to get dizzy and fall out a window."

Actually, it *was* too high up for Ben, not that he planned to admit it. Worse, the attic had huge windows on two sides. There was no direction he could turn to forget that he was not firmly planted on the ground. He tried to calm himself, recalling that he had once jumped out of an office window at least this high off the ground. Somehow, that only made him more nauseated.

The Hamels' attic was a junkman's dream. Almost every inch of floor space was piled high with mementos and castaways. The tremendous clutter guaranteed that this search would take several hours at least.

Most of the clutter derived from the man of the house. Incomplete projects filled the attic—a half-finished model train set, various model airplanes, a ship in a bottle. One corner was filled with fishing and camping gear. The only traces of Gloria he saw were a dust-covered dressmaker's dummy, a sewing machine, and various needles and threads—remnants of an avocation long since abandoned.

Well, there was no point in procrastinating. Ben chose the closest corner and plunged in. He tried to be as thorough as possible; he opened every drawer, every trunk, every cardboard box. He overturned every piece of furniture, carefully checking for hollowed cushions and the like.

An hour and a half later, he had tunneled a path to the first wall, and come up with nothing that cast any light on Hamel's death.

He patted down the wall, listening for a hollow sound that might suggest a secret room. All he heard was the consistent thud of plaster and wood.

You're losing it, Kincaid, he thought to himself. This is real life, not a Gothic romance.

Above him, Ben spotted a huge blue swordfish, stuffed and mounted on the wall. A small plaque informed him that Howard Hamel caught the fish off Padre Island on August 12, 1988.

The swordfish triggered something in the back of Ben's mind. It took him a moment to bring it back: *I love deep sea fishing,* Hamel had said. *If I could, I'd spend my whole life doing that and nothing else.*

Could it be? Ben pulled over a rickety chair and raised himself eye level with the swordfish. Maybe it was just his overactive imagination, but the fish seemed to be . . . smiling at him. Cautiously, Ben put his hand into the fish's mouth, stretched, and withdrew. . . .

Nothing. Ben jumped off the chair, utterly embarrassed. Who do you think you are, one of the Hardy Boys? he asked himself. First you look for secret passages, then you stick your hand into a swordfish. What did you expect? Golly, maybe we'll find a treasure map!

Then he recalled the remainder of what Hamel had said: *In fact, I'm going on vacation myself in a few days. Gonna catch some sun and some fish down at Key West. Get away from it all for a few days.*

Ben wondered if perhaps Hamel wanted to get away from a specific something. Or someone. If he had some kind of sensitive information, something someone else wanted intensely, Hamel would probably take it with him.

Ben raced back to the corner of the attic containing Hamel's fishing gear. He tore through the pile, uprooting rods, reels, nets, and sophisticated electronic gizmos. He found a tackle box and flipped open the lid. Lures, plastic worms, hooks, spare line—*yes*! He thrust his hand down to the bottom of the box and came up with a photograph.

"Mike!"

No response. He ran to the top of the attic ladder. *"Mike!"* he shouted again.

A few moments later, he heard, "What? I was in the middle of searching the half-filled paint cans. I love paint fumes. This had better be good."

"It is." As soon as Mike reached the top of the ladder, Ben thrust the photo into his hands. It was a small Polaroid, not very old.

"Do you have any idea who this is?" Mike said, after examining the photo.

"No. But people don't normally hide photos of naked

girls in their tackle boxes. I thought it might be important."

"Damn right it's important." The photograph showed a petite, blond teenage girl, nude except for a broken heart-shaped pendant on a chain around her neck. The expression on her face was difficult to read. But she was not happy. There was someone else in the foreground, facing away from the camera. The second person was impossible to identify; all that was visible was a bare shoulder and part of the back.

Mike flipped the photo over. On the back, someone had handwritten in a messy scrawl: *Kindergarten Club—#1*.

"See that strawberry birthmark on her left shoulder?" Mike said. "And two more below her breasts? I recognize the body markings. This girl was the serial killer's first victim."

Ben felt a sudden shortness of breath. "But—this photograph looks as if it was taken recently."

"I agree. There's very little fading or discoloration."

"What does it mean?"

Mike shook his head. "It means this case involving Howard Hamel and the Apollo Consortium just became a hell of a lot more important. And deadly."

* 26 *

Tomlinson walked The Stroll, his hands shoved into the pockets of his black leather jacket. It was tough—trying to keep up the Mr. Chameleon front, trying to look for someone without making it obvious he was looking for someone. Trying to get close enough to determine whether each bleached-blonde teen prostitute was the one with a scar across the bridge of her nose. Without getting beat up.

He moved briskly down the street, past the massage parlors and steam baths, the sex shops, and the lavender movie theatres. He approached two ladies occupying the corner of Eleventh and Cincinnati. The one closest to him was a big-boned black woman wearing a halter vest and a fake fur coat. The other woman was standing in the shadows; he couldn't see her clearly.

"Wanna date?" the black woman asked.

"As a matter of fact, yes," Tomlinson said. "But not with you, I'm afraid."

"Wassa matter with me, chump?"

"Nothing. Nothing at all."

"Do I scare you? Make you wanna run home to your mama?"

"No ... I'm just looking for someone in particular."

"I'll bet." She turned to her companion. "Gump with a tall bank."

Translation: homosexual with a lot of money. Tomlinson grinned. Wrong on both counts.

The companion stepped into the light of the street lamp. She had dark hair and was in her mid-thirties, probably. It was hard to be certain; they aged quickly on the streets. But she wasn't the one he was looking for.

"You ladies wouldn't know a girl named Trixie, would you? I'm told she works The Stroll, too."

"Why do you ask?" the black woman said. "Are you her daddy?"

"No. Just an interested party."

"Figures. That Trixie, she's more your speed. Tiny and unthreatening. And white."

"We have a prior relationship," Tomlinson explained, stretching the truth a bit.

"A repeat customer, huh? Well, ain't that peachy?"

She shared a laugh with her dark-haired friend. "Sugar, you just hustle on down three corners thataway. You'll find your dream girl. If she ain't busy at the moment. She'll be with Buddy, most likely. Come to think of it, you may like Buddy better than you do Trixie." They had another big laugh.

Tomlinson thanked them and headed in the direction the woman had pointed. He couldn't work up much irritation, much less anger, toward his informants. It wasn't their fault, this bizarre life they led. He knew from the days when he walked this beat regularly that prostitutes were almost always hardcore sexual abuse victims. And if they weren't when they came to the oldest profession, they certainly would be before they left. Talk about life on the edge. Most had daily contact with sex and needles, both of the most likely ways to contract AIDS, the twentieth-century plague.

It hurt worst when he saw the teenagers, the girls who for whatever reasons, usually compelling ones, had run away from home and joined the street culture. When he had walked this beat, he'd made a concerted effort to get as many of them off and out as possible. The hell with busting them—he just tried to get them into a life-style that wouldn't kill them before they were old enough to drive. He had some successes, too, but far more failures. It was a matter of timing. If he could catch them early on, say, during their first year, there was a chance he could get them off the streets, relocate them, find them another job. Over a year—forget it. They were here for life.

It was the newfound freedom that was their biggest enemy. The girls split from their homes and suddenly they could do anything they wanted. They could stay out all night, they could go to rock concerts, they could get dope without any trouble. Ts and Blues all night long. A dream come true, right? Until they were trapped. Until the pimp took control of their life, and the drugs took control of their life, and the booze took control of their life. Soon everyone and everything had control of their life. Except them.

A few blocks down the street, Tomlinson found her. She fit the description the man in the tattoo shop had given perfectly. She was extremely thin; something had been wedged in her bra to suggest a fullness she did not have. As he approached, he could see that her hair was not naturally blond, and he could see the adolescent acne that marked her skin. As if to confirm the ID, a pool of pennies lay scattered around her feet.

She was standing next to an older man with thinning reddish hair. The man wore tight leather leggings; he was obviously a male prostitute.

Tomlinson approached the girl casually. "Are you Trixie?"

She looked back at him, openly suspicious. "Who wants to know?"

He silently noted the small scar across the bridge of her nose. "I do. I've been looking for you for three days."

"Why me? I haven't done anything wrong."

"I didn't say you did. Why would you assume—"

"Because you're with the Fury, that's why."

Tomlinson was crestfallen; he knew the street slang for vice cops. Strike two for Mr. Chameleon. "Did someone recognize me?"

"Nah. It was just obvious. Wasn't it, Buddy?" The man in the leather leggings nodded his head.

"I thought I was blending in."

"Well, next time you want to blend in, leave the fancy blue jeans at home. They're way too new, not to mention too expensive, for anyone around here. And while you're at it, forget the penny loafers, too."

"I thought I had this down pat."

"That's the main problem. You're trying too hard. And you're looking for something specific, not just any port in the storm, like everyone else around here."

Tomlinson had to grin. Mr. Chameleon had been undone by Miss Marple in a halter top. "My name's Tomlinson. I understand you were a close friend of Suzie's."

"Do you know where she is?" Trixie said anxiously, stumbling awkwardly in her high heels. "I've been looking for her everywhere."

"I . . . may know where she is," Tomlinson said. "Can we talk privately?" After some initial hesitation, Trixie followed him to the steps of a nearby building. Tomlinson noticed that Buddy kept a close eye on them.

"I called the county jail," Trixie said, "but they told me they didn't have anyone by her description. I called the hospitals, too, but no luck. She's not in any trouble, is she?"

"That depends." Tomlinson saw that he was attracting attention from some nasty-looking men on the opposite side of the street. Chitchat was frowned upon; you were supposed to strike a deal and get off the street. "Do you know whether Suzie had a tattoo?"

"Of course I do. I was with her when she got it. I was against the whole idea. Suzie's only been on the streets about six months. I've been sort of her—well, I dunno, sort of her mother, I guess. I think tattoos are gross, but she'd met this guy, and he was a butterfly freak, and she thought—"

"The tattoo was a butterfly?"

"Oh, yeah. With lots of roses and stuff all over it. This john told her he loved her and he was coming back for her, and she believed him. When he didn't come back, she was all torn up. And she was stuck with the tattoo."

"Can you tell me . . . what part of the body she had tattooed?"

"What are you, some kind of tattoo freak?"

"No . . . I'm just trying to make a positive ID."

Trixie's face turned ashen. "Oh, my God. She's not . . . She isn't—"

"I'm not sure."

Trixie's lips did not move for a long time, as if she could not bring herself to speak the words that might clinch the identification. "It was on her boob. This one, I think." She touched her left side.

Tomlinson reached out to her. "I'm sorry. . . ."

"Oh . . . *no*!" Trixie bit down on her fist. "Oh, God! I should have been there."

"It's not your fault."

"Of course it is! I promised her! I promised I'd take care of her! I promised all of them!"

"All of them?"

"Oh, my God." She kept repeating the words, over and over. "First it was Angel. Then Suzie and Barbara. They say Bobbie Rae disappeared a few nights ago. That means I'm the last one."

Tomlinson was puzzled. "The last—what?"

"Don't you see? This can't be just a coincidence. One, even two of them—maybe. But not all. Not every one."

Tomlinson grabbed her by the shoulders. "Trixie, please calm down. You're not making any sense. Tell me what you're talking about."

She swallowed deep gulps of air. Her face seemed to go a million ways at once. "They're killing us all."

"Us all? Who? What do you have in common?"

She looked at him blankly. "The Kindergarten Club."

A sudden shout erupted from an open window in the building across the street. Tomlinson couldn't make out the words, but the tone was distinctly angry.

"Damn," Trixie muttered. "I'm in trouble now."

"What?" Tomlinson asked. "Who is that man?"

"That's my . . . boss."

"What did he say?"

"He's pissed because I've been standing here talking to a potential john for ten minutes, and we're still out on the street talking. As far as he's concerned, that's long enough to turn the trick and be back on the street waiting for the next one. Look, you need to get out of here."

"I can't do that."

"You have to."

"Trixie, if you're right, and someone is systematically killing people, and you're the only one left, you're in tremendous danger."

"If Sonny gets mad at me, he'll beat the shit out of me. Which is worse?" The tough facade melted away; a sad, pleading tone permeated her voice. "Please leave."

"I could arrest you."

"Sonny would have me out in two hours. And then he'd really beat the shit out of me."

"Fine. Then I'll, uh, hire you. Let's go upstairs."

"We charge thirty dollars, minimum. That's for just the basic service. Have you got that much on you?"

Tomlinson checked his wallet, embarrassed. "No."

"Then Sonny would beat the shit out of you."

Tomlinson stepped back and glared at the angry man across the street. Frustration seethed from his pores. "Trixie, I have to talk to you."

"Then come back tomorrow, when I have some time off. I have to work till morning, then I crash till the sun sets. Meet me at nine."

"Where?"

She pointed to a Denny's across the street. "There. We'll eat, we'll talk." She winked. "You'll buy."

Tomlinson bit down on his lip. He didn't like this arrangement at all, but it seemed to be the only solution. "Promise you'll be there?"

"Promise. Now clear out. You're blocking the window display."

Tomlinson slowly backed away. He found his car, then parked near a corner across the street from Trixie's post. He watched her for some time, maybe half an hour, until a tall man in a green flak jacket approached. She linked her arm through his and led him inside the building behind her. Half a minute later, a light came on in a small room on the second floor.

Tomlinson threw his car into first and drove away, disgusted and sick. Sick to his stomach, sick in his heart.

He'd have to get someone to cover for him on the switchboard tomorrow night, but he would definitely be here at nine.

In fact, he would be early.

* 27 *

Ben was sitting at his desk trying to make his computer do something—anything—when Christina popped her head into the office.

"Shouldn't you be in the main conference room for the staff meeting?"

Ben put down the mouse, irritated. "No. Staff meeting was canceled."

"Staff meeting was *postponed*, while Crichton visited his doctors again about his back. The meeting starts at ten o'clock sharp."

Ben checked his watch, then jumped out of his chair. "Hokey smokes. How did you find out?"

"I try to stay *au courant*. After all, one of us has to, and you're usually busy playing Sam Spade."

"You're a lifesaver, Christina. I'm out of here."

"Bon voyage."

Ben raced out of his office, down the corridor, and through the main conference room. Fortunately, he had some time to spare; the other lawyers (sans Crichton) were still milling about.

"Hey, Kincaid," Herb said. "Glad you could make it. We were beginning to think you were going to stand Crichton up. Boy, would he have been ticked off."

"I didn't know we were meeting."

"Really?" Rob said. "Herb sent us all memos."

Herb's brow furrowed. "That's right—I sent one to every lawyer in the department. Gosh, Ben, I don't know why you didn't get one."

Ben wondered.

"Ben, you have anything you want to take out of staff notes?" Chuck was standing behind him, holding another of his agendas. "We're trying to streamline the meeting."

"If you really want to streamline the meeting," Ben said, "teach Crichton how to pour his own coffee."

A smile played on Candice's lips. "You can't teach an old dog new tricks. Especially if he doesn't want to learn."

"I wonder what he would do . . ." Ben picked up the coffeepot on the credenza and filled the empty mug in front of Crichton's chair. "This may spoil his fun."

"By the way, Kincaid, I understand you were at Howard Hamel's house yesterday." It was Doug Gleason, perched safely behind his computer. "What on earth were you doing?"

"I was . . . helping the police search for information that might tell us what happened to Howard."

"Indeed. That's a novel approach. Make the prime suspect the detective."

"I am not a suspect." At least not officially, Ben thought. Yet.

Doug inhaled deeply on his cigarillo. "Well, if Howard had been found in my office, I bet the police would've had a few questions for me. Guess it pays to have friends in high places."

"What are you insinuating, Doug?"

"Oh, nothing. Nothing at all."

"How the hell did you find out I was at Hamel's house, anyway?"

He blew a perfect smoke ring into the air. "A little birdie told me."

"You know, Gleason," Candice said, "you are really an obnoxious twerp. I don't even like Kincaid, but I still think you're being a butthole."

"Oooh, retract those claws, Candy," Doug replied calmly. "No need for a conflagration with me. Everyone knows *I'm* not sleeping with you."

"What the hell is that supposed to mean?"

"Figure it out for yourself, dear. Buy a dictionary."

"You know, Gleason, I'd like to give you a swift kick between the legs."

"Is that what you're into? I'm not surprised."

Rob stepped between them. "Children, children, let's cool off." He held Candice and Doug arms length apart. "Why is it I spend half my time at staff meetings breaking up fights?"

"Because you haven't the sense to let nature take its course," Chuck answered. "Kincaid, do we really need the Nelson case on the agenda?"

"It's been very active this past week."

"But do we need to talk about it? Do you need our help?"

"Well—no, not particularly."

"Fine, it's off. Shelly?"

Ben heard a rustling on the other side of the room. She was sitting in a chair at the end of the table. Ben hadn't even noticed her.

"Shelly, I've got every goddamn project you've worked on for the last three months on the agenda. I hope you're ready to talk about each and every one of them. At length."

Shelly's face turned a sickly shade of yellow, but she remained silent.

"I was wondering," Ben said, drawing attention away

from her. "Maybe we should have some kind of memorial for Howard."

"Memorial?" Herb said.

"Yeah. Something to note his passing. Hell, one of our own was killed less than a week ago, and here we are going on as if nothing happened. As if he was never here."

"What do you suggest?" Chuck asked.

"I don't know—some kind of remembrance. Maybe you could put something on the agenda. We could each say a bit about what we remember best about Howard."

"What I remember best is how he stole the Kestrel case from me," Herb said. "And then, to make it worse, he screwed it up. That probably set my career back five years."

"I remember the time he came on to me at the summer retreat," Candice said. "He'd had way too much to drink. Kept babbling about how his wife was frigid and had I ever done this position or that position, the whole time staring at my—well, anyway. It was gross. He was practically drooling."

"I don't think this is the kind of remembrance Ben had in mind," Rob said quietly.

"Why not? This is fun." Chuck entered the fray. "Remember the departmental golf tournament, and how he kept shaving strokes off Crichton's score? Man, what a suck-up. If there was anyone in this department you had to be careful about, it was him."

"Remember the Alumco acquisition?" Doug said. "How he accidentally lost everyone's proposal but his own?"

"What is this?" a voice boomed from the doorway. "I thought we were having a meeting."

It was Crichton. Evidently, the fact that he was fifteen minutes late was of no importance. He expected everyone to be in their seats, lined up like obedient Boy Scouts.

As one body, they all scurried to the nearest available seat at the table. Once more, Herb outmaneuvered

Chuck and took the catbird seat next to Crichton. Once they were all in position, Crichton strode to his tall chair. He grimaced a bit as he sat down; evidently his back was still giving him some trouble.

Before he began, he reached out for his coffee mug. "Goddamn it, someone call Janice and—" He stopped in mid-sentence, as he saw the steam rise from the mug. "Someone already—but—" He sputtered another moment, made a growling noise, then grudgingly sipped his coffee.

Ben tried to hide his smile. What a bad boy he was, to spoil Bobby's fun.

"Chuck, have you got an agenda?"

Chuck slid the agenda down to Crichton. "First, I want to remind you all that we've got a softball game against the Memorex Telex legal department tomorrow, and I expect everyone to be there. Rain or shine, healthy or sick, and no matter how busy you are." Crichton scanned the agenda for a few moments. "Kincaid?"

Ben looked up, startled. "What?"

"Where's the Nelson case? It's not on the agenda."

"Well, that's because—"

"Didn't I tell you it was each lawyer's responsibility to submit each major project they're working on to staff notes?"

"Yes—"

"Did you think that case wasn't important? That case that could potentially cost this corporation millions of dollars?"

"It wasn't that. Chuck—"

"Damn it, when I give an order, I expect it to be carried out."

"I understand—"

"No exceptions."

"Really, the only reason—"

"Kincaid, I want you to submit a revised, all-inclusive agenda. And I want it on my desk by the end of the day. There's no excuse for letting a case of that magnitude slip through your fingers. I don't want this to ever happen again. Understand?"

Ben shot a fierce look at Chuck, who was conveniently looking the other way. The grins on the faces of the other lawyers were barely masked. They had known Chuck was setting him up from the start. Sabotage, corporate style.

"I understand, sir. It won't happen again."

"See that it doesn't." Crichton downed some more coffee, then, suddenly, his anger seemed to drain away. His flushed face resumed its normal color. "Good grief, Kincaid. I don't know what came over me. Imagine talking to a litigator of your caliber the way I did. And over a trivial matter like this. I don't know what gets into me sometimes. Could you possibly accept my apology?"

If the other lawyers in the room were delighted before, they were horrified now. It seemed that Ben Kincaid was impervious even to sabotage. The Teflon trial lawyer. "Let's just forget the whole thing, sir," Ben said softly.

"Done. So tell me what's going on in the case."

Ben reviewed the document production, the depositions he had taken of the plaintiffs, the hearing on the motion to compel, and the deposition of Andrew Consetti. "I'm planning to drive to Oklahoma City to talk to Al Austin and Bernie King."

Crichton's head rose. "Oh? Why do you need to do that?"

"Consetti identified both of them in his deposition."

"Al Austin is no longer with the company."

"Nonetheless, Consetti identified him as someone involved in the design of the XKL-1."

"Have the plaintiffs requested his deposition?"

"No. Not yet anyway."

"What about Bernie King?"

"Again, no."

"Then what's the point of talking to them?"

Ben shifted in his chair. "Mr. Crichton . . . I'm an officer of the court. I have an obligation to fully and fairly understand what took place. Plus, I have to know the whole story, to shore up any loose ends, to understand our weak points as well as our strong points, and to identify any exposure the Apollo Consortium may have."

"Bernie King is a very busy man. He's top dog in the OKC office. He runs a seven-hundred-man shop. He doesn't have time to play around with lawyers."

"I won't take any more time than neces—"

"Look, Kincaid, it's your case, but I don't think you should waste your time, much less the time of other important Apollo personnel. Find out whatever you can from the other side, then file your motion for summary judgment. I see no need for you to be investigating your own client."

He lowered his mug to the table, watching Ben very carefully. "After all, you already know what position you have to take."

* 28 *

Ben muttered most of the way to Oklahoma City, his hands tightly clenching the steering wheel.

"I got to hand it to you," Rob said. He was seated in the passenger seat of Ben's Honda Accord. "Most people would've backed off. Crichton made it clear he didn't think you should go to Oklahoma City, and here you are, doing it anyway."

"I have a long history of not being smart enough to take a hint," Ben said.

"Don't softsoap me, Ben. You're the kind of guy who believes that if a job is going to be done, it should be done right. You're going to handle this case properly, regardless of who or what gets in the way. I suppose that's why Crichton thinks you're such a super litigator."

"We'll see what he thinks after today."

Ben exited off Northwest Expressway. "What's the name of the place where we're meeting King?"

"It's called Knockers."

"Knockers? What kind of name is that for a restaurant?"

"Beats me. I've never been there. Crichton recommends it to everyone going to Oklahoma City."

A few minutes later, Ben pulled into the Knockers parking lot. The place had to be popular; almost every spot was taken.

"The food must be sensational to attract a crowd like this," Ben said. "I wonder if I can get some Buffalo chicken wings. That sounds great."

"Hope springs eternal." They climbed out of the car and walked to the restaurant.

Knockers probably did have some sort of decor, but whatever it was, Ben didn't notice. His eyes, like Rob's and everyone else's, were immediately drawn to the staff. The entirely and without exception female staff. The entirely and without exception young blond female staff. Bimbo paradise.

The "hostesses" all wore the same uniform: tight white T-shirts and pink spandex short shorts. The T-shirts were tied, quite snugly, around the midriff. The short shorts started low on the hips and ended high on the thigh. And as was immediately apparent, they weren't wearing anything else.

"Can we help you?" A nubile young hostess looped her arm around Ben's, giggling. "Can I show you to a table? A booth? Anything you want, I'll be happy to provide."

Ben noticed Rob had acquired a similar escort. "A booth will be fine. We're meeting a man named Bernie King. He may already be here."

"Oh, Bernie!" Rob's escort squealed. "We love Bernie. He's in the back."

Ben followed her swaying spandex to a booth in the rear. He marveled at how crowded the restaurant was; every office building in Oklahoma City must be feeding the place. He also noticed that every patron, without exception, was male.

Bernie's booth was in front of the big screen television. Another T-shirted waitress was standing on his table, a hula hoop revolving around her hips.

"All right, Jenny!" Ben's escort screamed. "Shake 'em!"

Jenny smiled giddily and accelerated her rhythmic revolutions.

Ben ducked under the hula hoop and tried to introduce himself. "Mr. King? I'm Ben Kincaid. This is Rob Fielder."

King shifted his glazed gaze slightly. "Happy to meet you." He returned his attention to the waitress on the table, then sighed. "All right, Jenny. That will be enough. I'm afraid we have some business to discuss."

"Aww!" the women wailed in unison. Jenny grabbed the hoop and stepped off the table. She grabbed Ben by the shoulders. "Can I show you my knockers?"

"What?"

Jenny handed Ben and the others small hand-sized wooden blocks. "These are my knockers. When you decide you're ready to order, just knock." She giggled. "Can I get you anything to drink?"

She took the drink orders—Cokes for Ben and Rob, two martinis for Bernie King—and scampered away with her friends.

King appeared utterly relaxed and at peace with the

universe. "I try to make it out here at least once a week. Robert Crichton first told me about this place. I consider it one of the few favors he's ever done for me. What do you think, Kincaid?"

Ben looked down at his silverware. "I don't think you want to know."

"If I didn't want to know, I wouldn't have asked."

"Well ..." Ben inhaled deeply. "Since you asked, I think this place is degrading to women, infantile, sexist, and all-around revolting."

King smiled. "That's what I would've said, when I was your age. The words would've been different, but the sentiment would've been the same." He stretched out, raised his feet onto the booth. "But I've mellowed with age. I don't get upset about the minutiae of political correctness anymore. If someone wants to make me happy, well, who am I to stop them?"

"Joints like this could set women back a hundred years."

"Perhaps so. And I wonder, would that be so horrible?"

"It would. Especially in the workplace. I've already seen behavior at Apollo—"

"Enough, enough. I'm not the CEO."

"That's the problem, as far as I can tell. No one wants to take responsibility. We have vice presidents for every conceivable aspect of Apollo's business policies, but no one is responsible for setting moral policies."

King smiled again. "Moral policy is not generally a principal concern of the stockholders at the annual meeting."

"Maybe it should be."

"Well, enough of this errant philosophizing. I understand you want to talk about the XKL-1 design project."

"That's correct." Ben brought him up-to-date on the litigation, including the discovery that had been conducted thus far. "Andrew Consetti mentioned that you were one of the principal designers on the project."

"That's true. Me and Al Austin."

"Right. That's one aspect of this affair that seems strange to me. After the completion of that project, you became a corporate VP with your own office in OKC, and Al Austin disappeared from the face of the earth."

"I like to think my promotion was based upon more than just one project. I've been working for Apollo for almost twenty years."

Ben tried to concentrate on what King was saying, but it was almost impossible with the big screen television flashing in front of his eyes. An exercise program was on, featuring four beautifully formed women in skintight exercise leotards bouncing around under the pretense of physical fitness. Ben liked lovely women as well as the next guy, but this big screen show of sweat and tights was beginning to have a Clockwork Orange effect.

"Can you describe the testing that was performed on the XKL-1?" Ben asked, forcing himself to look away from the screen.

"You name it, we did it. Stress testing, collision testing, front impact, rear impact—every test that could be performed, we performed."

"Well . . . I've searched the corporate records, as has my legal assistant, and we haven't found any test reports."

"Really?" King thought for a moment. "Well, it's a five-year-old project. They must've been thrown out."

"Hmm." Ben scrutinized King carefully. "And you're certain the design was thoroughly tested?"

"Absolutely certain."

"And the results were positive?"

He spread his hands across the table. "We put the product on the market, didn't we?"

"That doesn't quite answer my question."

"The quality control department would never intentionally release a product it didn't believe to be safe."

"That . . . still doesn't answer my question."

For the first time, King's dander appeared to be rising. "I've answered it several times."

"No, you haven't. My question is: did the testing prove the design was safe?"

"Yes, it was safe. It was incredibly, wonderfully safe. God spare me from the persistence of a lawyer." He leaned back into the corner of the booth. "I thought you were on our side."

"I am. I just want to know what happened."

King glanced absently at a group of hostesses building a pyramid with their bodies. "Well, that's what happened."

Rob seized the opportunity to jump in and smooth the troubled waters. "Do you have any explanation for what happened to Jason Nelson, Mr. King?"

"How could I know what happened? I wasn't there."

"But you are familiar with the case."

"I read the case summary Crichton sent over."

"Can you speculate as to what happened?"

"Well, anyone can speculate. Perhaps the kid was drinking. Perhaps he was necking with his girlfriend and lost his balance. Perhaps he just wasn't paying attention."

"The Nelsons strongly believe that what happened to their son was Apollo's fault."

"Because that's what their attorney has told them to think. You think they dreamed up this defective leaf spring theory on their own? Of course not. That's the lawyer's work. He's looking for a deep pocket. After all, if the accident was the kid's own fault, the parents are not going to get any money from anyone. And that lawyer is probably working on a contingency fee."

"The Nelsons don't strike me as particularly greedy—"

"It's not just greed. It's expiation. How horrible they must feel—they were with their son when it happened. They permitted him to ride on that flatbed—probably encouraged him to do it. Can you imagine the guilt they must feel? How much better if they can blame a third party, and transfer all their guilt to them."

Ben had to admit there could be some truth in what King said. He had seen attempts at absolution through litigation before. "Last question, sir. Do you know where Al Austin is today?"

"No," he said hastily.

"Any idea at all?"

"None whatsoever."

Was it just that Ben didn't like the man, or was there something more? For whatever reason, Ben had a distinct mental image of the man's nose getting longer with each denial. "Can you explain why he left Apollo?"

"I doubt that even Al could explain why he left. I liked Al, I really did, but he was the kind of guy who was never happy with whatever he was doing. Always looking for something better. For all I know, he left to discover America, or write the great American novel, or climb the mountains of Nepal."

"I hope not," Ben said. "I doubt if I can get a subpoena served in Nepal."

"Leave Al alone," King said wearily. "He's of no use to you."

"Yeah. That's what I keep hearing."

Jenny bounced back to their table. "What's wrong? You haven't knocked." She giggled and jiggled. "Don't you have an appetite?"

Innuendoes for an appetizer. Neat. "I do," Ben said. "I'd like some Buffalo wings."

"We don't have that," she replied. "But if you like, Megan will do the funky chicken on your table."

"That's quite all right. What do you have?"

"Hamburgers."

"What else?"

"Nothing else." She winked. "Except knockers, of course."

Ben sighed. "Hamburgers it is, then. By the way, is

there any chance you could change the channel on that television?"

* 29 *

Back at his office, Ben finished dictating his notes on his meeting with Bernie King. There was something there, but he wasn't sure what. One thing he was sure of, though—he was tired of all these calm, placid faces telling him not to worry, not to investigate, not to stir things up. Millions of dollars were potentially at stake, and everyone in the company was going out of the way to appear blasé about learning what really happened. That just didn't ring true.

After a few more moments' thought, Ben picked up the phone and dialed his old office on the North Side. Loving answered the phone.

"Loving? This is Ben. How's business?"

He heard a noise on the other end of the line that he took for sullen grunting. "Aww, I'm making ends meet, Skipper. Been tailing naughty husbands, mostly. It ain't the same since you left, though. You brought in such weird clients. There was always someone I could extract information from."

Usually by terrorizing them and threatening to make their lives a misery, Ben reflected. Ben had first met Loving after he'd represented Loving's wife in their divorce. Loving had burst into Ben's office one day, enraged, ready to do some damage. He was so grateful afterward when Ben didn't press charges that he offered to help Ben out with his fledgling practice. Eventually, he began working full time as Ben's private investigator. He was generally effective, although his methods were as a rule less than subtle.

"Did you ever figure out where the ex-husband in the Crawford case hid all his money?" Ben asked.

"Oh, yeah. Days ago. Piece of cake."

"What'd you do? Trace his bank transfers through computer networks?"

"Nah. I held him upside down over a swimming pool till he volunteered the information. You know, dip his head under for a minute, pull it out for a second. You'd be amazed how willing he was to talk after a while."

No doubt. "Well, I've got a new case for you."

"Really?" His excitement was evident. "You mean that hotshot corporation you work for is going to hire me?"

"You should just report to me. This is somewhat ... unofficial."

"Even better. Just like the good ol' days."

"This is a tough assignment, Loving. I don't know ... maybe I'm expecting too much from you. ..."

"Whaddaya mean? You saying it's too tough for me? Just let me at it."

Perfect. "I need you to find a man named Al Austin. All I know about him is that he used to work in Tulsa for the Apollo Consortium, in the engineering and design department. He worked on a suspension system design project called the XKL-1 about five years ago, but disappeared before the product was released onto the market. I don't know why and I don't know where he's gone. I'm sorry—I realize that doesn't give you much to go on."

"Apollo employee, huh? I know some Apollo guys. They like to hang out at the Bull-N-Bear on Harvard— you know, shoot some pool, have a few brewskies. I'll see what I can find out."

"Great. Call me as soon as you learn something."

"Will do, Skipper."

"You know, Loving, I'm not your Skipper—er, boss, anymore."

"Aww, heck. You'll always be the Skipper to me."

"Well, that's nice. I guess."

"We're keeping your office just like it was when you worked here. Kind of a memorial."

"That's really not necessary."

"We're still waiting for you to come back. Christina says it's just a matter of time."

"Oh, does she? Well, she may be in for a big—"

"I better get started on this. Thanks for calling."

No sooner had Ben hung up his phone than another familiar face from his previous life strolled through his office door.

"Jones! I wondered why you didn't answer the phone at the office."

"You called to check on us?" Ben's former secretary beamed. "Remembering the people you met on the way up. Who knows, you may need us again on your way down."

"My way— Have you been talking to Christina, too?"

"Face it, Boss. Christina is always right."

"Not this time. I'm very happy with my spiffy office and regular salary, thank you. The boss seems to respect me and I've successfully completed all my assignments. Look at this—I've even got my own desktop computer."

"I know. That's why I came by. Christina told me you've barely figured out how to turn it on."

"Well . . . I haven't had much time to devote to trivial office details."

"Uh-huh. That's why I'm here. Time for a primer. Computers 101."

"I hardly think that's necessary. . . ."

"Oh? Fine. Show me how you use your computer." Jones flipped the power switch on the back of the machine.

"Now where exactly is that switch?" Ben asked. "I couldn't find it before."

"Here, I'll put a yellow Post-it on it that says TURN ME ON." The monitor was illuminated with a blue screen. "This is your menu. It tells you what programs the corporation has already stored in your hard disk. What do you want to do?"

"Oh . . . I don't know. What are my choices?"

Jones rolled his eyes. "Sheesh." He brought the cursor to the top of the screen. "How about word processing? Lawyers do a lot of writing, right?"

"I've heard of that. That sounds good."

"Push *W*, and you've entered the word processing program, already installed on your hard disk. Now, you want to be able to store any documents you create. You can probably store them on the hard disk, but you should also keep an extra copy on diskette. Where do you keep your diskettes?"

"My what?"

Jones shook his head. "Lucky I came when I did. You're in sad shape, Boss." He rifled through Ben's desk drawers, eventually finding a box full of preformatted diskettes. He removed one small, square plastic 3 x 5-inch disk. "This," Jones said, "is a diskette."

Ben stared at the object in his hand. "That's it."

"I know it is. That's what I just told you. Ben, you're not paying attention."

"No, you misunderstand. That's *it*—that's what I saw but couldn't remember. That's what Hamel had in his hand when his body fell on top of me."

"Boss, are you on any medication?"

Quickly, Ben filled Jones in on what had happened during the past few days—finding Hamel's body in his office, then losing it, then finding it again in the alley behind his house.

"Boss, you're becoming the Typhoid Mary of premeditated murder."

"This is a major breakthrough," Ben said, ignoring him. "Why was Hamel clutching a diskette? And what was on the diskette? Was someone trying to get it?"

"But the police searched the area after the body disappeared, right?"

"Right."

"And there was no diskette?"

"Right."

"So whoever took the body also took the diskette."

"I suppose so. What kind of information can be stored on one of these, Jones?"

"Just about anything you want. Financial data, documents, lists, even entire publications."

Ben snapped his fingers. "Didn't you say documents could be saved on a computer's hard disk, then transferred onto a diskette?"

"That's the usual procedure. It's not mandatory."

"Then there's a possibility that whatever was in Hamel's hand is also stored on a computer somewhere."

"True. But where?"

"Well, we did find Hamel in my office. . . ."

Quickly, Jones punched a few buttons and brought up the document file on Ben's word processing program. It was empty. Jones spent the next ten minutes punching buttons, bringing up files from other programs. "Sorry, Boss. There's nothing here."

"If it isn't here, maybe it's stored in the main office computer. That would make more sense anyway—easier access for Hamel—and the computer room is just across the hall from my office." Ben snapped his fingers again. "Maybe Hamel was actually working in there. Then, when he heard Herb and Candice leaving, or when he heard Rob and me coming, he ran across the hall and hid in my office."

"Well," Jones said, wiggling his fingers, "shall I cross the hall and commence a search?"

"Not now. The computer room is well-staffed during the day. I don't think they'll let you sit down and start reading their confidential files. Besides, I don't want to tip anyone off. Remember, my theory is that Hamel's killer is someone in this corporation."

"What a pleasant thought. Well, I don't want to overstay my welcome. . . ."

"Okay. I'll call you later. Maybe we can arrange for a clandestine examination of the computer files. I'll need your help, obviously."

"You know where to call." Jones flashed a smile and headed out the door.

Ben pondered this new information. It seemed to confirm his theory that the killer was someone closely tied to the Apollo Consortium. Someone who had killed one person and tried to kill a second, if the attempt on Crichton's life was what he thought it was. Someone who in all likelihood would try to kill again, especially if he thought Ben was getting close.

Ben stood up and closed the door. Suddenly, his office seemed very small. The entire building seemed to be shrinking, as if the walls were slowly moving in on him. There he was, enclosed in a strange world filled with backstabbers, buttkissers—and someone who had killed one man and targeted a second.

And Ben could be next.

* 30 *

Ben drove his Honda Accord down the dirt road and parked well behind the bleachers, where he hoped his car would be safe from errant foul balls—mostly his, in all likelihood.

Everyone else was already on the softball diamond in Johnson Park, at the corner of Sixty-first and Riverside. Apollo's team was warming up. Each member was wearing an identical gray and red softball uniform with the Apollo logo on the back.

Christina tossed Ben a mitt and an official Apollo baseball cap. "Glad you could make it," she said. "I was afraid we'd have to hire a ringer to take second base."

"You'd have been better off," Ben replied. "I'm awful. I don't want to be here."

"Don't be such a grump. Show some *esprit de corps*."

Herb passed Ben while practice-swinging three bats forcefully through the air. Chuck and Candice lined up beside Ben and Christina and tossed a ball back and forth. Doug was rustling about, lining up the bats in order of length. Ben wondered where he had stowed his computer. Shelly was there, too, although she was sitting on the bench, quiet as always.

Crichton was behind the plate, making goo-goo faces through the chain-link screen. *Goo-goo faces?* Ben took a closer look. Yes, and goo-goo noises as well. The woman on the other side of the screen was holding a chubby toddler, maybe a year old, while a small girl a few years older sat beside them. Crichton was doing his best to entertain, and the whole family was laughing.

What do you know? Ben thought. The workaholic sexist pig really was soft on his family. Of course, Mussolini was a family man, too, he reflected. Still, it's hard to utterly detest someone after you've heard him sing "Itsy Bitsy Spider."

Ben noticed that he and Christina were conveniently positioned in the center of the group warming up. This presented an opportunity for schmoozing he thought he'd best not pass up.

"I hear the police are going to be visiting us in the next day or two," Ben said.

Chuck's ears pricked up. "The police?" He tossed the softball to Candice. "What would they want with us?"

"They're still trying to figure out who killed poor Howard."

"Christ," Candice said. "If they can't figure out who's mutilating all those teenage girls, they're never going to track down Howard's killer."

"Oh?" Ben said. "Why do you say that?"

"It's just a question of priorities, and it's obvious that the mutilation-murders have a higher one right now. I haven't heard Howard's name mentioned on the news once, but I hear an update every night about the latest grisly development in the teen serial slayings. The slaughter of little girls has so much more tragic appeal to middle America."

"I'd like to know what kind of questions the police are going to ask," Chuck said, reverting the conversation to the previous topic.

"The usual, I expect," Ben said nonchalantly. "Where were you the night Howard was killed? Did you know him? Did you have any reason to want him dead?"

Doug smirked. "I suppose we all had that, depending upon how petty you want to get about motives."

"The police can get pretty damn petty," Chuck mused.

"Why do you say that?" Ben asked.

Chuck shrugged and looked away. "Never mind."

"Well," Ben said, "I can account for where Rob was the day Howard was killed, and I know where Herb was shortly before I found the body."

"Really? Where?"

Herb turned and glared at Ben.

"At the office," Ben replied simply. "But everyone else is unaccounted for. Where were you, Chuck?"

"Who knows? I can't remember that far back."

"Surely you thought about it when you heard Howard was dead."

"I was at home that night watching television. By myself."

Christina made a tsking noise. "Not a very compelling alibi, Chuck."

"Sorry. If I'd known there was going to be a murder, I would have gone to the opera." He fired the ball back at Candice, throwing it so hard it smacked loudly against Candice's glove. Candice winced, took her hand out of the glove, and shook it out.

"Take it easy, Chuck."

"Sorry," he said. He didn't look sorry, though.

"What about you, Doug?" Ben asked. "I don't think I've heard what you were doing that night."

"I was writing," Doug replied.

"What a surprise," Chuck said with a wink.

"I didn't see you at the office," Ben commented.

"I wasn't there. I was at home."

"Took some files home with you?"

"I wasn't working on Apollo business. Some of us do have lives outside the office, you know." He hoisted a few bats into the air. "I was working on my novel."

"You're writing a novel?"

"What a surprise," Chuck repeated.

"What kind of novel?" Christina asked. "Adventure? Murder mystery?"

Doug peered down his nose. "Hardly. I'm writing a modern deconstructionist dialogue, encompassing the existential viewpoint and post–World War II logology, as viewed through the perspective of seventeenth-century poetry."

"Sounds fascinating," Ben said dryly.

"And this is a novel?" Christina asked.

"Oh, yes. But I've written it in sonnet form."

"Sonnet form?"

"Fourteen-line iambic pentameter, a-b-c-b rhyme pattern. It's a daunting project. But we all suffer for our art."

Ben suspected that there would be more suffering by

the reader than the writer. "When do you expect to have it completed?"

"Oh, it's done. I was just revising it a bit. Making some improvements."

"Then what?"

"Well . . . it's currently under consideration by various publishing houses."

"Oh?" Ben asked. "Like who?"

"Well . . . both Penguin and Vintage expressed interest. Unfortunately, the recession has caused them to make some difficult choices, sometimes favoring commercial tripe over significant literature. I've had some very favorable feedback from the University of Peoria Press."

"How much do you have to pay them to publish it?"

"Not as much as—" He stiffened. "I don't see as that concerns you."

"So you don't have anyone who can testify about where you were the night Hamel was killed?"

"No. I suppose not."

Ben shook his head. "You and Chuck are in a tough spot. The police don't have any real leads. And when they don't have leads, they start to get desperate."

"What do you think they'll do?"

"I don't know. Personally, I don't think the cops are going to solve this one unless they go back to . . . kindergarten."

The softball coming toward Chuck thudded against his chest. He grunted, but continued staring at Ben, his eyebrows forming a furrowed ridge over his eyes. "What do you mean by that?"

"I'm just saying they need to start fresh," Ben said, trying not to sound coy.

Chuck picked the softball up, but never stopped staring at Ben.

Rob strolled into the midst of the group and intercepted a softball on its way to Candice, much to her annoyance. He looked great in his uniform; he was obviously the only true athlete in the group.

"Everybody ready to play?" There was a spattering of well-tempered enthusiasm. "All right, let me pass out the assignments and the batting lineup. Anybody has any problems, let me know right away." Although Crichton was indisputably the coach, Rob was the manager, which meant Rob did all the thinking and all the work, while Crichton gave the pep talks and accepted the trophies.

The group stopped what they were doing and formed a huddle around Rob. "No problems? Okay. Now, listen up. Coach Crichton has a few pregame words for you."

Having been properly introduced, Crichton strode mightily into the huddle. "Listen up, team. I'll try to make this brief. I think you all know how important this game is."

Ben didn't. As far as he knew, this was the third game of the season and the team was one and one. So what?

"I know a lot of people disagree," Crichton continued. "A lot of people say, 'It's just the Lawyers' League. It's just for fun. Don't take it seriously.' Well, I'm here to tell you something different. Do you take your work seriously? Do you take your life seriously? My father used to say, 'Anything worth doing is worth doing seriously.' And he was right.

"Sure, we could just bumble through, drop pop flies, swill beer, act like asses. We could be cool and well-liked and friendly. And what would that get us? We're not here to hoist brews, damn it, we're here to play ball. Honest, proactive ball. And there's no point in playing the game if you're not playing to win. That's for losers. And we're not losers. *Are we?*"

The group answered with a rousing *"No way!"*, at least half the volume of which was contributed by Chuck.

Crichton huddled closer and grabbed the two players

on either side of him by the shoulders. "We're not just anybody, team. We're lawyers. Lawyers, damn it! We're the best there is, the cream of the crop. We're professionals. And that means more than just knowing how to file briefs and make convoluted arguments. It means we're professional about every aspect of our lives, and everything we do. Including softball.

"So when this game starts, I don't want to see a bunch of clowns and beer-guzzlers out there on the diamond. I want to see professionals. I want to see winners! *All right?*"

The team shouted *"All right!,"* slapped mitts, and ran out into the field of glory.

By the top of the fifth, Apollo was behind Memorex Telex by nine runs. Three more, and the game would be a skunk. And, sadly enough, there were men on both first and second, and it looked as if Memorex Telex would bring home the clinching runs at any moment.

The game had been a comedy of errors, except that thanks to Crichton's shouting, bellowing, and bullying, there was nothing funny about it. Tragedy of errors, perhaps?

Christina and Candice were both warming the bench, as they had been for the entire game. It would be difficult for Ben to say which was the more unhappy about it. Although this was purportedly a coed league, and necessarily so, the managerial team of Fielder and Crichton had not played a single woman yet.

Sexism carried to its most pathetic point, Ben mused. He could tell just from watching Candice warm up that she had a strong arm, and he knew for a fact that Christina was a much better player than he was. But here he was on second base, letting grounders bounce into his face and bumping into the shortstop, while Candice and Christina cooled their heels.

Shelly had been given the job of third base coach. Rob probably was just trying to get her off the bench, but this was a job for which she was ludicrously un-suited. She remained uncommunicative. She didn't un-derstand the rules of the game, or what she was sup-posed to be watching for, or what she was supposed to be telling the runners. As Chuck sailed toward third on his one hit of the game, he had yelled, "Is it safe? Is it safe?"

She shrugged her shoulders.

He was tagged out at home.

As he trudged back to the bench, Ben overheard Chuck doing a lot of muttering with Shelly's name in it. "Goddamn idiot. She's no better at softball than she is at law. I'm going to have another talk with Crichton about her, and soon. This is goddamn intolerable. . . ."

And so forth.

The next Memorex Telex batter hit a bouncing bunt right down the middle. It slipped past Crichton (who was pitching, natch) and headed toward Ben. It passed under Ben's glove, but he sat down on the ground and managed to block its progress with his posterior. He picked it up, then dropped it, fumbled around with it, bounced it off his chin, and eventually managed to throw it to the first baseman, much too late. The batter made it to first, the other two runners advanced.

The bases were loaded. Ben scanned the faces lining the infield. In the words of a great philosopher, it was Tension City.

Crichton marched toward the bench. "Time for my lucky glove!" he announced to no one in particular. He threw off his old glove, opened a wooden carrying case tucked under the bench, and removed a bright orange mitt.

"I've never lost a game with this mitt," Crichton said, as he returned to the mound.

Ben wondered if he had ever played with it before.

Crichton and Doug, who was catching, went through their usual series of signals. Doug told him to pitch wide outside; Crichton threw it straight down the middle. The batter got a piece of it, but fortunately for them all, it flipped backward. Foul ball.

Doug recovered the ball and, obviously annoyed, whizzed it back to Crichton. Unfortunately, Crichton was trying to intimidate the runner on third and wasn't paying attention. He turned around just in time to see the ball smash into the side of his face.

"Owww!" He fell to the ground, clutching his head.

Rob ran from first to the mound; Ben followed close behind. An extremely embarrassed Doug hobbled across home plate.

"Sorry, Mr. Crichton," Doug said, "I didn't realize you weren't watching."

Crichton didn't answer. He was lying prostrate across the mound, his eyes closed.

"I think he may be seriously hurt," Ben said.

"Oh, God," Doug said. "And just when I was about to get promoted."

"Rob," Ben said, "you know first aid. Check him out."

Rob hesitated a moment, then crouched over Crichton's body. "Damn. See that clear liquid in his ear canal?"

Ben looked over Rob's shoulder. "What is it?"

"I can't be certain. But it may be cerebral spinal fluid. And if it is, he's probably got a skull fracture."

Ben swallowed. That didn't sound good. "What does that mean?"

"It means he's hurt bad. May require surgery. Help me stretch him out." Ben took Crichton's legs and straightened his crumpled body.

"Now elevate his feet," Rob said.

Ben complied. As he did, Crichton began blinking his eyes rapidly. He was coming around.

"Thirsty," Crichton gasped hoarsely.

"Someone get him something to drink, okay?" Rob barked.

The repentant Doug hobbled to the sidelines,

snatched a beer from the thermos, then returned. Crichton greedily slurped it down, spilling half of it on his jersey.

"Help me up," Crichton whispered. "Got to finish the game."

"No way," Rob said. "You're hurt."

"Nonsense. I'm fine."

"Fine? You were temporarily unconscious!"

"Doesn't matter. The game isn't over."

"It is for you," Ben said firmly.

Crichton tried to sit up, groaned, then fell back onto the ground. "I never quit anything in my life, and I'm not quitting now."

"Look, sir," Rob said, "nothing personal, but we're getting beaten badly enough already. We don't need an incapacitated pitcher."

"Perhaps you're right." Crichton seemed relieved to have a graceful way out. "But who will take my place? We can't move any of the men from their positions."

"True. I think we have to ask Candice."

Crichton looked at Rob as though he thought this little better than putting in an inanimate object, but he grudgingly nodded.

"Candice," Rob yelled. "Take the mound."

Candice stood up, startled. "I've never pitched in my life."

"Well I *have*." Christina leaped off the bench and pushed Candice aside. She grabbed her mitt and marched toward the pitcher's mound. "I used to pitch twice a week when I played for Swayze & Reynolds," she said. "We were division champs."

Fortunately, Crichton's sneer was mitigated by his pain. "Was that in a . . . *ladies'* league?"

She shoved him off the mound. "Damn right. And every one of us could've showed you jokers a thing or two about softball. Play ball!"

Rob and Ben carried Crichton off the field. Candice

drove him and his family to the emergency room, and the game proceeded with Christina at the plate.

The batter was obviously amused at the prospect of having a woman pitch to him. He grinned at his team-mates, made a few suggestive remarks, and held the bat with one hand as the first strike whizzed across the plate. Even throwing underhand, Christina could pack a lot of punch in her pitch.

The batter's smile faded, and he paid considerably more attention as the second strike flew past him.

"All right, Christina!" Ben cheered.

The batter became serious. He hunkered down in a proper batter's crouch, held the bat with both hands and choked up. His brow furrowed as he watched the ball come toward him. He swung—after the ball crossed the plate.

"Strike three!" the umpire cried.

The Apollo team cheered, amazed by the sudden re-prieve. Rob started chanting Christina's name; Ben ran up and slapped her on the butt. It was a momentary high for all concerned.

Except Doug. He kept staring down the road, in the direction Candice had taken Crichton to the emergency room. He didn't appear happy at all.

* 31 *

Abernathy showed up for the hearing five minutes late, and the cause of his delay was immediately apparent. He brought his clients, Carl and June Nelson, with him.

That was extremely unusual. No witnesses would be called at the hearing; there was no reason for them to make the trip to the courthouse. Unless, Ben mused, Abernathy thinks Judge Roemer will be less inclined to dismiss the Nelsons' case if he sees them staring across at him with their grief-stricken eyes. That must be it—if Abernathy can't win the day by legal argument, he'll try intimidation and guilt.

Ben greeted the Nelsons as they took their seats on the front row of the gallery. They seemed subdued, reserved. Their attitude was probably influenced by whatever Abernathy had been telling them. He was very likely personalizing the litigation and blaming Ben for the fact that their case could be dismissed before trial. It was a shame; Ben hated to see the Nelsons distressed. They deserved much better than they were getting.

Rob sat in the back of the courtroom. Ben knew he would immediately report the day's events to Crichton, who was still in the hospital. Great, Ben thought. I was hoping for more pressure.

Abernathy tugged at Ben's suit jacket and pulled him to the side of the room.

"I don't suppose you've had a change of heart about

producing those ten documents to me?" Abernathy asked.

"The judge said no."

"I know, I know. I just thought you might be having pangs of conscience. I should've known better."

"My understanding is that those ten pages are just a lot of technical scribblings about an unrelated design project. Wouldn't help you a bit. I don't know why you're so anxious to see them."

"I don't exactly know why myself," Abernathy said. "But anytime a big corporation works that hard to keep something away from me, I start to get suspicious."

"I noticed you didn't file a brief in opposition to my motion for summary judgment," Ben said. "Does that mean you're going to confess judgment?"

"What it means is that I believe a lawsuit ought to be tried in court, before a jury of twelve peers, not on paper. I don't hold with all this motion practice you young kids go in for."

"If you're planning to submit evidence, I'd appreciate a chance to look at it in advance."

"I plan to submit my evidence at trial."

"If you don't come up with something today, Abernathy, you may never get there."

Abernathy placed his hands on his extensive belly. "Are you trying to tell me how to handle my lawsuit?"

"No. I just think the Nelsons are good people and I hate to see them screwed because their attorney isn't paying enough attention to their case."

"I resent that very much, Kincaid."

"I didn't mean to be rude. I just don't know if the Nelsons understand what they've got. How did they ever link up with you anyway? Surely they didn't respond to one of those TV ads."

"No." He bristled a bit. "It was a mail solicitation."

"You wrote them a letter?"

"In the normal course of business. I send out some twenty, thirty letters a day. I have a runner who examines police records every afternoon, getting the scoop on all the latest car wrecks. Then he visits the hospitals and examines the admitting records."

"I can't believe the hospital administration allows that."

"We ... have a special relationship with some of the desk clerks."

"You mean you pay bribes?"

"I wouldn't put it that way."

"This explains a lot. I had a minor fender bender a few months ago, and the very next day I got mail from four lawyers and two chiropractors. It was like a magic trick. Now I know how it's done."

"It's a very competitive market out there," Abernathy said. "A small practitioner has to protect himself."

"I've been a small practitioner," Ben said, "but I never haunted accident victims."

"Well, I can't afford to be quite as high and mighty as you. I have a family to feed."

"So you sent one of these solicitations to the Nelsons?"

"Actually, I sent three, staggered over three days, under three different trade names. Just to increase the odds that I'd be the one they chose."

"And now that you've badgered them into giving you their case, you haven't done a damn bit of work on it."

"I've been trying to urge an early settlement that would be to everyone's advantage. . . ."

"That's it, isn't it? You're just working on a percentage. You try to lure in as much business as possible, on the theory that some of those will settle profitably without any serious work. And the ones that don't settle—well, they just go down the tubes."

"You can't win every case."

"Especially if you don't try."

"Look, Kincaid, you're representing a big monolithic corporation. You're not supposed to care about regular people who suffer tragedy. I don't understand what you're getting so upset about."

"How can I put this to you, Abernathy? I think you epitomize everything that's wrong with the legal profession today. I hate lawyer jokes, I hate the bad press lawyers get, and I hate the lack of appreciation the general public has for what lawyers do. And then I meet someone like you, and I realize where people get these ideas. And it really depresses the hell out of me."

As if on cue, Judge Roemer sailed into the courtroom. "All rise," the bailiff intoned.

True to form, Roemer was in a no-nonsense mood. This could mean that he was familiar with Ben's brief and agreed with his argument. Or it could mean it was a sunny day and there was a golf cart at Southern Hills with Roemer's name on it.

"This is your motion, isn't it?" Roemer asked Ben. Ben nodded.

"Do you have anything you'd like to add?"

"Yes, thank you, your honor." Ben headed for the podium. He didn't actually have anything to add; his brief outlined everything he had to say. But he'd been practicing long enough to know it was a mistake to assume the judge had read the briefs.

"Under the standards adopted for summary judgment proceedings by the United States Supreme Court in the *Liberty Lobby* trilogy of cases," Ben began, "the plaintiff is required to come forth with some evidence to prove there are material facts in dispute that should go to trial. The evidence must be more than a mere scintilla; the evidence must be such that a reasonable jury could find there is some possibility that the plaintiff's position is correct. This is what the plaintiffs in this case have failed to do.

"Plaintiffs have reviewed thousands of Apollo documents, have issued interrogatories, and have taken depositions. They have forced the Apollo Consortium to expend thousands of dollars in legal fees and expenses.

And they have come up with nothing. This has been a gigantic fishing expedition conducted at Apollo's expense, and the plaintiffs haven't caught a single fish.

"Your honor, I have outlined the elements of the various claims plaintiffs have raised in our brief, and specified each requirement they have failed to meet. Plaintiffs claim there was a design defect in the XKL-1 suspension system, but they have no evidence. They claim there was negligence by Apollo, but they have no evidence. And they claim there was a failure to provide an adequate warning, but they have no evidence.

"Plaintiffs have brought an action for wrongful death, claiming that the acts of the Apollo Consortium caused the death of their son. But they have neither produced nor found any evidence to support this claim. Granted, the Nelsons have suffered a horrible loss, and I'm sure we all sympathize with them. But there is simply no connection between what happened to their son and the Apollo Consortium. Therefore, summary judgment should be entered against the plaintiffs."

"Thank you, counsel," Roemer said. He seemed pleased. Ben wasn't sure if that was because he liked what Ben had said or because Ben had said it quickly. Roemer was thumbing through the pleadings file, searching for something.

"Mr. Abernathy, I don't find a brief in opposition in the file from you. Did you reply?"

"Uh, no, sir."

Roemer frowned. "Would you like to reply now?"

"Yes. Thank you, sir." Abernathy fumbled with his papers and stumbled to the podium. Ben checked the Nelsons' expressions; they were obviously concerned.

"You know, your honor, I don't much hold with all this pretrial motioning."

Roemer's eyebrows rose slightly.

"I believe every man and woman is entitled to his or her day in court. Everyone is entitled to a fair shot at proving their case."

"If we followed your theory," Roemer said, "the courts would be so bogged down with trials we'd be backed up for years. Just dealing with all the lawsuits that do make it to trial is a nightmare."

"Still, your honor, every litigant deserves a chance to be heard—"

"We're not here to debate policy, Mr. Abernathy. The Supreme Court has given us our marching orders. Do you have any response to the defendant's motion?"

"Well . . . obviously I disagree—"

"Do you have any evidence to support your clients' claims?"

"Discovery is ongoing, sir. We still hope to uncover—"

"Perhaps you didn't understand me, counsel. I asked if you have any evidence. Now."

Ben covered his smile with his hands. This was going beautifully. He glanced at his colleague in the back row; he could tell Rob was pleased.

"Your honor, these are very complex, technical issues. We need more time—"

"There is no more time, Mr. Abernathy. Summary judgment is a put-up-or-shut-up motion."

"Still, your honor—"

"Mr. Abernathy, do you at least have affidavits from your clients? That might be enough to put a material fact into dispute. Surely you could get an affidavit from your own clients."

"I hadn't really considered that, sir. . . ."

Roemer threw up his hands. "This is absurd. You have no evidence. Furthermore, you have no likelihood of finding any in the future unless it walks up and clubs you in the face. This case is ripe for summary judgment."

"Judge, if I may—"

"In fact, it's more than ripe. This is a perfect example of what summary judgment was designed to preclude. A frivolous lawsuit alleging unsupported claims dragging a faultless defendant through pointless, expensive litigation. Summary judgment is hereby granted." He banged his gavel to solidify his decision.

Ben rose. "Thank you, your honor."

"You'll draft up the order and judgment, counsel?" Ben nodded. "I'll expect to see it in fifteen days. This hearing is dismissed." Everyone shot to their feet as Roemer exited the courtroom.

Ben whirled around, buoyant. What a coup. Even if Abernathy threatened to appeal, as he probably would, it would be futile. He'd been creamed.

The only thing that could be better than a major victory is a major victory while your boss's informant is watching. He started down the aisle toward Rob—then noticed the Nelsons sitting motionless on the front row.

June Nelson's lips were moving, but no words were coming out. Ben leaned in closer. She was murmuring something over and over, just on the edge of audibility.

"My son . . . my son . . . They took my son. . . ."

Carl Nelson gently took her by the arm. "The show's over, June. Let's move along now."

She did not respond. "Nobody cares. . . . They took my son. . . ."

Gently, Carl Nelson raised June to her feet and steered her toward the door.

"Is she going to be all right?" Ben asked.

"She'll be fine. She's just upset. It's hard, losing your son like that. And now, with the judge throwing our case out of court—" His voice choked. He paused, inhaled deeply. "It's as if the judge was saying it was okay. It was okay for them to do what they did. It was okay and nobody cares that our son is gone forever."

Ben was unsure whether he could maintain control of himself. "I'm sorry," he whispered.

Carl Nelson patted him on the shoulder. "That's all right, son. You were just doing your job."

They shuffled past Ben and left the courtroom.

* 32 *

Tomlinson waited outside the Eleventh Street Denny's, drumming his fingers on the steering wheel of his car. He'd been there since eight-fifteen. An overabundance of caution—perhaps. But he wasn't taking any chances. He was close—very close—to catching the killer, and proving to Morelli once and for all that he had the right stuff to play on the Homicide team. Now all he had to do was make sure he didn't fumble the ball in the last quarter.

He checked the clock on the dash of his car. It was five after nine. Trixie was late. He tried not to become concerned. She was a teenager, after all. When was a teenager ever not late? Still, it made him nervous. Too many potential witnesses had died already. He wasn't going to let this one slip silently into the grave as well.

He fingered the outline of the revolver in the shoulder harness under his jacket. He'd catch all kinds of hell if anyone knew he'd removed a weapon from the station arsenal—guns weren't generally required for switchboard duty. But Trixie needed protection, and he intended to provide it. She was a likable girl—charming, in her way. He hated to think about what could have driven her to the streets at her age. Her life had been tough enough already. It was going to stop here, if he had anything to say about it.

He hoped Trixie didn't take much longer. Nervousness aside, he'd promised Karen he wouldn't be out all night, as he had been last night, and the night before, and the night before that. He couldn't even remember the last time he'd spent a pleasant evening with Kathleen. These days, the only hours he was home were the hours she was certain to be asleep. He'd become exactly what he told himself he'd never be—an all-work, no-family fool. Just like his own father.

He rolled down the window of his car and listened to the dissonant sounds of the city. If he could just get past this one case, he thought to himself. If he could just get this psycho behind bars, get his promotion, and get on with his life. That was all he wanted. Why did it have to be so hard in coming?

At ten after, Trixie pushed open the front door of the building on the opposite side of the street. She was wearing tattered jeans with holes over the knees, a white T-shirt turned backwards, and gold hoop earrings. She looked almost normal—like any teenage kid you might see wandering around the mall. If only it were so.

She passed between two parked cars and started crossing the four-lane street. Just as she made it to the center, Tomlinson heard the squeal of tires. A large black van pulled away from the curb and peeled across the street. It careened down the center at an impossible speed; its target was obvious.

"Trixie!" Tomlinson screamed out.

Trixie looked up just in time to see the van's headlights bearing down on her. She staggered backward, confused.

"Trixie! Move!"

Trixie skittered clumsily back the way she had come and jumped onto the hood of one of the parked cars. The van whizzed by, scraping the parked car as it passed. There was an electric, burning sound; sparks flew between the cars. The parked car shuddered. Trixie rolled with it and landed on the sidewalk.

"Trixie, wait! *I'm coming!*"

Trixie did not wait. She fled back inside the building. A few moments later, Tomlinson saw all the lights shut off.

Tomlinson ran across the street. There was no point in trying to follow the van; it could be halfway to Joplin by now. He entered the tall, narrow building Trixie and her buddies called home.

The entire house was dark. Faint traces of moonlight filtered through a few high windows, but provided precious little illumination. He couldn't see a foot before him.

"Trixie! It's Officer Tomlinson!"

There was no response. Of course not. She didn't know who was prowling around down there. She hadn't known him long enough to recognize his voice. For all she knew he was the maniac driving the van. Maybe she thought he had arranged this meeting so he could kill her. No, she wasn't going to come out for anyone.

"Is anybody else in here?" If so, they weren't answering. Probably there was no one—the other girls would be working, and their pimp lived across the street. In all likelihood, it was just him and Trixie.

Slowly, his eyes began to adjust to the darkness. He could see the dim outline of a staircase leading upstairs. Through the foyer, he saw a parlor—nothing elegant, just a television and a ratty old sofa. He passed through the parlor, then through the kitchen, then back into the foyer, without finding anyone.

He mounted the staircase. The steps creaked beneath his feet. In the blackness, the effect was eerie. He watched his feet, trying to make sure he didn't slip through a crack or fall off the edge. Even in the dark, he could tell this house was a rathole. Unclean, unfit, poorly ventilated—and Trixie's boss probably charged her more for it than Tomlinson paid on his mortgage. Another piece of the boss man's percentage.

He reached the top of the stairs. He spotted a light switch and flipped it; nothing happened. Trixie must've cut the breakers. She was taking no chances on being caught.

The top of the stairs unfolded upon a long hallway

that stretched in two directions. Tomlinson saw several doors on both sides; the rooms must be the size of closets. Enough room for a cot and a change box—that was all that was required.

He opened the door to the first room on the left. "Trixie? Trixie, I promise I'm not—"

There was a sudden shrieking, and something hit him in the face. He staggered back, disoriented, panicked. Whatever it was, it was still there, clinging to him. Something cut him; he could feel blood trickling out. He flailed desperately, trying to break free, trying to see, reaching up for—

It was a cat. He grabbed the furry beast and tossed it across the room. He had to laugh, despite the fact that he was dripping with sweat and trembling from head to toe. It was just a damn cat, for Pete's sake. A cat had jumped up and scratched him. And he'd practically had a cardiac arrest.

The darkness was definitely getting to him. He was breathing in short raspy breaths, and his shirt was clinging to his skin. If he could just find some candles, or a flashlight. Maybe he should go back to his car—

But if he did that, Trixie would leave, and he might never find her again. He had to track her down now, while there was still some hope of regaining her trust.

He heard a noise downstairs. He couldn't quite identify it—probably the cat racing outside, trying to escape the tall, dark monster it had encountered in the dark. It couldn't be Trixie. He would've heard her going down those creaky stairs.

"Trixie! Please come out. Turn the power back on so we can—"

And that's when it occurred to him. Maybe that hadn't been the cat he heard downstairs. Maybe—

He froze. His chest heaved, but other than that, he couldn't move. Maybe the noise hadn't been the cat slipping out, he thought. Maybe it had been someone else slipping in.

Tensing all his muscles, he forced himself into action. He ran to a window overlooking the front door. Sure enough, a black van with smoked glass windows was parked not twenty feet down the street. He couldn't read the license plate.

He cursed himself bitterly. The driver hadn't sped off. The driver was right here with him. In the dark.

As quietly as possible, Tomlinson sidestepped back into the hallway. It was so quiet—was there something outside, some noise, some hint, some echo? Something soft and regular? Footsteps? Breathing? Or just his imagination?

"Trixie?" he whispered. "Is that you? If it is, please come here. We're safer together. I can protect you."

Abruptly, the soft sound stopped. It was the absence that proved its existence; Tomlinson was only certain he had heard a noise when it ended.

"Trixie?" he repeated.

If it was her, she wasn't coming any closer. Could it be—the other? He was sure the driver of the van couldn't be upstairs yet. Those stairs creaked so badly; he couldn't possibly have come upstairs without being heard.

Tomlinson placed one hand on the handle of his revolver. He pressed himself flat against the wall. He scanned the hallway as well as possible in this killing obscurity.

There was nothing there. Nothing, nobody. He released his breath in an outpouring of relief. How long had he been holding his breath? He walked to the head of the stairs. That would be the safest, smartest place. The driver couldn't get upstairs without being heard, and Trixie couldn't leave without going through him.

His confidence began to return. This was a workable plan. Foolproof, really. He was embarrassed for not thinking of it sooner. He'd been letting the dark get to him, letting it affect his performance as a police officer.

There was nothing here to worry about. Nothing that could hurt him—

The hands wrapped around his neck in a tight choke hold, cutting off his breath. Something hit him hard in the stomach. Tomlinson grabbed his gun, but one of the hands applied crippling force to his palm. He heard his fingers snap; his gun fell to the floor. The pain was unbearable. He felt dizzy and sick.

Suddenly, it was even blacker than before. Something had been pulled over his head, something cold and thin. It crinkled like plastic. He tried to catch his breath, which made the plastic cling to his mouth and choke him all the worse. He tried to struggle, to move, to get away, but his assailant held him tight. Whoever it was must be incredibly strong; Tomlinson couldn't move at all.

He lost his footing and stumbled off the top stair. It didn't matter. The strong hands held him upright.

He felt something tighten around his throat. He knew he was fading. He tried to kick, but his feet only touched empty air. He tried to shout, but he couldn't make a sound. He was absolutely helpless.

Trixie! he wanted to cry out, but the words would not come. He could barely think, his chest throbbed so. He felt his consciousness escaping as the world swirled around him. Bright white lights flashed before his eyes. What would happen to Karen, and Kathleen? He fell to his knees, wanting to cry, wanting to beg for mercy, but helpless to do anything at all.

And then everything turned to black.

PART THREE

*   *

Toward Chaos

* 33 *

The driver of the van exited on the Eleventh Street side of the corner. His black boots tapped along the pavement, clickety-clack, clickety-clack. The wind tousled his meticulously styled hair. Annoyed, he pushed the errant strands back into place.

He opened the glass door to Denny's and approached the counter. He waved at the waitress, smiling a handsome smile.

"Excuse me. Did you work here last night?"

"That I did." She placed her order pad inside her apron and leaned against the counter. "Why? D'you fall in love and come back to marry me?"

"No," the man said, grinning. "But I may yet. I'm looking for someone."

"'Zat right?" She wiped her hands on a dish towel. "Why would you be doing that? You're not a cop, are you?"

"No. Not by a long shot." He took a Polaroid photo out of his pocket and passed it to the woman. "This is the girl I'm looking for. I believe she goes by the name Trixie."

The woman glanced at the photo, then passed it back. "What you be wantin' with Trixie?"

"I owe her some money. See, I'm a . . . well, a former customer, if you know what I mean. Kind of a regular, actually. I was short of cash last time, and I wanted to make up the difference."

"Sonny let you leave without paying in full? That's not the Sonny I know."

"Exactly. That's why it's so important that I find her quickly. I don't want her to get into any trouble."

The woman's eyes narrowed. "Are you sure that's all you want?"

The man hesitated before answering. "I guess I can't fool you, can I? It's not just the money. I thought I might arrange another . . . date."

"You got the money this time?"

"Gobs. I was hoping I could arrange one of those pricey picnic jobs. Thought we might go to The Playground with a few of my friends."

"The Playground. What on earth would you be doing out there?"

"Searching for eternity," the man said. "Scaling the final barrier. Achieving a sense of closure."

"Sounds weird to me."

"I'm sorry. I tend to wax metaphysical from time to time. Do you know where I might find Trixie?"

"Normally, I'd say right across the street, but she doesn't seem to be there tonight. Come to think of it, she wasn't there last night either."

"Any idea where she went?"

"'Fraid not. She don't check in and out with me."

"Well, if you do see her, tell her a friend is looking for her. I'll check back here tomorrow."

"You do that, lover boy. I'm sure she hasn't gone far."

The waitress watched as the handsome man walked out of the diner, his heels clickety-clacking on the linoleum floor. He climbed into his van and drove away.

A few moments later, after she was sure he was gone, the waitress crouched down and whispered, "Did you hear all that?"

Trixie crawled out from under the counter, brushing the dirt from her knees. "Yes. Every lying word."

"Did you see what he looked like?"

"No. But I heard his voice."

"You should have seen his eyes. Most of the time, he seemed perfectly normal—handsome, in fact. Friendly. But for just a second there, when he was talking all high-toned and fancy, he let his mask drop, and I looked into his eyes. There was something real disturbin' about him, Trixie. Somethin' scary."

"You're giving me the creeps, Marge."

"Good. What you going to do, child?"

"I don't know. I can't stay around here, that's obvious."

"What's Sonny say? He's supposed to take care of you."

"Sonny only takes care of himself. He thinks I should be back on the street."

"That man would find you in a heartbeat."

"I know. I need somewhere to go, someplace to hole up."

"Got any family?"

"Not around here. And I'm not going back to my father's house, no matter what."

"Maybe you should take a vacation. Got any money?"

"Not enough." She stretched out her legs, careful to make sure she was not visible through the front windows. "Marge, is there any chance you could put me up? It would only be for—"

"I'm sorry, Trixie. I'd do almost anything for you, you know I would. But I've got two children of my own at home. I can't be luring some sicko to my place."

"But he's going to *kill* me!" Tears began to well up in her eyes. "Did you hear about what he did to that nice cop?"

Marge nodded grimly. "I heard. And that's all the more reason I can't be inviting that man to my house." She paused. "Honey, maybe you should consider talking to the police."

"Get serious."

"I am."

"Why? So I can get another bust on my record?"

"They might be able to help."

"I've gone to the police before, and all I got for it was beat within an inch of my life. When did the police ever help any of us? Think about it, Marge. There's four of us gone now. *Four of us.* In less than three weeks. And the police haven't done a damn thing."

Marge tossed down her dish towel. "Well, you're going to have to do something, honey. And the sooner the better."

Trixie remained on the floor, her arms cradling her knees, rocking back and forth. "I know, Marge. I know."

* 34 *

Ben, Christina, and Jones rode the glass elevator to the top of the Apollo headquarters building. It was almost one in the morning. The night was overcast; there was no moon, no stars. The effect was breathtaking; it was as if they were flying into the heavens. Oddly enough, Ben thought it much less unsettling than most elevator rides. Perhaps the darkness obscured his sense of height.

"I'm still not sure this is a great idea," Ben said nervously.

"Getting cold feet, Boss?" Jones asked.

"Don't worry about Ben," Christina said. "He's a scaredy-cat from way back. Nonetheless, he always manages to pull off these escapades with great finesse."

"And," Ben added, "I always seem to be pulling them off with you. I thought we swore off break-ins for all time."

"This hardly counts as a break-in," she replied. "After all, we do work here."

"Yeah, but no one expects us to be skulking about at one in the morning. And no one would ever permit us to sift through the computer records."

"If we asked them." Christina smiled. "Don't let him scare you, Jones. Break-ins are Ben's métier. And who's going to catch us at this time of night?"

"I'm not worried," Jones replied. "If I get nabbed, I just plan to blame everything on the Boss."

That caught Ben's attention. "Oh?"

"I'll say I had no idea we were doing anything wrong. Ben hired me to do some computer research, that's all. I had no way of knowing everything wasn't on the up-and-up."

The elevator dinged and the doors opened. "Well, I feel much better now that I know you've got your butt covered," Ben said. "Let's go."

They crossed the elevator lobby and turned the corner toward Ben's office and the computer room. They were all wearing sneakers, broken in and nonsqueaky.

Ben suddenly heard a loud pounding noise. He froze, motioning the others to stay put. "What is that?" he hissed.

"It came from down the hall."

"Oh, great. Just where we're headed." Frowning, Ben crouched and tiptoed down the hallway. The pounding repeated. Ben saw the closed door to Herb's office quiver and shake.

He crept closer and saw Herb standing outside his office, pounding on the door—buck naked. Herbert the Pervert strikes again.

"Goddamn it!" Herb yelled at the closed door. "This isn't funny! What if someone comes?"

Ben heard a reply from the inside, but it was muffled

and he couldn't make out what was being said. The voice was definitely female, though. Perhaps he'd called Candice a nasty name one time too many.

"Let me in!" Herb repeated, pounding again and again on the door. "I mean it!" The door did not open. "Look, I'm sorry I said you'd put on a few pounds. I was just teasing. You look great."

He waited, but there was still no response from the other side. "I can't believe you'd take advantage like this, just because I had to go across the hall to the crapper." He shook with frustration. "Honey, what if someone comes through the front door—"

He gestured toward the front door, and in so doing, saw Ben crouched on the floor. "Too late."

Herb ran behind a secretarial station and tried to hide himself behind a typewriter. "Kincaid! You again?"

Ben stood up. "This is becoming a distressingly familiar event. What's the problem, Herb? Can't you afford a hotel room like everyone else?"

"That's none of your goddamn business. What are you doing here, anyway?"

"I . . . had some work I wanted to finish before tomorrow morning's staff meeting."

"Sounds suspicious to me."

"Says you. At least I have my pants on."

Herb made an evil, growling noise. "Look, I don't want this story going around the office, understand? Especially not to Crichton."

"Really? I was thinking about putting it in staff notes."

"Hardy har har. Cut me some slack, Kincaid. Guy to guy."

"Well, since you put it like that." Grinning, Ben headed back the way he had come. He heard Herb do some more pounding, then finally heard the office door open. He hated to think about what Herb must've promised her.

To his surprise, Ben hadn't walked halfway down the

hallway when he saw Candice approaching from the other direction. And heading toward Herb's office.

"Candice!"

"True. What of it?"

"But I thought—I mean—I assumed—"

"Pull yourself together, Kincaid. You're not making any sense."

"I—never mind. What are you doing here this time of night?"

"I'm looking for that asshole Herb. Have you seen him?"

Ben felt beads of sweat forming on his forehead. "I think he's in his office."

Her eyes became tiny slits. "Is he alone?"

"No, I don't think so."

"That son of a bitch." She collapsed against the secretarial station. "I might have known."

"For whatever it's worth," Ben said, "I think the less you have to do with Herb, the better."

"Easy for you to say. You were brought in at an Attorney Four level."

"At what?"

"Attorney four. Two levels and twenty thousand dollars above me. Since I started working here five years ago, Crichton has promoted every man in the department on a regular basis. But not me."

"Why?"

"I didn't play the game. Didn't communicate my ideas via male intermediaries. Didn't sit back and let men take credit for my work. And there was the Herb problem."

"I'm not sure what you mean."

"Herb had been coming on to me since day one. Suggesting that I should dress *like a woman*. Asking what I'd be willing to do to keep my bosses happy. Touching me when he talked. Making off-color jokes. Then he got bolder. He started asking if I wanted to come over to his place and watch porn movies. Asking if I ever got the *urge* to fuck various Apollo employees. Did I like to do it with other women? Did I like to do it with myself? He was disgusting. I rebuffed him at every turn."

"Good for you."

"Easy to say. Soon Herb was badmouthing me to everyone in the department, including Crichton. I confronted Herb, asked what the hell was going on. He hinted strongly that I wasn't going to rise in this organization until my male colleagues—like him—stopped reporting that I was an unpleasant bitch. But he had a price for his positive recommendation."

"Surely you didn't—"

"I resisted for years. But after awhile, after I saw assholes like Chuck and idiots like Doug make Attorney Three and Four while I was still Attorney One, I thought, what the hell. Sure, it was a compromise, but ..." She waved her hand shakily in the air. "I started giving Herb what he wanted."

"And?"

"And, just four months ago, I made Attorney Two. First and only woman in Crichton's department to be promoted. Of course, it was just a token promotion; even Crichton knew he might have legal problems if he didn't toss a bone to one of the women in the department."

"So that's how it started with you and Herb. . . ."

"Yeah. Herbert the Pervert." She laughed bitterly. "I hate him. All those fights between Herb and me that you thought were fake? They were only fake on one end. Maybe not even that. I came here to tell Herb it was over. I know Herb could still crush my career in an instant, but I just can't stand it any longer."

"I don't think you want to go in right now."

"No, this is fine. He's made it even easier for me—if I catch him in the act, maybe he'll feel guilty. Or maybe I can blackmail him. You wouldn't happen to have a camera on you?" Ben shook his head. "Anyway, I'm going in there."

"Do you really think that's—"

Ben's words were useless; she had already passed him and was practically in Herb's office. Ben decided to move quickly in the opposite direction. A few moments later, he rejoined his group.

"What's all the commotion up there?" Christina asked.

"I'll tell you later."

"Later, schmater. I want to see for myself." She started down the hallway.

Ben grabbed her arm. "Believe me, Christina. You absolutely, positively do not want to see for yourself. I have a hunch that in a few moments the whole corridor is going to go ballistic." He swung her back toward the elevator lobby. "Let's go around the other way."

They tiptoed through the elevator lobby and emerged on the other side of the floor. Ben thought he heard a sound ahead of him—some kind of movement. He approached the corner cautiously, his back pressed against the wall.

"Be careful," Christina whispered. "I heard it, too."

Ben breathed in and out, trying to slow his racing heart. All this creeping around was starting to get to him. But why should he be afraid? Who hadn't he met up here already? He spun around the corner.

"*Ahhhhhh!*" the man on the other side cried out.

"*Ahhhhhh!*" Ben cried back, startled.

After the initial shock, Ben pulled himself back down to earth and focused. *"Loving?"*

It was in fact Loving, Ben's private investigator from his previous life. Loving was dressed in a T-shirt and blue jeans.

"What are you doing up here?"

"Covering your backside," Loving answered. "I thought you guys might need some protection."

"If you're covering our backside, why are you in front of us?"

" 'Cause you keep changing directions!"

"Oh. Sorry. How did you get up here? I didn't hear the elevator."

"I didn't take the elevator. I took the stairs."

"All the way up? You must be exhausted."

"Piece of cake," he said, trying to conceal his gasping for air.

"Look, why don't you sit down and catch your breath? We have to move on."

"No way. You guys might need some muscle. I'm sticking to you like glue."

Ben resigned himself to the inevitable, and motioned for Loving to follow. Down the chain of hallways, Ben led them to his office and, on the other side of the hall, the main computer room. Various computer terminals and printers lined the walls, while one much larger terminal rested in the center.

"That one must be the big mama," Jones said. "It probably controls the entire LAN."

"Think you can get in?"

Jones wriggled his fingers. "Let's find out." He sat down before the terminal and turned on the CPU. "It boots directly into a Wordperfect database. Let me review these files and see if there's anything that might've interested Hamel."

Jones reached for the keyboard—then realized that it was locked in a wooden case. "Uh-oh," he said. "Someone doesn't want unauthorized personnel playing with the computer."

"Does this prove they have something to hide?" Ben asked.

"Not necessarily. Corporations are notorious for going to great lengths to keep secrets. After all, if their records were open to any hacker in town, they'd soon have no secrets at all."

Ben examined the rectangular pine box. "It's locked up tight. I don't see how we're going to get in without a key."

"Allow me," Loving said. "This is where you need

some muscle." Loving extended his fingers, concentrated, then brought his hand down hard on the top of the box.

"Owww!" he cried out. "That smarts."

"Have you ever studied karate?" Ben asked.

"No. But that's how those guys do it in the movies."

"Ah. Jones, did he do any damage?"

"Well, not to the box."

"Blast," Ben said. "We're never going to get in there. All this risk, all this sneaking around, all for nothing."

"Don't give up yet, o intrepid adventurer," Christina said.

"Why not?"

"Look what I found." She dangled a single key hooked around a brass ring.

"Where'd you get that?"

"From the back of the storage cabinet. That's where they keep the spare."

"How'd you know that?"

"Well . . ." Christina glanced at the ceiling. "I just happened to invite Marilyn from Bookkeeping out to lunch today, and we got to talking about the Apollo computer system, and one thing led to another. . . ."

"You sly dog," Ben said. "You were way ahead of us."

"What else is new? I thought our plan should be more detailed than, 'Let's sneak in and see what happens.' "

"Thank goodness you were here." Ben unlocked the box and withdrew the keyboard. Jones took control and began punching buttons.

"Great," Jones said. "Every file is identified and listed in alphabetical order. I'll just scan them and see if there's anything that might've gotten Hamel killed."

Christina gazed over his shoulder. "There are hundreds of files in there."

"True," Jones said. "Maybe you'd better have a seat."

* * *

An hour and a half later, Ben and Christina were still sitting on the floor watching Jones's fingers fly over the keyboard. Not exactly the most stimulating way to pass the early hours of the morning. Ben had to fight to keep his eyes open. Loving had posted himself outside the door, to "keep an eye out for trouble."

"Seen anything interesting?" Ben asked.

"To tell you the truth," Jones said, "I'm more interested in what I can't see. All the files on this system are subject to easy access, except one. That one file is locked up tight; you can't get in without a password."

Ben scrutinized the computer terminal. "Think you can break in?"

"Only if we figure out the password. I'm not equipped to generate random letter combos or do any serious hacking."

"What can we do?"

"I've been trying obvious possible passwords, but so far, I haven't had any luck. I tried *Apollo*, *Consortium*, *Howard Hamel*, and several others."

"Try *Crichton*," Ben suggested. The man was just egotistical enough to use his own name.

Jones typed it onto the screen. Nothing happened.

"What about *Herbert*? Or, if he was feeling romantic, perhaps *Candice*."

Jones tried both. Still no results.

"What about something more generic," Christina suggested. "Try *Lawyer*. Or *Legal*. Or *Murder*."

Jones tried all her suggestions, and several others that followed, but nothing cracked open the file.

"Wait a minute," Ben said, snapping his fingers. "Try *Kindergarten Club*."

Jones gave him a strange look, but obediently typed the words onto the screen.

A split second after Jones hit the Enter button, the screen faded. A blue blip was followed by page one of a new document.

"It worked!" Jones said jubilantly. "Great work, Boss."

"Lucky guess." He scanned the document. It appeared to be an address list containing about fifteen names.

"They're all Apollo employees. See?" Christina pointed to the screen. "It identifies their departments and phone extensions."

"But look here," Jones said. "Up at the top. See the empty space? Someone has deleted a name."

"Curiouser and curiouser." Most of the names were unfamiliar to Ben. "What do they have in common?" he wondered aloud.

"Apparently," Christina said, "they're all members of the Kindergarten Club."

"Yes," he said, nodding his head thoughtfully. "But what in God's name is that?"

* 35 *

Later that afternoon, as Ben struggled to keep his eyelids open, he was relieved to see Christina walk into his office. Not only was he desperately sleepy—he was bored. While the Nelson case was pending, he'd been in constant motion. Now that the case was over, he had nothing to do. He had assumed he would get another case, but so far, nothing.

"Have you heard anything about Crichton?" Ben asked.

"I heard he's going to be released from the hospital

soon. Knowing him, he'll probably be back in the office the next day."

"Probably right." Ben pressed a finger against his lips. "Isn't it funny? Since you and I came here, we've been on two of these macho corporate outings, and both times Crichton has managed to get hurt."

"I was thinking the same thing myself," Christina said.

"Almost as if someone was out to get him, isn't it?"

"Yeah. Almost."

"Had any luck with the Kindergarten list?"

She shook her head no.

"Blast. Tomorrow's my deadline with Chief Blackwell. If I don't have something concrete for him, he's going to bury me so deep you won't be able to visit me without a warrant."

"I'm doing everything I can," Christina said. "I pulled the personnel files on the fifteen employees on the list. They're in different departments, answering to different bosses, doing all different kinds of work. I can't find any connection among them, other than that they're all Apollo employees, most of them at a fairly high level."

Ben slapped his palm on his desk. "Hell. Maybe we should just *ask* them what the Kindergarten Club is."

"Right. That's likely to produce results. 'Excuse me, we've uncovered evidence that you're involved in some kind of weird organization linked to the mutilation-death of four teenage girls and possibly Howard Hamel. Would you mind talking about it?' And then we could just sit back and watch the attorneys congregate."

"I suppose you're right."

"Your problem, Ben, is that you're just too honest. Instead of making some gigantic frontal assault, let's try something with a bit more élan. Something more ... surreptitious."

"I'm not breaking into any more offices!"

"I'm not saying you should. All I'm suggesting is that you take a profitable walk down the hallway."

"I don't follow."

"Look, everything we've learned about this case points right here, inside the legal department. All our best suspects are just down the hall. Hamel seems to have known something that someone else did not want to get out. If Hamel had some sensitive information pertaining to this Kindergarten Club, maybe some of the other lawyers do, too."

"Makes a certain twisted sense," Ben admitted. "But I don't see how it gets me a course of action."

"Go forth and investigate," she whispered. "Search their offices."

"During office hours?"

"Well, as we've discovered, these offices are never entirely vacated. And it will be considerably more suspicious if you get caught rummaging through someone's office at two in the morning."

"This is true." Ben thought for a moment. "But I can't just go wandering around, poking into desks and file cabinets. I need some kind of excuse."

"Easily contrived. What are you working on right now?"

"Well, actually, nothing."

"Nothing at all? Have you talked to Rob? He's acting as Crichton's messenger."

"Crichton hasn't given me an assignment since the Nelson case ended."

A deep furrow crossed Christina's brow. "Is that a fact? Well, all the better. Since we came here Crichton's been griping that he can't tell what cases are pending and what cases aren't. I think you, the bright hardworking young lawyer, should seize the initiative and compile a litigation calendar."

"A litigation calendar?"

"Sure. Identify pending cases, list any pressing deadlines, future plans, that sort of thing. Of course, you'll have to get information from the other lawyers about their cases. And if they're not in their offices at the time . . . you might have to hunt around a bit to get what you need."

"And if they *are* in their office?"

"Make sure they aren't."

"I dunno, Christina. Sounds dangerous."

"True, this is a risk. But Chief Blackwell is a certainty unless you come up with something in the next twenty-four hours."

"Well, since you put it like that . . . let's get to work on the calendar."

* 36 *

Ben decided to start with Shelly's office. His first choice had been Doug's, but Doug was poised squarely behind his computer and appeared unlikely to move unless a power shortage blanketed Tulsa. Shelly was much easier—she was out of her office, and probably wouldn't cause trouble in any event.

Ben picked up a small framed photo on Shelly's desk. The picture was of a cute, chubby-cheeked redheaded infant, perhaps three months old. Must be Shelly's daughter, Angie. Ben could see the resemblance. Very cute. He scanned Shelly's desktop calendar and saw the usual appointments and deadline ticklers. No references to a Kindergarten Club—not even a cryptic *K.C.* She did have an unusually high number of doctor's appointments, but that could probably be explained by the fact that she had so recently given birth.

He checked the hallway. Still no sign of Shelly. He opened her desk drawer. Pencils, pens, rubber bands, paper clips—so what? He closed the desk and opened the top drawer of her credenza. It was cluttered with files going two different directions; organization was obviously not Shelly's strong point. He found a half-empty box of Snickers bars tucked away in one corner and more baby pictures in another. Ben thumbed through the baby pictures, and to his surprise, found a wallet-size photo of Howard Hamel.

He held the Hamel photo next to one of Angie. Come to think of it, there was some resemblance there, too.

He returned both photos and began rifling through her files. Nothing caught his eye—until he spotted one labeled Nelson. He pulled it out. Sure enough—it was the same Nelson case Ben had just managed to win.

"Are you looking for something in particular?"

Ben jumped a foot into the air. He slammed the drawer shut.

Shelly was standing in the doorway.

"I . . . er . . . I was just looking for . . ."

"Yes?"

"I just happened to notice that you had a file pertaining to the Nelson case. I've been trying to close out the case but I noticed some of the pleadings were missing. When I saw this file, I thought maybe you had them."

She relaxed a bit. "I was involved during the preliminary negotiations, before the lawsuit was filed. I don't have any pleadings."

"So I see. Sorry about that." Ben stepped away from her desk. "How did you get strong-armed into that case?"

"I was just back from maternity leave. Crichton dumped the case in my lap the day I returned, then took it back the very next day. Apparently Chuck told him I didn't have my head together yet."

"I thought Rob worked on that case before I came."

"Oh, Rob was only assigned to the case a day or two before you arrived. The case was originally assigned to Howard Hamel."

"Hamel?"

"Yeah. Crichton added me when he saw how much work would be involved. Then Chuck got me kicked off the case, and when you were hired, Howard got kicked off the case. And you and Rob were put on."

"Huh." Ben pointed to the picture on her desk. "By the way, adorable baby."

For the first time, Ben actually saw her smile. "Yeah, she is, isn't she?" She picked up the photo.

"*Shelly!* I thought I gave you something to do!"

Chuck was hovering just outside the door.

Shelly dropped the photo like a hot potato. "You did, Chuck. It was five minutes ago, remember?"

"Yes, and I expected you to get to work, not to screw around with baby pictures."

"I was not—" She shifted from one foot to the other. "I was just helping Ben with his case."

"That's not how it looked to me. Damn it, I don't know why Crichton hires women on the mommy track who pretend to want to be attorneys."

"That's not fair—"

"Maybe we should all just throw away our cases and hold a great big baby shower!"

"Chuck . . ." Ben said softly, ". . . I really think you should clam up."

"Butt out, Kincaid. This is none of your business."

"I disagree. I'm an attorney representing the Apollo Consortium, and I feel duty-bound to prevent you from engaging in any activities that could subject this corporation to liability."

"Shove off."

"You are engaging in classic Title VII sex discrimination and sexual harassment, federal offenses for which Apollo could be held liable for hundreds of thousands of dollars, especially if a pattern of discriminatory conduct is discovered. If that happens, you'll be the biggest pariah in the company. Frankly, I think Shelly already has more than enough ammunition to file suit."

"You don't know what you're talking about—"

"Oh, but I do. I know the Supreme Court held back in 1986 that sexual harassment claims fall under Title VII of the 1964 Civil Rights Act. I'm familiar with the EEOC guidelines on sexual harassment and sex discrimination, and I've seen you violate about ninety percent of them!"

Chuck fell silent.

"I think it's fair to say the only thing that's keeping you in your job is Shelly's patience and restraint," Ben continued. "Of course, that could disappear at any moment."

Shelly and Chuck exchanged a pointed look.

"If I were you," Ben added, "I'd start behaving civilly to Shelly. If you like your job, anyway."

Chuck's fists balled up. His face flushed red; he looked as if he might explode. He started to speak, then whirled around and stomped down the hallway.

"Thanks," Shelly said softly.

"I'm not sure I did you much of a favor. Probably just infuriated him. I'd keep a close eye on him."

"I will. Still, thanks."

Ben left her office. He was glad he'd been able to help her out, however temporarily. And more importantly, he was glad he'd been able to get out without explaining what he was doing in her office.

* 37 *

Ben spent the rest of the afternoon combing through offices. His encounter with Shelly inspired him to be more careful; he didn't go in unless he knew the attorney was in a meeting that would ramble on for at least half an hour. By the end of the day, though, he'd managed to search every office.

He'd searched every attorney on his level or lower—Herb, Candice, Chuck, Doug. He'd even searched Rob's office, though he knew Rob had been with him the entire day Hamel was killed. During his search, he'd learned that Doug was a fan of *The Executioner* novels, which was a surprise, and that Herb kept a pack of condoms in his desk, which wasn't. But he didn't find anything that brought him closer to understanding who killed Howard Hamel, or why, or what the connection to the murdered teenage girls could be.

Ben sat in his office, feet propped up on his desk, trying to solve the puzzle. Unfortunately, he couldn't come up with anything. The solution seemed just as elusive as it had always been.

He looked up from his desk blotter and was startled to see Crichton standing not two feet away.

"Swamped, Kincaid?"

Ben straightened up and put his feet on the floor. "I was just thinking something over . . ."

"I can come back if you're too busy."

"No. To be honest, I don't have a thing to do. Ever

since the Nelson case concluded, my assignments have dried up."

Crichton declined to comment. "Here's a new case I want you to work on." He tossed a file Ben's way. It smacked heavily on his desk. "It's extremely urgent. I want a thorough analysis and litigation strategy prepared in writing by tomorrow morning."

Tomorrow morning? "Uhh . . . what time will you be in tomorrow?"

"I don't want to know anything about it. You'll report directly to Harry Carter."

Carter? The hatchet man Christina warned him about? "May I ask why?"

"This is more his field of expertise than mine. And I'm too damn busy to get caught up in something like this."

"Sir, excuse me for asking, but shouldn't you be at home resting?"

Crichton released a short *pfui* sound. "That was much ado about nothing. Bunch of ball players acting like old women. Just a bump on the head. Nothing to get excited about."

"Sir . . . I heard you had a skull fracture."

"Very minor. Nothing that could take me out of commission. Work is really the best thing for it. You can't let incidents like this slow you down. You've got to get right back on that horse again and ride."

Ben wondered if Crichton subscribed to some sort of cliché service. "Surely you should at least try not to move any more than necessary. . . ."

"Can't be helped. I've got work to do." He pointed toward the imposing file on Ben's desk. "And so do you." He pivoted abruptly and left.

Ben fingered the manila folder on his desk. For a new case, the quantity of paperwork was immense. He scanned a few of the documents. It was an antitrust case involving dozens of parties, price fixing, RICO, and restraint of trade. Ben was stunned—he didn't know anything about antitrust litigation, an incredibly rarified, specialized field of practice. There were probably half a dozen people in Crichton's department better qualified to handle this case. Why on earth would he give it to Ben?

Before Ben had a chance to dwell on this new mystery, he saw a familiar figure in an unseasonably heavy overcoat step into his office.

"Mike! Glad to see you. I tried to call you last night but—"

Ben froze in mid-sentence. Chief Blackwell followed Mike into the office.

"Greetings, Kincaid. I came to check on your progress."

Ben rose. "Now, wait a minute. You gave me a week. I still have another day."

"I know, I know. I just wanted to see if you were making progress. After all, if you haven't gotten anywhere yet, what's the point of waiting till the last moment?"

"Especially when you've been unable to come up with a suspect on your own, right?"

Blackwell made a snarling noise. "You're treading on thin ice, Kincaid. I've already got more than enough to bring you in."

"I thought we had a deal."

"We did." He strode forward. "I just want you to understand that I'm serious."

Mike edged in between them. "I got the message that you tried to call me, Ben. Why don't you tell us what you've got?"

Ben told them about the computer file Jones discovered. "I've made a copy for you."

Mike scanned the list. "And you and Christina haven't found any connection linking the names on this list?"

"Other than the fact that they're all Apollo employees, no."

"Hmm," Blackwell said. "Maybe we should interview these jerks."

"I think that's a bad idea," Ben said. "No one is going to tell you anything unless you have more ammunition to throw at them than we have at the moment. All you'll do is raise their defenses."

Mike nodded. "I concur. I'm going to put a tail on each of them, though, if we can spare the manpower. Maybe we can learn something from where they go, what they do. Maybe they'll hold a meeting of this Kindergarten Club."

"That would be great," Ben said.

"I'm not convinced there's any link between this so-called club and the murders," Blackwell said gruffly, "and I'm not going to divert men from proven police procedures to chase some wild goose."

"I showed you the photo we found at Hamel's home," Mike said. "What more proof of a connection do you need? Surely we can spare a few men to follow up on this. We already have so many undercover officers planted in the red-light districts they're picking up one another."

"Red-light districts?" Ben said. "What's this about?"

Mike eyed Blackwell. Blackwell hesitated a moment, then shrugged. "Go ahead."

"This is top secret stuff," Mike said. "It has not been released to the press yet."

"I can keep a secret," Ben said. "Shoot."

"We've found the link between the victims. They were all teenage prostitutes."

Ben nodded appreciatively. "That should advance the investigation. How did you figure this out?"

"Through one renegade sergeant who couldn't follow orders," Blackwell cut in gruffly.

"That one renegade sergeant came up with more dope than the rest of us have in three weeks," Mike said curtly. "Ben, have I ever introduced you to Sergeant Tomlinson?"

"I don't think so."

"Decent guy. Real straight-shooter. Very by-the-book. Lovely wife, cute daughter. I liked him."

"You had a funny way of showing it," Blackwell said.

Mike twisted his neck uncomfortably. "I was just giving him a bad time, trying to make him work harder. He's dedicated, but a bit pedestrian. I was trying to make him stretch."

Blackwell smirked. "You were riding him like a saddle."

"He had applied for a transfer to Homicide," Mike explained. "He was qualified, sure, but I didn't want him to think it was easy. So I spun him around some. Just to push him."

"And now he's in a hospital bed," Blackwell said. "Practically dead."

"What!" Ben's eyes widened. "What happened?"

"We think he had a run-in with our killer," Mike said. "Someone had him in a choke hold—plastic trash bag tied around his head with a silken cord. One of the residents of the building they were in—a lady of the evening—happened to walk in on them before Tomlinson was altogether dead. The killer had to flee. But before he did, he tossed Tomlinson down a flight of stairs, just for good measure."

"Oh, my God," Ben said. "And he's still alive?"

"Just barely. The woman who walked in on them had the guts to call the police, even though she risked being picked up herself, and an ambulance took him to St. John's. He's still on a respirator and he hasn't regained consciousness. There's a chance he never will, or that when he does, he'll have severe brain damage from oxygen deprivation."

"Jesus." Ben steadied himself against his chair. "Do you have any idea what he was doing? How he tracked down the killer?"

"He made some notes we found in his desk. They're

sketchy, but they're better than nothing. Apparently Tomlinson recognized a tattoo on the second victim's body and traced that back to a red-light district. We're not sure which district, though Tomlinson used to work Eleventh Street, so I'd say that's our best bet. Anyway, he started investigating and eventually deduced that all the victims were teenage prostitutes. He seemed to think there was a pattern to the killings, a connection other than the fact that the victims were hookers. Unfortunately, he doesn't explain the connection in his notes. Like I said, they were very sketchy. All the last entry says is that he's looking for someone named Trixie."

"So you have a name? Great! Then all you need to do is round up every teen prostitute in town named Trixie."

"Believe me, Ben, we've tried. We've systematically quizzed every streetwalker we could find. No one fesses up to being Trixie. In fact, no one will even admit to knowing someone named Trixie."

"She must be hiding. She may have left town."

"That's possible, but I think it's unlikely. We've been watching the traditional exits carefully, and besides, most teen hookers are on a very short leash. I think she's still here. She's just keeping a low profile."

"Any idea why?"

"Only speculation. It's not all that unusual for a teen prostitute to keep her distance from the police."

"Good point." But, Ben thought silently, it's just possible someone not associated with the police might have better luck. His eyes met Mike's. He could tell he wasn't the only one in the room having the thought.

"Do we have a description of Trixie? Or the killer?"

"I'm afraid not. I've been assuming the killer is a man—because the murders and mutilation required strength and because all the victims have been female prostitutes—but I could be wrong. And it could be a man working for someone else. Serial killers come in all shapes and sizes."

"Are you sure it's a serial killer?"

Mike hesitated for a moment, then cocked an eyebrow. "Funny you should ask that. Just between you and me?"

"I'm not likely to report to *The New York Times*."

Mike glanced at Blackwell, then continued. "I'm certain all the murders were committed by the same person. The MOs are too similar; even an eyewitness couldn't duplicate the crime with such perfection. The phrase *serial killer* suggests a loony tune—a psychotic, or sociopath, or sexual deviant. Someone who kills with no motive other than what his twisted mind may invent. But there's something eminently ... logical about this killer."

"You find something logical in the mutilation of four helpless prostitutes?"

"That's just it. Why the mutilation? It doesn't seem to reflect gender hatred, or cannibalistic tendencies, or sexual obsessions, or any of the other traits you'll find in the FBI profiles. And why no threats? Why no sexual assaults? Why no taunting letters to the police? It's as if the killer is duplicating the eccentricities of a serial killer, but lacks the core madness of a true psychotic."

"If that's true, Mike, then we're looking for someone with—God forbid—a logical reason for committing these murders."

Mike pursed his lips. "I'm aware of that. What's more, I think Tomlinson was convinced of it."

"Well, pardon me if I'm not convinced. Anyone who would commit crimes like this is a nutcase in my book, *per se*. Surely you'll catch him soon if you continue this all-force full-court press."

"I'd like to tell you we're getting closer, Ben, but I'd be lying. This case is the living embodiment of the third law of thermodynamics: all things tend toward chaos. The harder we look, the less we find. The longer it takes, the more it gets away from us."

"Well, thanks for the info, Mike. Let me know if you

learn anything about the people on the Kindergarten list. I'll be sure to call tomorrow."

"Don't bother," Blackwell said. "I'll be back here the second your week is up. The press are hungry for a suspect. And I'm going to give them one."

"One way or another, huh?"

Blackwell stepped forward and stood so close that Ben could feel his hot unpleasant breath on his face. "That's exactly right, Kincaid. One way or another."

* 38 *

A few minutes after Mike and Chief Blackwell left, Christina breezed into Ben's office and seized her favorite chair. "Janice said you were looking for me."

Ben bit his knuckle pensively. "Christina, I need your help."

"Okay. Don't look so distressed. Have I ever denied you anything?"

"There's always a first time. I want to mount an undercover operation. Just you and me. Tonight."

"Tonight? That's not much advance warning. What if I have plans? What if I have a big date?"

"Then you need to cancel it. This can't wait."

"Why not?"

Ben tugged at his collar. "I just had a visit from Chief Blackwell."

"That blowhard? Let him arrest you. He'll never make it stick."

"Oh? The police are experts at making charges stick, especially when they're desperate, as you of all people should know. Besides, the arrest alone would kill my professional reputation, and if I'm behind bars how am I ever going to find out who killed Howard Hamel?"

"Okay, okay. How much time do you have?"

"Less than twenty-four hours."

She gulped. "Tonight it is. Give me the précis."

Ben recounted the new information that Mike had provided about Sergeant Tomlinson's private investigation. "The knowledge that the victims are all teen prostitutes is the wedge we need to crack this case wide open. We've been pumping away at our suspects here in the office and coming up empty. Now I think we need to come at it from the other end—from the victims' side of the mystery. Maybe we'll uncover something that will tie this whole mess together."

"Well ... it's worth a try. Especially since you're desperate. So what do you want me to do?"

Ben hemmed a bit and traced the pleat in his slacks. "Like I said before ... I want you to go undercover."

"Where?"

"Eleventh and Cincinnati. Walking the streets."

Christina drew herself up in the chair. "Now wait a minute, Ben. There's no chance in—"

"It's the only way."

"There must be an alternative."

"There isn't."

"I absolutely, positively refuse."

"Why? I've gone along with your schemes in the past."

"Never anything like this. Forget it, Ben. This is not going to happen."

"Please, Christina. It's important."

"Ben, you've been watching too many *Charlie's Angels* reruns. I am not going to masquerade as a prostitute."

Ben frowned. "A prostitute? No, you misunderstand. I don't want you to masquerade as a prostitute. I want you to masquerade as a customer."

* * *

Christina strolled leisurely down Eleventh Street, try-ing not to look back over her shoulder. Ben had prom-ised to follow in his car at a discreet distance, but you could never be sure about Ben. Sometimes he got lost walking from his kitchen to the living room. Or he might step up on a curb and get vertigo.

She hated these heels that he had insisted she wear. She'd only bought them at the resale shop as a joke; they tilted her feet up at ninety degree angles. Ben had turned her clothes closet upside down looking for "suit-ably sleazy clothes," and complained that there were too many possibilities to choose from. The billowy "bimbo top" he'd chosen, along with the hip-hugging miniskirt, certainly filled the bill. He'd even accesso-rized it for her: hoop chain belt, red glitter purse, and long dangling earrings.

Truth be told, the feather boa was her own idea, but she still wasn't fond of the general premise. Why did they have to go the cheap and tawdry route? Why not a Utica Square society matron on the make—fur coats and long glittery evening gowns? Oh, well—she proba-bly couldn't afford the costuming.

She'd been on the street for over an hour, chatting up every streetwalker, male or female, she'd met. Ben had been right about one thing; they seemed more willing to talk since Christina looked like she belonged there. They seemed perfectly relaxed around someone who they perceived as an insider looking for some action. Talk they did, but they had precious little of value to say. No one admitted to knowing a girl named Trixie, and there were some who wouldn't discuss the matter at all. She'd flashed some cash, hoping to attract some co-operation, but ended up only attracting an acne-pocked weasel who wanted to know if she "wanted some grass to go with her ass."

A very deep debt was accumulating on Ben Kincaid's

ledger, and she planned to make damn sure she collected.

Three women were huddled around a lamppost on Detroit, displaying their wares. Christina knew that society was usually the ultimate cause of poverty, addiction, and prostitution. It was wrong to belittle women who were forced to make these difficult choices. Nonetheless, as she approached the street corner, it was difficult to keep the word *floozies* out of her mind.

Christina strode in for a closer look. All three appeared too old to be teenagers. Come to think of it, she had seen precious few teenagers all night. Maybe one happy result of this horrible tragedy would be that teenagers finally figured out that this was a dangerous profession.

A large black woman wearing an uncommon amount of lipstick addressed Christina in a tone far from friendly. "What d'you think you're doin', honey?"

"I'm looking for . . . someone."

"Aren't we all?" The woman laughed, a coarse, heavy braying. "Run along, Betty Sue. This corner's taken."

"These here blocks belong to Sonny," another woman said. "He don't care much for competition."

"Especially dressed like her," the third commented. "Really brings down the neighborhood."

"I do like this wrap, though," the black woman said. She began to tug Christina's boa off her neck. "I like this a lot."

Christina clamped down on the boa. "What'll you give me for it?"

The woman smiled. "How 'bout I just ask Sonny not to carve you into little pieces?"

Christina's throat felt very dry. She peered across the street. Was it just her imagination, or did she feel Sonny's eyes bearing down on her?

"Run along now, sugar. We don't need another working girl around here."

"But I'm not—" Christina scanned her attire. "Ben assured me that I did not look like a—a—"

"Honey, why else would you be here?"

"Well . . ." Christina felt her face beginning to turn crimson. "Maybe I'm shopping."

"Oh, honey, we don't do none of that weird stuff. Maybe up on Fifteenth."

"No, you don't understand. I'm not interested in other women."

"Then you's on the wrong block." The tall woman pointed down the street.

"But I *am* trying to find a particular young woman," Christina insisted. "Someone named Trixie."

The three women all exchanged a quiet glance. "You ain't the first."

"Do you know where she is?"

"No. We don't know nothing."

"Don't try to con another woman. I saw the way you all looked at one another. You must know something."

"Nope. Never heard of her."

"Are you sure?"

"Absolutely positive."

"No way I could change your mind?"

"Not a chance."

"I'll let you have my boa."

The woman's chin rose; her eyes fell upon the long white fluff. A moment later, she placed her hand on the boa and slowly pulled it away from Christina's neck.

"I still can't tell you nothing," the woman said. But Christina noticed that she was staring across the street and down a block. "Follow the pennies."

"What does—"

"That's all I know. Now *git*!"

Christina took the hint and left. Across the street and one block down, she found two men in their early thirties dressed in tight jeans and fringed jackets. Obviously hooking. She took a deep breath and plunged ahead.

The man closer to her cocked an eyebrow. "Wanna date?"

Christina tried not to barf. "As a matter of fact, I do."

The man stepped closer and placed his hand on her waist. "You've come to the right place, baby. Thirty dollars and you'll be in paradise."

Christina's teeth set on edge, but she kept smiling. "Actually, I had something specific in mind."

He ran his hand through her hair. "I'm flexible."

She laughed nervously. "No, you misunderstand. I'm looking for a particular person."

He pressed his legs and groin against her. "I'll make you forget him. I'll make you forget everyone you've ever known."

"Well, how nice." Christina cleared her throat and straightened her skirt. "Seriously, though—"

"You'll feel ecstasy like you've never felt before. Your body will tremble; your thighs will ache. You'll have a hurt that only I can fix." He leered at her. "And the wonderful thing is, I'll be right here the next time you need me."

"Boy, that's ... really ... some kind of deal." Christina was uncommonly warm, and the fact that his breath was smacking her in the face didn't help any. "But I'm actually looking for a woman. Someone who works here, or used to. Her name is Trixie."

The man disentangled himself and backed away, a snarl on his lips. "Shit! Is everyone in town looking for that stupid bitch?"

"You know her?"

"You're talking to the wrong person." He gestured toward his companion. "You should—"

The other man glared at him, silencing him with a look.

"I should what?" Christina faced the other man. "I should ask you? Do you know where Trixie is?"

The second man practically spit at the first. He shoved him aside roughly.

"Hey, Buddy, watch it. I didn't say nothing."

"You said too much, you stupid-assed whore." Buddy stepped into the streetlights and ran a hand through his thinning red hair. "I don't know anything about this . . . Trixie." His voice was thin and nervous. "No one does. You might as well go home."

Christina gave him a quick once over. Buddy had a pasty white complexion and a pudgy figure; he lacked the harshness of most of those she had spoken to tonight. This tough guy routine did not appear to come naturally to him.

"Why is Trixie hiding?" Christina asked. "Why are you protecting her?"

"The street people got to look out for one another. No one else will."

"The police are trying to help her."

"Like hell. The Fury almost got her killed. Twice. Least that's what I heard," he added hastily. "They can't help her any more than they helped the first four. They couldn't care less about us. They've been screwing around, asking stupid questions, doin' strip searches and dicky checks on everyone they find. Sick bastards. That's why all the sickos and perverts come here to do their hurting and killing. No one cares. We're the invisible people."

"Could I at least get a message to Trixie?" Christina asked. "It's very important that I reach her."

"Wouldn't know how. I told you—I don't know where she is. In fact, I don't know who you're talking about. Now get off our corner."

"It's a free country."

"Not here it ain't. Here, everything costs." He glanced across the street. Two flamboyantly dressed men were leaning out the open window of a brick building. Something glistened in one of their hands. Something that bore an unsettling resemblance to a knife.

"Time for you to shove off, lady."

"Yeah, fine." Christina edged away, careful not to

turn her back to them or the men in the window. She hurried back the way she had come, watching for Ben's Honda. She tried to remain rational, but she couldn't shake the feeling that someone was closing in on her, lurking over her shoulder, watching her every move.

She saw a dented front grill that positively identified the car as Ben's and crossed toward it. Thank God. She couldn't get off this street fast enough.

* 39 *

"Stay down!" Ben whispered harshly. "He might recognize you."

"I'm down, I'm down," Christina muttered. She was crouching in the floor of Ben's car. "How long do you think I can stay scrunched up here?"

"As long as it takes. No one ever said a stakeout would be comfortable."

"Just as well. I'd sue for breach of warranty." She raised her head slightly. "How much longer are we going to wait?"

"Not long. He's starting to move." Ben eased the transmission into drive. "Come on, Buddy. Take us home."

Ben watched the pudgy man in the fringe jacket cross the street and walk north on Cincinnati. He was moving at a brisk pace, without hesitation.

Ben followed as far behind as possible, lights off. He took a pair of binoculars out of the glove compartment and focused on Buddy. He stayed just close enough to keep his quarry in binocular range.

"Do you know what you're doing?" Christina whispered. She wasn't sure why she was whispering; it just seemed appropriate somehow.

"Of course I do. I've been on stakeouts before. And Mike once showed me how to tail a suspect in a car."

"Mike did?"

"Yeah. What of it?"

"Just doesn't sound like Mike. I'd expect him to grab the suspect, snap on the cuffs, and haul out the rubber hoses."

Ben smiled. "Mike does have his subtler side."

"Very subtle. In fact, almost invisible."

Ben watched Buddy hesitate on the corner of Eighth Street. Buddy seemed to be waiting for something. He checked his watch, then tapped his foot nervously. He glanced back over his shoulder, then up and down the street. Eventually, he continued walking north.

"Good thing you were out of sight," Ben commented.

"What was he looking for?"

"Beats me. He acted as if he thought someone might be following him. And of course, he was right."

"He acted nervous the entire time we talked," Christina said. "As if someone might be lurking just around the corner. He didn't even want to say Trixie's name aloud. It was as if the evocation of her name might put her in danger."

"Perhaps it might," Ben said. He let his car inch forward, maintaining a constant distance between himself and Buddy. "Are you sure he knows where she is?"

"I'm not sure of anything," Christina replied. "But he did act strange when Trixie's name came up. Defensive—in fact, almost protective. His friend suggested that Buddy knew something about where she was. And of course, the lady of the evening now modeling my feather boa also indicated that Buddy was the key to finding Trixie."

"Let's hope she's right. I'm not sure we could repossess your boa."

"I'm not sure I'd want to."

Ben continued his surveillance for about ten minutes. Buddy turned left, walked about five more minutes, then took another left.

"I think this is it," Ben said.

Buddy approached a small two-story house with a white brick exterior. It was not in the best condition, but that lent it a certain charm, Ben thought. It looked as if it belonged in this neighborhood, but in a different time.

There were no lights on inside the house. Buddy fumbled for his keys a moment or two, then opened the door.

As soon as he was inside, Christina sat upright. "Elegant pied-à-terre. You think that's where he lives?"

Ben shrugged. "He seems to have his own keys."

"I thought all the prostitutes lived on The Stroll. Under their pimp's thumbnail."

"I don't know. Maybe it's different for guys. At any rate, he appears to be here for a reason."

"Great. Now what do we do?"

"We wait."

And wait they did. They followed the trail of lights that showed Buddy moving into a small room on the ground floor (bathroom, Ben guessed), then up the stairs. Lights came on in a larger room, and Ben saw Buddy's silhouette pass across the windows.

"Bingo," Ben muttered under his breath.

"What? What's going on?"

Ben grabbed the binoculars and trained them on the upstairs window. "There's a second silhouette in there. He's not alone."

"Can you tell who it is?"

"Not without X-ray vision. But there is definitely a second person in there—a smallish person, on the short side."

"Like a teenage girl?"

"My thought exactly."

Ben kept his binoculars trained on the window for a

few more moments, then put his car back in drive and cruised down the street.

"Where are we going now?" Christina asked. "I thought we were going to watch him."

"We found out where he lives. Time to get you back home."

"Home? Who says I want to go home?"

"I do."

"What is this, some macho protect-the-damsel-from-distress routine?"

"It's nothing like that—"

"You're just getting rid of me because you think there may be trouble."

"Someone needs to fill Mike in on what we've learned. And cover for me at the office." And yes, he thought but would never say: there might be trouble.

Christina laid her hand on Ben's shoulder. "You're going in there, aren't you?"

Ben nodded.

"Ben, five people have been killed already. Be careful."

He placed his hand on hers. "Believe me, I'll do my damnedest."

About an hour later, Buddy exited the front door of the house. He was dressed as before, except that he had added a scarf wrapped several times around his neck. Protection against the chill of the night, Ben thought. He wished he had one himself.

Buddy rounded the corner and headed back toward Eleventh Street. As soon as Ben was certain he was out of sight, he eased quietly out of his car and approached the house.

The lights in the house were off, but he knew there was still someone in there. He passed through the white picket gate that provided access to the front door. There was a doorbell just beside the mailbox. Ben pushed it twice.

There was no answer. He didn't detect any movement inside.

Could he possibly have been wrong? He thought he had seen a second figure through the window curtains, but perhaps it was a trick of the light, or a reflection in the mirror.

He knocked on the door, loud enough to be heard in the attic. But there was still no response. Well . . .

He tried the doorknob. To his astonishment, the door was unlocked. He pushed the door open, just a crack.

"Hello? Is there anybody there?"

His voice echoed through the empty house.

"Anybody there?" he repeated.

Still no answer. Ben pushed the door the rest of the way open and stepped inside. The house was dark. He searched for a light switch, then thought better of it. Maybe he shouldn't make it obvious that someone else was here.

He scanned the living room area as best he could. The furniture had a musty, grandmotherly feel about it; most of it appeared at least fifty years old. Lace doilies on the sofa and faded burnished curtains on the windows. An old piano in the corner. But no trace of a human being.

On the far end of the living room, he spotted a swinging door. Probably leads to the kitchen, he mused. He pushed open the door and walked inside.

The instant he passed through the door, something dropped out of the darkness and grabbed him by the throat.

* 40 *

Ben whirled, trying to loosen the grip of whoever or whatever had descended upon him. He felt fingers clutching at his neck—it was definitely a person. He threw his shoulders back, trying to dislodge his attacker, without success. He grabbed the hands, trying to pry them off his throat. He felt something jab him in the side. Something sharp.

"Ahhhhh!" He wanted to clutch his side, but knew if he loosened his grip on the hands around his throat he'd be history. He had to do something quick; he couldn't breathe at all. His vision was getting spotty and it was difficult to think. He needed air, badly.

He careened backward into the swinging door, using the person on his back as a battering ram. They smacked the door solidly, but the impact threw Ben off-balance. There was nothing he could do to regain his equilibrium. He fell over and smashed down on the pinewood floor.

The shock of the fall loosened the grip of the hands around his throat. He managed to roll away, gasping desperately for air. He felt the oxygen coursing back into his lungs, clearing away the cloudiness that was already fogging his brain.

He tried to focus on the bundle he had so gracelessly deposited on the floor. Whoever it was was already gone. He squinted into the darkness, but couldn't find a trace.

"Look," he said, breathing heavily, "my name is Ben Kincaid and I—"

The shadow lunged at him before he could finish his sentence. The sharp instrument again jabbed into his side, just below the ribs. He fell sideways, collapsing onto a love seat. The pain was even worse this time.

He felt something wrap around his mouth, then his throat. He was fighting gravity as well as his assailant; the person choking out his breath had the power position.

He felt the air draining from his lungs. He had to stop this now, or he would absolutely never have a second chance. He pushed against the arms bearing down on him. They barely budged.

In desperation, Ben released his grip and jerked his arms away. His attacker was caught by surprise; the body hovering over him fell to one side. Ben wriggled away. The person in the darkness started to bolt, but Ben grabbed the narrow shoulders and shoved them back as hard as he could. The figure tumbled over a coffee table and fell onto the sofa, lace doilies and all.

"Look," Ben shouted, "I'm not armed, I'm not dangerous. I'm not going to hurt you!"

The figure on the sofa leaned forward. Ben saw a hand snake out and grab something long and thin and sharp from the coffee table. It caught the moonlight and glistened. Like a knife.

Ben ran to the front door and flipped on the overhead lights. The sudden shift in visibility was blinding. He squinted to block out the sudden glare, then gradually reopened his eyes.

The person on the sofa was a teenage girl. Fifteen, sixteen tops. She was clutching a letter opener.

"You must be Trixie," Ben said, trying to keep his voice calm. "My name is Ben Kincaid."

Her eyes were wide and scared. Her hands trembled, but continued to clutch the letter opener. Ben wanted to approach her, but he wasn't taking any chances. Teenager or not, this girl had almost strangled him to death.

"I'm here to help you," he said, still gasping. "I'm not the one who's been killing your friends."

The girl seemed frozen, unable to move.

Ben yanked his wallet out of his pocket and tossed it to her. "See for yourself. Check the bar card. I'm a lawyer. Someone in my office was killed and somehow it's connected to the murders of the four teenage . . . girls. If you want, I can give you the number of a friend of mine at the police station. He'll vouch for me."

Keeping a close eye on Ben, she snatched the wallet off the floor and examined each ID, membership, and credit card. After she had seen everything there was to see, she tossed it back to him. "How did you find me?"

"I followed Buddy."

She nodded. "What do you want?"

"I want to know whatever you know. I want to find out who's doing all this killing. And I want to help you."

"Help me?" She laughed hollowly. "No one ever helps me. No one but Buddy."

"I can," Ben said. He took a cautious step forward. "I can get you police protection. Or nonpolice protection, if you'd prefer. I can keep this maniac who's trying to kill you from succeeding."

Ben saw her shudder. Her eyes were desperate and pleading. He could almost see her deliberating over how much she could afford to trust.

"How can you help?" she said, barely audibly.

Ben stepped forward, reached out, and gently took the letter opener from her hands. "First things first," he said. "What can you tell me about the Kindergarten Club?"

* 41 *

At Ben's suggestion, they washed the dirty dishes in the kitchen—at least a week's worth. Ben washed, Trixie dried. He hoped to catch her up in the rhythm of an ordinary, mundane chore, something that might distract her and allow the words to flow more freely.

It seemed to be working. Half an hour later, she was talking almost without hesitation.

"You're from St. Louis originally?" Ben asked.

"Uh-huh."

Ben sank his hands beneath the suds. "How did you end up in Tulsa?"

"It's . . . a real long story."

"I'm in no hurry."

"Why do you care?" A tinge of bitterness crept into her voice. "No one else ever did."

Ben rammed a sponge down a dirty highball glass. "Maybe you never told the right person."

"I told everyone I knew. It never made any difference. Everyone always sided with my stepfather."

"You didn't get along with your stepfather?"

"My stepfather hurt me. And molested me. Several times."

Ben set the glass down on the towel. "Oh."

She looked up at him. "You know, that's the first time I've ever said that aloud. Using those words, I mean. When it was happening, I didn't know what he was doing, or why, or what to call it."

"When did this start?"

"Right after he married my mother and moved into our house, three years ago. He was always touching me when he shouldn't, and where he shouldn't. Making dumb jokes. Asking if I wanted to shower with him. Wink wink. Jab jab.

"It just got worse and worse. One night he had this big party for all these big shot male friends of his. They were drinking and smoking shit, acting really rude. He asked me to come out of my room and join them. I didn't want to, so he forced me. Mom wasn't home, naturally. He dragged me out, and they gave me booze to drink, the first time I'd ever had it, and they let me gag trying to inhale their grass, and before long they were all passing me around, pawing me, feeling up my dress, feeling . . ."

She looked away. "They were gross. But I was so out of it, I didn't realize what was happening. I mean, I did, but it was like it wasn't really me, or like it was me in a dream, you know? Anyway, I must've passed out eventually. I didn't wake up until the next morning."

She picked up the glass and applied the towel furiously, long after it was dry. "I woke up and found I was naked, not a stitch on me. And no, in case you're wondering, I didn't normally sleep that way. Then I noticed the surroundings were all wrong. I wasn't in my room; I was in *his* room—in his bed. And then—" She set the glass down on the counter. "And then I noticed that he was lying next to me, and he wasn't wearing anything either."

Her eyes closed, fighting back the tears. "I thought it couldn't get any worse than that. But it did. I sat up, and I saw one of my stepfather's friends in bed on the other side of me. And he was naked, too."

Ben felt his stomach tighten. He dropped a few more plates into the sudsy dishwater.

"I didn't know what to do, but I knew I had to get out of there. I got dressed and ran out of the house. As far as I was concerned, I was running away and never coming back. But where could I go? I didn't have any money, not a dime. I didn't know anything about buses, or trains, or shelters. I just wandered around the streets aimlessly. Couple of hours later, he found me. He grabbed me by the hair, slapped me a few times, and dragged me into his car. When he got me home, he beat me up but good. I had bruises, a black eye, welts. That's how I got this scar across my nose. My mom was home the whole time, but she never said a word. I screamed out to her, but she wouldn't interfere. She was scared of him, too."

"You should have gone to the police," Ben said.

"I did, about a week later. My stepfather told me he was having another party and he wanted me to be there. To entertain, he said. I just couldn't let it happen again. If it did, I'd be more than just sick. I'd *die*—I was certain of it. So I ran to the police station and told them what he did to me. They put me in a tiny room with four male officers, and I told them everything, over and over again. I was amazed—it just came pouring out of me. I told them everything about my stepfather."

"And?"

Her lip curled, then trembled. "They didn't believe me. Not one of them. They said I was making it up."

"Whether they believed you or not, they had a duty to investigate."

"Yeah. And they did, in a way. They called my stepfather. I begged them not to, but they did. He came in, furious, and they put him in the same tiny room with me, and—what a surprise!—he denied everything."

"Did you have a chance to call any other witnesses?"

"Who would I call? No one else knew, except his buddies and my mother, and I knew they wouldn't say anything. It was just him against me. And they believed him."

"Did they hold a hearing?"

"Yeah." Her hands gripped both ends of the kitchen counter. "My stepfather showed up with some fancy lawyer and a buddy from the police station. Some clown I'd never seen before in my life came in claiming to be my guardian or something. What a joke—he didn't even talk to me. My stepfather's cop friend got the whole thing fixed. He talked to the judge privately and he talked to the other officers who were going to testify. He convinced them I was a troublemaker. A discipline problem, that's what they kept calling me.

"The judge said a lot of stuff I didn't understand about how I hadn't proven a right to be emancipated and ordered me to go back to live with my stepfather. Can you believe it? No matter what I did, I couldn't get away from him. A *judge* ordered me to go back and live with the man who . . . who . . ." She turned away from him and dabbed her eyes with the dish towel.

Ben cleared his throat. He wanted to comfort her, to tell her that he understood, but he didn't know how to begin. "Sometimes there are some . . . problems with the juvenile justice system."

"Justice?" She was crying full out now. Ben took the plate from her hands, turned off the running water, and led her back to the living room. She crumpled onto the sofa and continued to cry. Ben sat next to her and waited.

After a long while, Trixie composed herself enough that Ben felt he could ask another question. "Did you go home with your stepfather after the hearing?"

"I had no choice. They literally put me in the car with him. As soon as we were out of sight, he hit me in the face. With his fist. And promised he'd do a lot more when we got home."

Ben swallowed. He was afraid to ask what happened next.

"We walked through the front door. He turned toward me, his face all twisted up real mean, like he could kill me with his bare hands, and I kicked him right between the legs. Just like that, before he even had a chance to think about it. Hard. While he was down, I grabbed his wallet from his coat pocket and ran out the door. I ran to the bus station, got on the first bus that left and didn't get off till I was in Tulsa."

"Do you have relatives in Tulsa?"

"No. I don't have relatives anywhere, at least not that I know of. I was just out of money. Someone picked me up at the bus station, though. Someone who was scouting for Sonny."

"Sonny is your . . . boss?"

"Right. I had no hope at all at this point, and my stepfather's money was almost gone. I was certain I was going to starve to death, or freeze to death, or die some other horrible painful way. Or get sent back to my stepfather, which would be worse. Sonny offered me hope. He offered to take care of me."

"If you'd work for him."

"Right. I didn't like it, but what could I do? I couldn't even get a job at McDonald's at my age. I almost didn't get a job from Sonny."

"I didn't realize he was all that particular."

"He requires all his girls to have a physical regularly, especially before they start. Says he doesn't want them spreading diseases that might put off his customers. I couldn't get a physical, though, without some kind of ID. Thank God for Buddy. I guess you've met him; he works the other side. He's the best friend I've ever had. Only friend, really. He pretended to be my stepfather and got a copy of my birth certificate."

"And you passed the physical?"

"Of course. And I've been hooking ever since. Maybe it's not my dream come true or anything, but I had to keep on eating somehow. So I made a compromise."

"Another compromise." Ben was quiet for a moment. "Seems awfully risky."

"Hey, life is risky. If you don't believe me, just try crossing the street in these heels sometime."

"How long has it been since you left home?"

"Over a year now."

Ben felt himself sinking into the sofa. Over a year. Twelve months. Three hundred and sixty-five days on the street. "Trixie, I'm so sorry. I just wish—"

"I'm the one who should be sorry. What a whiner I am." She brushed away her tears and grinned. "You're a nice guy, you know. Sweet."

"Well, anyone else would feel the same—"

"I know that's not true. Boy, do I know it." She nodded toward the upstairs bedroom. "You wanna . . . you know, go upstairs?"

Ben closed his eyes. "No, Trixie. I don't think that would be . . ." He struggled to find the right words. "We still need to talk. I know this has been hard for you. But I need to know how you became involved with this Kindergarten Club."

She shrugged, disappointed, but unwilling to show it. "The Kindergarten Club was around long before me. I was a late entry. They drafted me to replace Carol Jo after she went back to L.A."

"What exactly is it?"

"A bunch of gross old guys who worked together looking for some cheap easy thrills. They didn't like to be seen on The Stroll or any of the usual places you'd go to pick up a . . . date for the evening. So they had this one guy, kind of the head creep, he made all the arrangements. He sent another guy out to gather us up and drive us to The Playground—that's this place north of the city where no one else ever goes, including cops. The five of us girls would go out there, and then the men would show up, and we'd do . . . whatever."

"What's whatever?"

"Whatever they wanted. It changed from one night to the next. Usually some kind of weird show to get them worked up, then we'd finish off with the usual orgy."

"The usual orgy?"

"That's what they liked to call it. It really wasn't an orgy, 'cause most of those guys weren't good for more than one time, and only about thirty seconds at that."

"What kind of a show?"

"Oh, we'd dress up in costumes, or we'd make a big deal of undressing. One time we stripped down and kind of messed with each other. They really liked that. Another time we let them pee on us. They got a big charge out of that, too. One time we tied some of them up and, you know, kind of teased their private parts. I wouldn't let them tie me up, though. I drew the line there."

Thank God. Ben's teeth clenched tightly together. He wasn't sure which was worse—thinking about her committing these acts, or hearing her recite them in such a matter-of-fact manner. "Why did you do this?"

"Because Sonny told me to. Besides, it paid very well. Every time the Club met, I could afford to take a night or two off, and sometimes Sonny would let me." Her voice grew quieter. "That would make almost anything worthwhile."

"This one guy you mentioned—the head creep. What did he look like?"

"I don't know. I heard about him, but I never saw him."

"Could you recognize these men if you saw them again?"

"Oh . . . possibly. You know, we're told not to look the johns in the face, and I think that's usually sound advice."

"Do you remember any of them?"

"I recognized one of them when I saw his picture in the paper. The one who got killed."

Ben leaned forward eagerly. "What was his name?"

"I don't remember, but he was the one who used to drive us out to The Playground." Trixie crossed the room and took a folded newspaper out of the coat closet. "Here it is. I saved the paper."

Ben glanced at it; he didn't have to look long. It was the *Tulsa World* article about Howard Hamel's murder. Hamel's picture was on the top left corner of the page.

"When you saw this, didn't it make you suspect you were in danger?"

"I already knew. I suspected when Angel disappeared." Her eyes reddened. "He got her the day after her birthday. I'd given her a present—one of those necklaces with a gold heart torn in half. You know, she'd keep one half, I'd keep the other. It was supposed to symbolize being friends for life." Her eyes focused on the carpet. "Some friendship. The next day, she was gone. And now she's dead."

"What did you do next?"

"Like I said, I was suspicious when Angel disappeared. But I was certain when they got Suzie and Barbara. I tried to save Bobbie Rae, but I was too late. And then he came after me."

"Who?" Ben grasped her firmly by the shoulders. "Who came after you?"

"I don't know. I never saw him. But he tried to kill that policeman, and the next day he was all over The Stroll looking for me."

"That's why you went into hiding. It wasn't the police you were hiding from. It was the killer."

"Right. But I didn't have anywhere to hide out. Sonny was no help—he wanted me back on the street. I didn't know where to go. I sure as hell wasn't going to trust the police again. Buddy was the only person who offered to help. He has this place his grandmother left him. He said I could stay here."

"Thank goodness," Ben said under his breath. If Buddy hadn't gotten her off the street . . . well, he preferred not to think about it. "Does Buddy live alone?"

"Yeah, other than me. He used to have this boyfriend,

but it didn't work out. So he had plenty of room for me."

"When we were looking for you, we were told to follow the pennies. If you don't mind my asking, what's the deal with the pennies?"

Her face flushed; for the first time, she seemed embarrassed. "Oh, that. That's . . . nothing important."

"I'm curious."

"It's just . . . see, I try to do nice stuff for people whenever I can, you know? Little rays of sunshine, I call them. Everything is so bad around here, it just seems like . . . well, any dumb thing might help. Sometimes I swipe change from a john's pockets and buy flowers for the other girls. Or sometimes I whip up breakfast in bed—I do decent scrambled eggs. And whenever I get pennies, I throw them on the ground. You know, so other people can find them."

" 'See a penny, pick it up, and all the day you'll have good luck.' "

"Exactly." Her cheeks were a bright crimson. "Super dumb, I know."

Ben smiled. "I don't think it's dumb at all."

She shifted awkwardly on the sofa. "Well, we all do what we can."

"Let me ask you one last question." Ben touched his side gingerly. "What was that you stabbed me with?"

"Oh!" She reached under the sofa cushions. "I was in the kitchen when you came in. I just grabbed the first two things I saw—the blade from Buddy's electric mixer, and the extension cord."

"That blade really stung," Ben said. "I'm glad you didn't have time to get to the cutlery."

"Gosh, I'm sorry I hurt you. I really am. I was just so scared." She placed her hand on his leg. "Are you sure there isn't some way I can . . . make it up to you?"

"I'm sure there is." Ben gently removed her hand and dropped it in her lap. "From now on, lock your front door."

* 42 *

Ben talked with Trixie for almost three solid hours, until he had all the information he thought she could offer. Most of it didn't pertain directly to the case. He knew from past experience, though, that sometimes the facts that turn out to be the most telling don't even seem relevant at first. He tried to learn everything he could about Trixie, the Kindergarten Club, and life on The Stroll.

"Trixie, I have to leave for a short while, but I don't want you to be here by yourself. How long till Buddy comes back?"

Trixie glanced at the clock on the wall. "He's already late. Probably stopped for coffee or something. I'm sure he'll be here any minute."

"I'm not leaving you alone," Ben said flatly. "I'm going to call a friend of mine to stay with you until I return."

A fearful expression returned to her face. "Not a cop. I don't want any cops."

"Trixie, it's for your own protection."

"That's what they said before. And the next thing I knew I was getting beat up again. For all I know, this killer is some sex pervert cop."

"Trixie, I don't think—"

"If you call a cop, I'm running out of here as fast as I can. And you won't be able to stop me."

Ben sighed. "All right. How about a woman, then? Not a cop. Someone I know we can trust."

Her head tilted a fraction. "That might be all right. Who is it, your girlfriend?"

"Just a friend. But a very good one."

Christina arrived about half an hour later. Her eyes were cloudy, and her strawberry blond hair was a jumbled mess, but she was there. She was wearing a gray sweatsuit and sneakers.

"Ben, do you have any idea what time it is?"

"Of course I do. It's almost four A.M."

"It was a rhetorical question, Ben." She nodded toward the girl eyeing her carefully from the sofa. "Is that—?"

"Yes. The long-sought Trixie."

"I figured as much. I'm impressed. Regular Dick Tracy you're turning into."

Ben introduced them, then let them chat a few minutes until Trixie appeared reasonably at ease with Christina. Christina soon had Trixie thoroughly engaged in an animated discussion of rock groups and music videos. Ben wrote out his name and his home and office phone numbers and addresses.

"I'm going to my apartment," he explained to Trixie. "I need to call my office and tell them I won't be in today, and then call . . . a friend of mine and tell him what I've been doing. And I need to feed my cat. As soon as I've taken care of all that, I'll be right back here."

"Great." Ben was pleased to see Trixie smile a bit. She was beginning to trust him.

On his way out, Ben motioned for Christina. "She's scared to death of the police," Ben whispered. "That's why I haven't called Mike yet. But I will as soon as I get to my place. If you see anything suspicious, or anyone other than Buddy tries to come through that door, I want you to call the police immediately, whether Trixie likes it or not."

"Understood."

"Don't take any risks."

"The biggest risk here, Ben, is that I'll return to the slumber my body so keenly craves."

Ben pointed at Trixie. "If Christina's eyelids begin to droop, poke her with that mixing blade." Ben grinned at Christina. "Take my word for it. You won't fall asleep."

Night still blanketed the streets of Tulsa. As Ben headed home, the lights surrounding the TU campus cast a blue glow across his windshield. What a night it had been! Ben couldn't believe he'd been up so long. It was worth it, though—the pieces were finally starting to come together. Hamel, the Kindergarten Club, the accident at Camp Sequoyah—it was all beginning to make a twisted sort of sense. He still didn't know who the killer was, but the choices were definitely narrowing. . . .

He turned onto Lewis. A few minutes later, he pulled up to the curb just outside his boardinghouse. Not a legal parking place, but who could be particular at this hour of the morning? He got out of his car and stretched; he was stiff from stem to stern. Maybe he would indulge in a shower and shave before he called Mike, just to clear the cobwebs out of his brain.

He froze halfway across the front yard. That was odd—the window to his upstairs room was open. He didn't remember doing that. In fact, he never opened it; among other reasons, he didn't want Giselle to get out. Would Mrs. Marmelstein have opened the window? As far as he knew, Mrs. Marmelstein never even went in unless he was home.

He approached the house and stood directly under the window. That's when it became clear: the window wasn't opened; it was smashed.

Ben raced through the screen door and bolted up the stairs. He hesitated for a moment in the hallway—what if the intruder was still there? Never mind. He would just have to take his chances.

He turned the doorknob and flung the door open. And gasped.

His apartment had not been ransacked. He had seen places that had been ransacked before, and this was not what they looked like.

His apartment had been destroyed.

* 43 *

Buddy awoke to find himself strapped to a chair. His hands were tied down on something—a table, perhaps? It was dark and he couldn't tell for sure what it was. Or where he was. Or what the hell had happened to him on his way home from The Stroll.

"Ah. Sleeping Beauty awakes."

Buddy heard the steady clickety-clack of heels crossing the floor, drawing closer to him. "What's going on here? What happened to me? Why am I tied up?"

There was a click, and then the room was flooded with light. Buddy still couldn't tell where he was. A cheap motel room? He couldn't be certain. A man Buddy had never seen before in his life hovered over him. The man was dressed entirely in black, down to the tips of his cowboy boots.

"Taking your questions in reverse order," the man said, "you're tied up so that you can't get away; I clubbed you over the head when I saw you on Eighth Street; and you're about to tell me where Trixie is."

"Trixie? Who is this Trixie? People have been asking about her all week, and I don't know the slightest thing about her."

The man smiled handsomely. "My sources say otherwise."

"Well, your sources are screwed in the head. I don't run with women. Especially hookers."

"Really. And how did you know she was a hooker, since you don't know the slightest thing about her?"

Buddy hesitated for just a second. "Well, it stood to figure—"

"Don't bother. Your face betrays you. And your mouth."

"Look, I know a guy on The Stroll who knows every hooker who's been through here for the last twenty years. I'll fix you up with him and—"

"Shut up." The man leaned across the table. "Are you right-handed, or left?"

"Left. Why?"

The man took Buddy's left hand and grasped his middle finger. "Where's Trixie?"

"I told you, I don't know any—"

The man pressed the finger back as far as it would go without breaking. "One last chance. Where's Trixie?"

Buddy's breathing quickened. He tried to block out the pain, the fear. He tried to wrest his hand free, but it was not possible. "I told you. You need to talk to—"

The man pressed the finger all the way back. The tiny bones shattered, and Buddy's finger dangled limply in the middle of his hand.

Buddy screamed. The pain was excruciating. He had never felt such agony before in his life, never even imagined that anything could hurt so much. His entire left arm began to shake; he couldn't steady it. Every nerve ending was on fire. He screamed again and again and again until he was breathless from screaming.

The man sat on the other side of the table and waited patiently. "Ready to talk yet?"

Buddy stared helplessly across the table. He couldn't speak, even had he wanted to. His lips mouthed words, but no sounds emerged.

"No?" The man shrugged. "As you wish." He took Buddy's right hand and grabbed the middle finger. "You may wonder why I've switched hands. Truth is, I believe your left arm is already as convulsed with pain as it could possibly be. There are limits to the amount of pain the brain can process, the amount of shock the nervous system can endure. And we don't want you passing out prematurely. So it's time to start fresh."

He leaned into Buddy's face. "That way you can feel twice the pain you feel now."

Buddy shook his head back and forth, his eyes pleading, mouthing the word *no*. Tears were streaming down his face.

"Losing your enthusiasm for secrecy? I don't blame you. No cheap piece of teenage twat is worth this." He pressed the middle finger all the way back. The bottom knuckle strained against his white flesh. "Where's Trixie?"

Buddy began inhaling raspily, breathing in quick short gulps. "Please, no. Please—"

The man pressed even harder. Buddy could feel the tension on the bone, could feel it beginning to snap.

"Last chance. Where's Trixie?"

Buddy cried out, a loud piercing wail. He was making short whimpering noises, like a pathetic oil-slicked seal. "Don't . . . know. . . ."

The man broke his finger. Buddy shrieked, a loud hideous endless cry. The pain was unimaginable, unendurable. He prayed for unconsciousness, for anything that would remove him from this living nightmare. But there was no release. Nothing except the man in the black boots, his malevolent smile, and the unbearable pain.

"Still not ready to talk? Amazing. The systemic shock must be incredible." He reached down toward Buddy's face and laid his fingers over Buddy's eyes.

Buddy twisted away from him, throwing his head to one side. It was no use—he was firmly tied down. He

could not get away. He had no use of his arms whatsoever; both were shaking uncontrollably.

"Please stop. *Please* . . ."

"I will stop, Buddy. I will." The man caressed the
side of Buddy's face. "I want to stop. Truly. Do you
think I enjoy this? I don't. It's just that I need information, that's all. And I need it quickly. Too many people
are poking their noses into my affairs. If I don't address
the Trixie situation soon, there could be some serious
complications. Do you understand?"

He leaned forward and kissed Buddy on the cheek.
"Won't you please tell me where she is?"

Buddy looked back at the man through blurry,
clouded eyes. He couldn't control his own hands, much
less wipe the tears from his eyes. The pain was not sub-
siding. No, it was getting worse with every passing second. Blood drained out of his veins; his hands were
swelling and felt as if they might explode.

"Please," Buddy whispered. He was begging. "Don't
hurt my fingers. . . ."

"Worried about the fingers, eh? 'Doctor, if I survive,
will I be able to play the piano? Oh yeah? I never could
play the piano before!' " He laughed uproariously, then
slapped Buddy on the back. "Funny, huh? I didn't see
you laugh, though. I like it when people laugh at my
jokes."

Buddy tried to smile, but found he hadn't the
strength.

The man's grin faded. "I'm not going to hurt your
fingers, Buddy, because I don't think they can take any
more pain without inducing unconsciousness, and I very
much want you awake. So I'll take a different approach."

The man reached into his jacket, unsnapped a holster
and withdrew a long, thick knife. "I'm in the mood for
a little surgery, Buddy. Nothing too major. Just the re-
moval of a few unimportant organs. Nothing you're
likely to miss."

He pressed his nose against Buddy's. "I'm not going to bother asking anymore. You know what I want to hear. When you're ready for me to stop, just start talking."

He reached down and loosened the belt around Buddy's pants. "Let's see. Where shall I begin?"

Buddy sobbed and shrieked, venting his anger and desperation. His entire body was cold and trembling. He felt horrible. It wasn't the pain, although the pain was agonizing.

He felt horrible because he knew he was going to tell.

* 44 *

Ben stared at his apartment in amazement and dismay. It was a shattered arena of destruction and debris. Everything that could be broken had been broken. Chipped pieces of Plexiglas from his stereo system littered the floor. Sofa cushions had been ripped open. The lid of the piano was up. He looked inside. Sure enough—the son of a bitch had gutted it.

His bedroom was just the same, and the kitchen was even worse. There were so many easily broken objects in the kitchen. And yet, through all the rubble, he saw precious few indications that his apartment had been searched. He knew the usual signs—rifled drawers, dumped files—and he didn't see any of them.

This wasn't a search. This was a warning.

Ben slapped himself on the side of the head. *Giselle!*

"Giselle? Sweetie?" He made a clicking sound with his tongue. "C'mere, kitty."

No response.

"Kitty kitty kitty. C'mon. Daddy's home."

He watched for some stirring, some indication of life. Nothing.

Ben felt a deep hollow in his heart. That poor cat. He bent over and crawled through a stack of broken records, ripped books, and torn linens. Maybe she was buried under here somewhere. Maybe she was pinned and couldn't get out.

Wait a minute. He shouldn't jump to any conclusions. He knew how to test for cat life. He ran into the kitchen, burrowed through the cabinets—now a jumbled mess—and retrieved a can of Feline's Fancy. Giselle's favorite.

He opened the can and waited as the aroma filled the apartment. Not that it ever took more than a few seconds. She was normally prancing around beneath his feet before he had the lid off. He waved the can around the kitchen, trying to deny the obvious, trying to pretend it hadn't been too long yet.

Until it was. Even he had to admit that she would've been here long ago. If she could.

He fell back against the refrigerator and brushed a tear from the corner of his eye. He just couldn't believe—just couldn't believe—

He heard something. Something barely perceptible, just outside the range of his hearing. What was it?

He stood, trying to trace the source of the sound. It seemed as if it had come from—where?

He whirled toward the kitchen sink. And the window just above the sink. The broken window he had seen from outside the house.

He crawled up on the sink and pressed his head through the broken window, careful not to cut himself on the jagged pieces of glass. The window overlooked a short ledge of the roof, a narrow shingled eave. And in the corner was a huge black cat huddled against the edge, as far as she could go without falling off the roof.

"Giselle!"

He wrapped his hand in a towel, knocked out the loose pieces of glass, then raised the window. "Giselle! It's me!"

Giselle slowly moved her paws away from her eyes. She was terrified, but not so much that she couldn't recognize the putative master of the house. Her head perked up. She slowly padded back to the window.

Ben scooped the cat up and brought her inside the kitchen. "You smart kitty. You must've crawled out there to get away." He cradled her in his arms and hugged her close. "What a smart little kitty."

Giselle purred and snuggled against the crook of Ben's neck. She stayed there for at least ten seconds, until she noticed the open can of Feline's Fancy on the floor. She leaped out of Ben's arms and started munching.

Ben smiled, but the smile only lasted a moment. In the back of his mind, he was still thinking about what had been done, and why . . .

And when.

It must've been during the day. Otherwise it would've been impossible. Too many people would've been in the building in the evening or night. They would've heard and come to investigate. But if this destruction had occurred during the day . . .

Mrs. Marmelstein would've been home.

He shut Giselle in the bedroom so she couldn't get out again, then ran downstairs and pounded on his landlady's door.

"Mrs. Marmelstein? It's Ben!" he shouted. "Are you okay?" He continued to pound on the door.

No one answered.

He pounded some more. The door popped open a crack. It must not have been closed securely.

He shoved his way into her room. That son of a bitch. That miserable goddamn son of a bitch. If he hurt Mrs. Marmelstein—

From inside her bedroom, Ben heard the sound of . . . Paul Harvey?

"Mrs. Marmelstein? It's Ben Kincaid!"

The sound of the radio evaporated. Ben recalled that Mrs. Marmelstein left the radio on all night—not to help her sleep, but to keep her company. He heard some heavy footsteps on the carpet, and a few seconds later, Mrs. Marmelstein poked her head through her bedroom door. She had obviously just awakened. "You're not a tenant here any more, Mr. Kincaid."

"What?" Now he was thoroughly confused. "Are you all right?"

"Of course I'm all right. I'm as all right as any woman could be who just had the worst day of her entire life." She stepped into the parlor, tightly bundled up in a pink woolly robe. "It's a wonder I could sleep at all last night."

"I don't understand. What happened?"

"Don't act innocent with me, Ben Kincaid. I heard all that noise you were making up there yesterday."

"You did? And you didn't call the police?"

"Hmmph. For all I knew you were with the police. Partying with those hooligan police friends of yours. Making all kinds of noise. Breaking furniture. Don't think I don't know you did. My hearing's not as bad as you think."

"Mrs. Marmelstein, it wasn't like that at all. Someone—" He cut himself off. On second thought, maybe it was better to leave her with the illusion of drunken revelry than to let her know her home had been invaded.

"I heard some squealing and shrieking, too. Harlots, no doubt." She sniffed. "I suppose I shouldn't be surprised."

Squealing? Must've been Giselle, poor thing. She wasn't friendly with strangers under the best of circumstances, which these weren't.

"I told you a long time ago I wouldn't put up with

that sort of immoral behavior. I'm sorry to do this, Ben. I'll miss you, and I don't know how I'll manage without you looking after my estate. But I'm evicting you."

"Mrs. Marmelstein—"

"Don't try to talk me out of it. My mind's made up."

"Mrs. Marmelstein—" He stepped closer and took her hand. "I don't know what came over me. You know how men are sometimes."

"Hmmph. Indeed I do. And I—"

"Then you can surely find it in your heart to forgive me. Just this once. If I promise never to do it again. Never ever ever." He plastered his most contrite expression on his face. "Pretty please?"

"Well . . . I don't know. . . ."

"I promise I'll pay for all the breakage."

"Still . . . I don't—"

"And I'll handle your financial affairs for the next year for no charge." What a sacrifice—he'd never charged her in his entire life.

"Well . . . I suppose I could give you one more chance."

"Thanks, Mrs. Marmelstein. You're a doll." He kissed her on the cheek and hurried toward the door. "Sorry, but I have to run. Immediately."

Ben bolted back up the stairs and into his apartment. Hell with the shower and shave—he had to call Mike, and he had to get back to Trixie, pronto. If this maniac was on the rampage—and Ben was ankle-deep in proof that he was—Ben couldn't afford to leave Trixie and Christina alone.

Who knew where the killer might be at this very moment?

* 45 *

"Then where the hell *is* he?"

The switchboard operator on the other end of the line assured Ben that she had no idea where Lieutenant Mike Morelli was at this particular moment.

"It's almost five o'clock in the morning!" Ben shouted. "If he's not at home, he must be out on police business."

"I'm sorry, sir. I have no information as to his current whereabouts."

"Can you at least take a message? Tell Mike I've found Trixie, and the murderer has found me. Tell him Trixie and Christina may both be in danger. Tell him to meet me at this address as soon as possible."

Ben gave the operator Buddy's address, and the operator promised she would convey the information as soon as Mike called in.

Ben slammed down the receiver and hurried out the door. He just hoped he hadn't wasted too much time already. If the killer could find him, it only stood to reason . . .

He jumped into his Honda and blazed down the street. The traffic at this time of the morning was perfect: there wasn't any. He was speeding and probably violating several other provisions of the municipal code, but he didn't care. On the contrary, he hoped he did attract some police attention; he could use all the help he could get.

In less than ten minutes, Ben made it to Eleventh

Street. Two minutes later he pulled up in front of Buddy's house. He parked his car on the opposite side of the street and crossed over to the house.

The front door was wide open, flapping in the breeze.

He knew Christina well enough to know that she never would allow that to happen. If she could help it.

He ran toward the door, then heard the sudden squeal of tires as another car raced around the corner. Ben ran to the side of the house and hid behind a tall hedge.

He parted the branches slightly and watched. He didn't recognize the car, and he couldn't see through the smoky windows. Was the killer returning to the scene of the crime, or just now arriving? He felt his heartbeat racing, his palms sweating. Why didn't the driver get out of the goddamn car?

A few more tense moments passed; then the passenger door swung open and Ben saw a familiar dirty overcoat step out of the car.

"Mike!" Ben ran out to meet him. "What happened to the Trans Am? Where'd you get this car?"

"Belongs to the department. I was cruising Eleventh Street, hoping I'd stumble across a clue. I came as soon as I picked up your message on my radio. How long have you been here?"

"I just arrived. This is where Trixie has been holed up with her pal Buddy. I left Christina with her about an hour ago. Then I found my apartment had been demolished, and I'm not exaggerating. I called you and raced back here as soon as I could."

"The front door is open," Mike observed. "Was it that way when you left?"

"No way. The last thing I said was for them to be sure the doors were locked tight."

Mike looked at him grimly, then reached inside his car for the radio. After he finished his call for backup, he reached inside his overcoat and withdrew a Bren Ten automatic from its holster. "Is there any way out other than through the front door?"

"Yes. There's a back door in the kitchen."

Mike nodded. "I'm going in now. You stay here."

"You may need help."

"Don't be silly. I can handle this alone."

"I bet that's what Tomlinson thought, too."

Mike frowned, but didn't argue. He approached the front door, gun held in both hands, shoulder high. Ben followed close behind.

As they passed through the doorway, Ben saw the splintered lock in the jamb. Someone had forced his way in. The living room was essentially as Ben had left it, except that Trixie and Christina were both missing. The lights were turned off. Ben saw the mixing blade on the sofa. On closer examination, Ben noticed that one of the footstools had been overturned, suggesting that someone had gotten up in a great hurry.

He heard a sudden noise from the kitchen that he couldn't identify.

"Christina!" Ben called out. "Trixie!"

No answer.

"What's in there?" Mike asked, tilting his head.

"The kitchen."

Mike pushed through the swinging door, gun first.

The kitchen was just as Ben remembered it, except that the faucet over the sink had been left running. Mike picked up a towel and turned it off. He examined the back door. It was closed and locked. From the inside.

"I think you should stay by the door," Mike said.

"Stop trying to get rid of me."

"This isn't an excuse. This is important. If the killer is in the house, I don't want him to slip out the back door while I'm prowling around somewhere else. There's no point in me risking my neck if he's just going to get away."

"I think we should stay together."

"Why? My backup should arrive within minutes. Just make sure the creep doesn't escape in the meantime."

"Mike, I really think—"

"Ben, for once in your life would you just do as you're told!" His head shook, and Ben could see beads of sweat trickling down his temples. The tension was obviously getting to him, too.

"Fine. I'll stay put. But just until your backup arrives. If you find Christina or Trixie, call out."

Mike nodded. Ben watched grimly as Mike passed through the swinging kitchen door and out of sight.

* 46 *

Mike paced himself as he did a clean sweep of the downstairs. He moved cautiously, step by step. It took him about thirty seconds to circle through the living room and dining room; it seemed like ten years.

Damn it, get a hold of yourself, Morelli! You're a police officer! It isn't supposed to get to you like this.

Mike wiped his brow and clenched the gun all the tighter. The sorry truth was that he was scared to death.

The killer was in the house. He was certain of it. The same sick bastard who nearly killed Tomlinson and did kill all those girls was in this house. He had seen the black van with the smoked windows on the street as he came around the corner, but it wasn't just that. It was more a matter of instinct than detection; he *knew* the man was here, he could *feel* it. He would never admit to anyone that he was proceeding on such a wild hunch. But he was certain, nonetheless.

That's why he'd gotten rid of Ben. If Tomlinson couldn't take this creep, Ben didn't have a chance. He would just be in the way. No, this was going to be between Mike and the bastard who'd tried to kill his sergeant.

Mike mounted the stairs, taking them slowly. The air conditioner cut on and he jumped, startled. Jesus, he was keyed up. If he didn't get killed by the murderer, he would probably die of a heart attack.

Mike stood at the top of the stairs, trying not to look back. It had not escaped his memory that the killer had tossed Tomlinson down a flight of stairs, almost breaking his neck in the process. Mike wasn't going to give him a chance to try it again with a different victim.

There were three doors in the hallway, all of them shut. Two bedrooms and a bath, most likely. Well, if Muhammad wouldn't come to the mountain . . .

Mike said a silent prayer to the guiding spirit of William Faulkner and stepped into the hallway. He decided to try the doors in order. He crept across the hardwood floor to the door on the far left. He pressed himself against the wall, then swung around and kicked the door in.

"Freeze!" Mike crouched in the doorway, scanning the room as quickly as possible. No one was visible.

He inched forward, checking every nook and cranny. The room was very orderly; the bed had not been slept in. If anyone used this room, it must be someone extremely fastidious. He looked under the bed, then opened the clothes closet. No skeletons, no killers. And no clues.

Mike stepped out of the room and into the hallway. He approached and entered the bathroom in the same manner. The door thudded back and forth between the wall and his foot. Well, if the killer didn't know he was there before, he certainly knew now.

Mike scanned the small bathroom. No one was there, unless they were hiding in the medicine cabinet. What the hell! He checked the medicine cabinet. Nothing. He pulled back the shower curtain; no one was lurking within.

Mike returned to the hallway. Only one room left. If his instincts weren't completely off base, the man he wanted was behind that last closed door.

Mike pressed himself against the wall, then swung forward. Just before his foot connected with the door, he felt something wrap around his throat and jerk him backwards.

He stumbled, lost his balance and dropped his gun. Only the grip around his neck kept him from falling. He reached up and grabbed the thin—cord?—wrapped around his throat. He tried to pull it away, but he wasn't strong enough. It was already wound twice around. The cord was pressing into his neck, cutting as well as choking. He gritted his teeth and pulled with all his might, but he couldn't even budge it.

The lack of oxygen was already affecting him. He needed air and he needed it fast. He reached behind his head and grabbed his assailant's arms. He tried to heave him over his shoulders. No luck—he just couldn't get enough leverage. The killer must be made of concrete; Mike couldn't move him an inch.

He began to feel lightheaded. He didn't think it would happen this fast, but it did. He fell to his knees, no longer able to stand. He looked into the bathroom and saw an inner door standing open. Of course—an adjoining door connected the bedroom to the bath; that's how the killer got behind him. Stupid fool—he deserved to be strangled.

His strength was fading fast. Mike knew he only had time for one last gambit. He suddenly threw his entire weight to one side. It caught his attacker off guard; he lurched forward. Mike saw his opportunity. He slammed his elbow back, catching the killer in the stomach. He heard a satisfying *oof!*, then grabbed the cord and tried to pry it loose.

The attacker recovered quickly. Much too quickly. He slapped Mike's hands away and pulled the cord even tighter around Mike's neck. Mike fell forward, the air drained from his lungs. His lips parted; his tongue fell out of his mouth. He could barely think, barely see. He had tried everything he had and come up short. It was over. Worst of all, he knew Ben would be next and . . . he didn't even want to think about it.

Fortunately, a few seconds later, he wasn't able to think about anything at all.

* 47 *

Ben just couldn't stand it any longer. He knew Mike was right; if the killer escaped through the kitchen door the whole exercise would be a waste of time. But he couldn't bear to stand idle while Mike took all the risks. He couldn't even hear Mike move since the air conditioner had come on.

Of course, Mike would be furious. . . . Screw it. Mike's backup should be here by now anyway, but since it wasn't, Ben was appointing himself.

The instant he entered the living room Ben heard something upstairs—a heavy thumping sound. He walked around and peered up the stairs. Through the bannister, he saw Mike down on his knees, and someone else, someone Ben could only see from the waist down, standing behind Mike, holding something tight around Mike's neck.

Ben checked his instinctive impulse to dart upstairs. He needed a weapon if he was going to stand half a chance. His eyes swept over the room, but he didn't see anything, not even the proverbial poker. His eyes lit upon the mixing blade, still on the sofa where Trixie had left it. That would have to do. Ben scooped it up and ran upstairs.

The other man heard Ben coming, but not in time to prevent himself from being tackled. Ben hurled himself against the back of the man's legs, sending him flying into the wall. The man released his grip on the cord; Mike's head thudded down on the hardwood floor.

Ben followed the man to the wall and stabbed him in the side with the mixing blade. The man let out a shout. Ben came at him again, but the man grabbed Ben's arm and tossed the blade aside. This man was strong—incredibly strong.

In no time at all, he had twisted Ben's arm behind his back. He pushed Ben against the banister, trying to shove him over the top. Ben struggled to get free, to get a look at his assailant's face. He wedged his feet between the rails of the banister to lock himself down. The man pushed even harder. Ben felt the tendons in his legs straining; he knew he couldn't resist for much longer.

Suddenly, they both became aware of a siren wailing in the distance. Thank God, Ben thought—the backup finally made it. The man shoved Ben onto the floor, then flew down the stairs. A second later, Ben heard the kitchen door open and slam shut.

Ben pulled himself to his feet. There was no point in trying to catch the assailant; he was far ahead and considerably faster, and besides, Ben was worried about Mike. Ben crouched beside his friend's motionless body. Mike's eyes were closed; his face was a ghastly color. There was a long, jagged cut across his forehead and it was bleeding profusely. Ben grabbed him by the shoulders and shook him. No reaction at all.

Ben placed two fingers against Mike's throat and felt for a pulse. It was faint and irregular but, by God, it was there. He was still alive. Ben saw a pool of blood on the floor where Mike's head had fallen. Damn, damn, damn—he might have a concussion or skull fracture, on top of being nearly asphyxiated. If Mike didn't get some help fast, his chances were slim to none.

Ben ran down the stairs, planning to call an ambulance. To his surprise, he saw a white and blue EMSA ambulance pull up in the driveway. The siren they heard hadn't been the police after all.

Ben ran out on the porch to meet them. His amazement doubled when the passenger door flung open . . . and Christina jumped out.

"Christina! You're all right!" He grabbed her by the shoulders and hugged her tight.

"I was worried about you, too, Ben. What happened?"

The paramedics ran up to the front doorstep. "He's at the top of the stairs," Ben said, pointing. "He's banged his head and may be suffering from oxygen deprivation." The paramedics clambered up the stairs.

"Who? Mike?" Christina asked.

"Yes. The murderer got him. And he almost got me." Her eyes widened. "Did you see who he was?"

"No, damn it. I never got a look at his face, and I think he was wearing a stocking or mask anyway. I never even got a good look at his body. Christina, where have you been?"

"I got a phone call about half an hour ago saying you had been brought to St. Francis's emergency room. I tried to get Trixie to come with me, but she refused— said she had to wait for Buddy. When I arrived at the hospital, and no one there had even heard of you, I became suspicious. I ran down to the ambulance bay, told them I had an emergency situation, and rode back here with them."

"You probably saved Mike's life. I think he needs immediate attention." He looked up the stairs and saw that the paramedics had applied an oxygen mask to Mike's face.

"If you're not in the hospital, Ben, who called me?"

"Must've been the killer."

"How did he get the number?"

"I don't know. Has Buddy come home yet?"

Christina shook her head.

"That may answer that question."

"But why would he make a false phone call?"

"To lure you away—" Ben suddenly turned white as a sheet. "Oh, my God! Trixie!"

Ben flew into the house and bolted up the stairs, avoiding the paramedics hovering over Mike. He could see into the two upstairs rooms with open doors. One was a bedroom, the other a bathroom. No one was in either one.

Ben approached the third door, the closed one. Taking a deep breath, he grabbed the doorknob and flung the door open.

There she was.

* 48 *

Trixie's body hung limply over the edge of the bed. Her head nearly touched the carpet; her face was a ghastly blue. Her neck was lacerated with deep, bloody abrasions.

This time, Ben didn't bother searching for a pulse. Her condition was obvious.

Ben crumpled against the wall. His legs were like jelly, useless appendages. He pressed his hand against his face, still staring at her lifeless body. He felt sick.

He stiffened his legs and forced himself to stand. Then, after a long pause, he stumbled through the connecting door into the bath and lowered himself over the toilet.

After he was done, he wiped his face and tried to speak. "In there," he shouted hoarsely.

One of the paramedics looked up.

"There's another one." He pointed into the bedroom.

The paramedic peered through the door, then grabbed his bag and ran inside. Ben braced himself against the porcelain and waited for the confirmation.

A few moments later, the paramedic feeding oxygen to Mike shouted, "You need any help in there?"

"No," the man in the bedroom replied. "Stay with him. This one's already gone."

Ben slumped onto the bathroom tile and cried.

Ben didn't remember anything else until he felt Christina's hand on his shoulder. "It's not your fault," she said firmly.

Ben stared up at her but didn't answer. He couldn't.

"Look, if it's anyone's fault, it's mine. I'm the one who left her."

"If it hadn't been for me," Ben said hoarsely, "you never would've been involved."

He pushed past her and walked as best he could back into the bedroom. The paramedic was tending to the body; Ben tried not to look. He focused on the walls, the desk, the clothes closet. There had to be a clue, damn it! There had to be something, some trivial detail that would give him the information he needed to stop this fiend before he killed anyone else.

Ben searched through her clothes, but saw no clues to anything other than Trixie's obvious occupation. He searched the desk; it was practically empty. On the bookshelf, he found a small blue plastic recipe box. He popped it open.

The first thing he saw was a glittering gold half-heart necklace: the other half of Trixie's birthday present to

Angel. He also found a strip of four photos of her and Buddy, probably taken at a carnival or fair.

He withdrew a large green document and unfolded it. He saw the notary seal at the bottom, but it took him a moment to realize what it was. Ben bit down on his lower lip; the tears began to flow once more from his eyes.

It was Trixie's birth certificate, the one Buddy had obtained so she could get her medical examination.

She was thirteen.

* 49 *

Ben took Christina's hand and let her lead him out of the bedroom and downstairs. He didn't want to go; it seemed like one more betrayal, one more desertion. But he also knew the room was now a crime scene, and disturbing it wouldn't help anyone.

"I repeat," Christina said, as they walked downstairs, "it wasn't your fault. You did everything you could."

"It wasn't enough," he replied bitterly. "It never is."

"What difference would it have made if you were here? I'll tell you—the only difference would have been that your corpse would be strewn on the floor, too."

"Maybe it should be."

"You had your shot at him, Ben, and he flung you around like a rag doll. If you and Mike couldn't take this butcher, there's no way you and Trixie could have. The only one who was deprived by your absence was the killer."

She turned to face him. "Ben, you need to be careful.

This killer, whoever he is, is a desperate man, or a raving lunatic, or both. He may have seen you. He may know who you are."

"He does," Ben said flatly. "He's been in my apartment. Tore it upside down. Scared poor Giselle out of three of her lives." He touched Christina's arm. "And if he knows about me, he may know about you, too."

"Ben, I think we should both consider hiring some protection. Professionals."

"For this maniac, we'd better hire a frigging battalion."

"Where am I? Where is he?"

They both heard the weak but familiar voice from the landing at the top of the stairs. "Mike!"

Ben bounded up the stairs, Christina close behind.

Mike was still lying in the hallway, his head raised onto a pillow. One of the paramedics was monitoring his vital signs.

Mike focused on Ben's face and frowned. "What are you doing here? You're supposed to be guarding the kitchen door."

"Go to hell," Ben replied.

"A fine way to talk, you AWOL ass." Mike smacked his lips. "I'm parched. Can you get me something to drink?"

The paramedic shook his head. "Sorry. We have to avoid any chance of you aspirating on your own vomit. Besides, with a head wound, you may require surgery."

"Do you think it's a skull fracture?" Ben asked.

"That's a nasty burst laceration on his forehead, but I don't think it's too profound. Head wounds always bleed a lot. Still, we need to check for hematoma and contra coup injury."

"Would you two stop talking about me like I wasn't here!" Mike growled.

"Judging by his rude tongue," Ben said, "it appears he has regained consciousness."

"True. But he still may have sustained injuries. We're

going to take him to the hospital as soon as he's stabilized a bit."

"I see." A line creased Ben's brow. Something was bothering him. But what was it?

"I take it the son of a bitch with the strangulation cord got away," Mike whispered.

"I'm afraid so," Ben replied. "If it makes you feel any better, I managed to hurt him before he escaped, though not nearly as much as he hurt me."

"Maybe these goddamn medics should be bothering you instead of me. Give me some air." Mike tried to push himself up.

"Just stay where you are," the paramedic said. "Try to relax."

"I don't want to relax, damn it! I'm fine."

"That remains to be seen. In the meantime, I want you to stay calm."

Mike grimaced. "Bully."

"That's it!" Ben snapped his fingers. "That's the answer."

Mike and Christina stared back at him. "What are you talking about?"

Ben didn't hear them. He was busy thinking it through. Now that he realized what he had missed before, everything else seemed to fall into place.

"Can you guys take care of Mike from here?"

The paramedics nodded.

"Okay. I've got to leave."

"Now just a cotton-pickin' minute." Mike braced himself with his arms. "What's going on? What's all this sudden urgency?"

"I know who the killer is," Ben said. "And I think I know how to prove it, too."

"Well then stop being so damned mysterious and tell us!"

"You need to go to the hospital. I'll check in with you when I'm finished."

"Where are you going?"

"Believe it or not—the High Course at Camp Sequoyah."

Mike and Christina yelled at him, but he ignored them both. He flew down the stairs and out to his car. If he was right, he didn't have any time to spare. His chance to nail the person who had committed all these murders had finally arrived. All he had to do was something that made his entire body quiver just thinking about it, something that instantaneously filled him with dread.

And not get killed in the meantime.

* 50 *

Ben drove under the archway that identified Camp Sequoyah, doing seventy miles an hour on the narrow one-lane dirt road. Caution to the wind—this time he was not going to fail.

He drove through the parking clearing, then over the small embankment that served as a curb. His Honda shuddered and squealed as he took the car onto the uncleared grass and down a steep hill. What the hell! The car was about to fall apart anyway.

He parked his car outside the closed circle of oak trees he remembered from the weekend before. This was as far as he could possibly travel on wheels. He jumped out of the car and raced into the forest. The sun was just rising; the orange corona was visible above the treetops.

The High Course had been taped off, but Ben didn't have any trouble crawling under. The police had closed it off as a crime scene, but there was only so much that could be done to restrict access to a forest. The guards had left long ago. Since access had been restricted, though, there was still a chance he could find what he wanted.

He was now certain that Crichton's belay line had been cut. Problem was, the police had combed the grounds and searched everyone before they left the site. If the line was cut, what happened to the knife?

It must've been left somewhere on the High Course, he reasoned. The police probably didn't search sixty feet up in the air. The most likely hiding place would be the big oak tree that connected the giant's ladder to the Burma bridge. If Ben could find the knife, it might bear the fingerprints of the person who had left it there. That would provide the proof Ben needed to confirm his theory.

Problem was, the High Course was ... high. Sixty feet high, to be exact. Ben didn't have any belaying equipment, and there was no one here to spot him even if he did. He was going to have to go up without a net, so to speak. Alone.

He felt himself dizzying, just thinking about it. How could he possibly climb that high by himself? His stomach was fighting him, threatening a repeat of the upheaval he had experienced before. When he found ...

And that was the answer. Trixie. This might be his only chance to catch the bastard who killed Trixie. And Hamel. And almost killed Mike. He'd climb fucking Mount Everest if necessary; that sadistic butcher was not getting away.

He stood on the stump and hoisted himself onto the first rung of the giant's ladder. His arms ached with the strain. He'd been hurt more in his scuffle with the killer than he'd acknowledged. And he wasn't exactly in primo shape to begin with.

Didn't matter. None of it did. He was going up.

He balanced himself carefully on the first rung of the

ladder, trying to remember everything he had been told when he tried this the first time. Don't look down, Crichton had said, and that seemed like eminently practical advice. He placed his foot on the metal joint of the connecting wire. Didn't much matter if Crichton thought he was a wimp now—he just wanted to get to the top without dying.

He hoisted himself up till he was lying flat on the second rung. He clung to the wooden beam, holding on for dear life. Two down, seven to go. He tried to pull himself upright, which was tricky enough on this narrow beam without the additional complication of having his eyes clenched tightly shut.

He tried to establish a rhythm: reach, pull, hoist, and balance. Reach, pull, hoist, and balance. It should become a routine, something he did without even thinking about it. Slowly, methodically, and please God without looking down, he pulled himself up to the third rung, then, in rhythmic succession, the fourth, fifth, and sixth.

After the ninth beam, Ben grabbed the vertical wire and stretched himself upright. He'd made it. The giant's ladder was by far the part of the course that required the most physical strength. If he could climb it, he could finish the whole course. He grabbed the high wire with both hands and started inching his way toward the oak tree and the Burma bridge. A sensation of pride swelled through his body. By God, he'd faced the demon head-on and conquered it. Fear of heights or not, he'd made it to the top, something a lot of people couldn't do even with a belay line. Feeling fearless, he opened his eyes and looked down toward the ground.

Someone was there, watching him. The killer.

"Bravo," the man said, clapping. "Quite a performance. All the way to the top in less time than it would take some grandmothers. The older ones, anyway."

Ben clenched the overhead wire tightly. "What are you doing here?" he shouted down.

"Looking for you, of course. Did you think I would

just run away and hide until you came after me the next time? Not my style, I'm afraid. After I left the house, I parked on Eleventh Street, waited for your car, then followed you out here. It was easy, despite the fact that you drive like a maniac."

"You should know," Ben said. He gripped the wire even tighter. His hands were dripping with sweat, which he knew would not improve his grip. "What are you planning to do?"

The man smiled maliciously. "Well, I really can't let you fill out a police report, can I?" He seated himself on the ground. "I'm very patient. You have to come down to earth sometime."

"You're too late. The police are on their way. They should be here within the hour."

"Hmm. Probably a bluff. Still, I can't afford to take the risk." Rob Fielder stood up, brushed off his hands, and gripped the first rung of the giant's ladder. "Very well. I'm coming after you."

* 51 *

Ben was paralyzed with fear. He didn't know which he was most afraid of—falling sixty feet to the ground or coming within an arm's reach of Rob Fielder.

He'd already tangled with Fielder back at the house. For that matter, so had Mike and Tomlinson, two men vastly better-qualified to defend themselves than he. If Fielder laid his hands on him, Ben didn't stand a chance.

Ben watched Fielder climb steadily upward. In the

few seconds Ben had spent thinking, Fielder had already made it to the third rung. Another minute or two, and they'd be standing side by side.

Ben sidestepped toward the oak tree, his only chance. He had to keep moving forward, to get to the end of the course and ride the zip line down. In his heart, Ben knew Fielder would catch him before he reached the end. But there was no turning back now that Fielder had the giant's ladder covered. Ben had to keep plowing through the course. The smartest thing he could do was keep Fielder distracted in the meantime.

"The way I figure it," Ben said, as he inched toward the tree, "you lied. Hamel wasn't dead at all. At least not when we first found him in my office."

Fielder paused on the fourth rung. "Pretty smart, Kincaid. And it only took you a fucking week."

"You lied about being a first-aid expert so I would let you take Hamel's pulse and you could tell me he was dead. Then, after I ran for help, Hamel got up and simply walked away. Later that night, you killed him. And since you knew the police suspected me already, you dumped the corpse in my backyard and smeared some blood in my car."

"All true, I'm afraid," Fielder grunted, as he pulled himself onto the fifth rung. "How did you figure it out?"

"A paramedic reminded me that you never give a head injury victim anything to drink. He might aspirate on his own vomit. Plus he might require surgery. Then I remembered that you did just that—you gave Crichton a drink after he was clobbered by Doug's wild throw. Beer, no less. At first I thought you just didn't know, but a trained first-aid expert should be better informed. Then I started to think: maybe you were lying about having Red Cross certification. Maybe it was important that you be the one who checked Hamel's vital signs. Then it all made sense."

"Very smart," Fielder said. "Bravo."

"And it relates to the Kindergarten Club, right? You're the member whose name was deleted from the list."

"Guilty as charged. That list never should've been put on the central computer. Only an idiot like Hamel would've done such a thing."

"I assume Hamel downloaded a copy onto the floppy disk. Then, when he saw us on his way out of the computer room, he hid in my office. When I opened that door, he played dead. And you covered for him so he could get away. Temporarily."

"Too true. By the way, Ben. Your shoestring's untied."

Ben stiffened. "Nice try." He returned his attention to the tree, almost within his grasp.

"The Club was my brainchild. I set it up for Apollo perverts who were too cowardly to handle their own procurements. I made a lot of money at it, too. A lot of money. Hamel was sort of the secretary of the Club. I gave him a share of the profits, and in exchange, he set up appointments, made reservations, and arranged for the personnel."

"A regular Boy Scout."

"Yes. He liked the money and the house it allowed him to buy. Everything was dandy, until he panicked. Was certain the police were closing in on us. Threatened to turn state's evidence to save himself. I assume that's why he wanted the address list—so he could turn it over to the police. Or a newspaper reporter. Obviously I couldn't allow that to happen."

Ben grabbed the tree with both hands and hugged it tightly. He'd made it. He lowered himself down to the wooden platform, then started across the Burma bridge.

He couldn't resist looking back over his shoulder. Fielder was almost on the top rung of the ladder; he'd be on the bridge in no time at all. Keep him talking, Ben. Keep him talking.

"But why the girls? Why did you have to kill them?"

Fielder paused reflectively. "Hamel's irrational threats made me aware of the danger the continued existence of the Club presented to my career. Not to mention my freedom. I decided it was time to eliminate all possible witnesses. Especially the cheap whores who would tell everything they knew for ten bucks."

Ben walked toe-to-toe across the bridge, pushing his arms out, smooth and steady. "If you wanted to eliminate all possible witnesses, you'd have to kill all the members, too. Every name on the address list."

"The thought had occurred to me," Fielder said, with astonishing detachment. "But the girls were a higher priority."

Halfway across the bridge, Ben felt it begin to shake. He glanced over his shoulder; Fielder held the ropes and was swinging them violently back and forth.

"Don't let this throw you, Ben," he said, laughing. "The principles are all the same, even if the bridge is sideways. Or upside down. Just don't fall out. It's a long way to the ground." He laughed again, a sickeningly merry tone to his voice.

Ben clung to the ropes for dear life. The ropes burned into his hands, reopening the wounds that had only superficially healed from the weekend before. *Hang on, damn it.* Fielder had him practically horizontal now. It would be so easy to fall, to just let go and . . .

Ben's right foot slipped off the balance rope. He fell forward, but held tightly onto the ropes in his hands. Swinging himself backward, he managed to fall inside the triangle, onto the balance rope.

Fine—any port in a storm. He'd crawl the rest of the way.

"Good show!" Fielder yelled. "Admirable recovery. Slow way to proceed, but feasible. If I weren't coming after you." Fielder pushed away from the tree and started across the bridge.

Ben reached out with both hands and hauled himself forward. He wasn't going to try to stand up. It would take too long and it was too risky—one misstep and the bridge would toss him to the ground. He struggled along, trying to close the gap between himself and the next tree, trying not to think about how close Fielder must be behind him.

"Twenty feet and closing!" Fielder shouted. "I'm excited about this. Aren't you?"

Ben pulled himself through the last foot of the bridge. He was drenched in sweat; he felt as if he had just stepped out of a swimming pool. He was breathing much too rapidly and had burns and bruises in a hundred places. Nonetheless, he managed to pull himself erect beside the next tree, the one connected to the horizontal telephone pole.

"So you started killing the prostitutes even before you killed Hamel?" Ben shouted.

Fielder stopped again, apparently pleased to tell his colorful story. "True. They were the most likely to talk, the most easily bought, the ones with the least to lose. Fortunately, Hamel, always the deviant, had taken photos of them. I searched his house trying to find a missing photo, without success. Didn't matter. I found most of them in Hamel's briefcase, and I had all of the girls' names. They were easy to kill. All you had to do was drive down the street, pick them up, and take them to a hotel."

He gazed contentedly toward the sky. "Slip the bag over their heads, tighten the cord around their throats, and wait. It didn't take long. And the whole time, I was in complete control. I dominated—I was God to them. It was fabulous. I usually kept a souvenir, just to remember them by. And then I eliminated all the clues. And dumped the bodies on The Playground.

"Of course, I removed their heads and hands to slow identification. The beauty of it was—even when the police learned their identities—who would care? The police don't care about a bunch of sleazy prostitutes; the vice squad probably considered it a favor. My chances of getting caught were nil."

He paused, and his eyes narrowed to tiny slits. "Until that stupid plainclothes cop blundered in. And then you."

Fielder was getting too close; Ben had to start across the horizontal telephone pole. Just pretend like you're on the ground, he told himself. It's just like walking on a curb, except that the telephone pole is actually much wider. Piece of cake. He closed his eyes and pushed.

Halfway across, Ben was startled by a tremendous scream. He opened his eyes, waving his arms to recover his balance. He sat down quickly and straddled the pole. Somehow he managed to keep himself upright. He scooted across the rest of the pole.

Fielder was almost across the Burma bridge, laughing uproariously. "Made you flinch," he said, grinning.

"Son of a bitch," Ben muttered. He clung to the tree and scrutinized the next leg of the High Course. It was the wire track—one above, one below. If he could just make it across without falling, he could ride the zip line down to the earth. Terra firma. Best of all, he could tie the zip line down at the bottom so it wouldn't return to Fielder. Fielder would have to go back through the course and descend on the giant's ladder—and that would give Ben enough time to get away. If Fielder didn't catch him first.

Ben stepped sideways across the wires. "Killing the girls wasn't a piece of cake, though," Ben said. "At least not the last one."

"True enough," Fielder admitted. "I did have trouble locating ... Trixie." He let the name drip off his tongue. "Sneaky cunt took to hiding, had half the whores in town covering for her. Bitches. I found her, of course, courtesy of that faggot she holed up with."

"What did you do to Buddy?" Ben asked. "Is he still alive?"

Fielder ignored him. "Don't worry. I had my revenge

with Trixie. I didn't kill her fast, like the others. I dragged it out and enjoyed it."

Ben felt his sickness returning. His eyes were watering up. *Just ignore him,* he told himself. You can't afford to be distracted now.

Ben watched Fielder float effortlessly across the telephone pole. He seemed to have no fear at all; he acted as if it really was just a curb on the ground. A heartbeat later, Fielder was on the wires and moving steadily toward Ben.

"End of the chase," Fielder said. "Strap on your parachute. What—you don't have one? Pity."

Ben moved as quickly as he could without plummeting to the ground. It was no use. Fielder moved more than twice as fast as he did.

"Why did you try to kill Crichton?" Ben asked.

"Crichton?" He seemed genuinely puzzled. "He wasn't in the Club. He was never on my list. On the contrary, his stupidity has been quite useful to me."

Ben reached the end of the wire track and clutched the final tree. He tried to take the zip line, but Fielder grabbed him by the shoulders and yanked him back.

Ben pressed his hands against Fielder's chest, trying to hold him off. Fielder slammed down hard on Ben's elbow, trying to break his arm. Ben cried out, then wrapped his arms around Fielder. Fielder twisted back and forth, trying to get free. Ben held tight. Snarling, Fielder butted Ben with his head.

Ben fell to his knees, his arms wrapped around Fielder's legs. "I'm not letting go!" Ben shouted. "If I fall, we both fall!"

"I'll see about that." Fielder reached over Ben's head and grabbed the zip line seat. Bracing himself, he drove his knee under Ben's chin. A second blow thudded against Ben's chest.

Ben felt the wind rush out of his lungs. He was out of breath, heaving, trying to maintain his all-important balance. Freed from Ben's grasp, Fielder swung his leg back again and kicked hard.

This blow caught Ben in the stomach. His head slammed back against the tree. He fell to one side. At the last possible moment, he clutched a limb of the tree, desperately trying to keep from falling. He knew he wouldn't be able to withstand another kick like that.

"You're history," Fielder said. He reared his foot back for the killing blow.

A gunshot rang out from somewhere below them. Fielder stopped, then, a second later, twitched strangely. Ben saw the wound on Fielder's right shoulder.

"Stay right where you are or I'll fire again!"

"Chicken shit assassin," Fielder mumbled. He lurched forward suddenly and embraced Ben. "He'll have to shoot us both."

Ben struggled, but couldn't break Fielder's grasp. He raised his fist and pounded Fielder's shoulder, just over the bullet wound. Fielder shrieked in agony and fell backward, just enough. Another gunshot rang out, this time catching Fielder dead center in his chest. He staggered backward, teetered for a moment, and fell.

Ben watched Fielder's body plummet to the earth. He smashed onto the ground with a sickening thud.

Ben grabbed the tree behind him and pulled himself to a more stable position. He inhaled and exhaled evenly, trying to slow his racing pulse.

"Are you planning to stay up there all day?" Mike called out. He was standing on the ground, bracing himself against a tree trunk.

"Just for a little while," Ben said between gasps. "Till I'm certain I'm not having a cardiac arrest." He took a few more deep, drinking breaths. "I thought you were going to the hospital."

"While you rushed out and played the daring young man on the flying trapeze? Not a chance. I gave the paramedics a rain check."

"Just as well, under the circumstances."

"So, are you planning to come down or what?"

Ben wiped a quart of sweat from his forehead. "Maybe. Someday. No hurry."

"I thought you were afraid of heights."

Ben tried to smile. "I'm becoming acclimated."

233   William Faulkner

5.   "It's yourself you don't think you'll fool."
            Hightower

PART FOUR

* *

What We Can

* 52 *

Ben poured cups of coffee for himself and for Christina. The Apollo legal staff meeting had already run over an hour long and they weren't done yet. Mercifully, Chuck had suggested a break.

Ben picked up the two hot Styrofoam cups, then winced. His hands were still raw and tender from his race through the High Course.

"Here's the java," Ben said, passing Christina her cup. Because of the importance of the subject matter of the meeting, legal assistants had been invited for the first (and probably last) time.

"Thanks. How are your hands?"

"Not bad. Sore enough to give me an excuse to retire from the High Course forever."

"Retire? Just when you were getting the hang of it?"

"Believe me, I was awful."

"Ben, last week you couldn't complete the High Course in full regalia. Two days ago, you completed it without any belay support. I'd call that significant progress."

"Well, my progress was forced somewhat by the circumstances."

She grinned. "Are these meetings always so gloomy?"

"Only when the main topic of conversation is how one member of the staff murdered another member of the staff and five other people as well." During the past hour, the staff had been informed of the horrible secret buried inside their department. Mike was the official leader of the meeting, but Ben was filling in most of the details. Ben had tried to explain the whole plot as he now understood it—how Fielder had formed the Kindergarten Club, how he'd enlisted Hamel as secretary, and how together they had raked in the dough.

Ben noted several macho grins and sneers as he talked about teen prostitutes and kinky group orgies, but the snickers faded when he began describing the multiple strangulations and dismemberments. He told them how Fielder panicked and began killing off the girls, one after the other. How that had caused Hamel to download the address list so he could turn state's evidence. How he'd been caught in the act by Fielder, which had caused Hamel to become Fielder's next victim.

Christina nudged Ben's shoulder. "Look at Shelly." Shelly was solemn and silent, even more so than usual. "She really seems to be taking this hard."

There may be a good reason for that, Ben thought, but he kept it to himself. "Herb seems a bit upset, too."

"Yeah, but that's probably because all these orgies were going on and he never got invited."

Ben smiled, but again he could think of another possible explanation. He noticed that Herb and Candice were not seated together, and had not spoken to (or shouted at) one another since they entered the room.

Crichton was sitting at one end of the long conference table opposite Mike. Crichton appeared to be taking the news worse than anyone. Understandable, Ben thought. Not only had he lost another member of his staff; he'd been made to look a blundering fool. He was staring down at the black enamel table. His coffee cup was empty, but he hadn't even called for Janice.

"If you don't mind," Mike said loudly, "I'd like to finish this up." Mike had looked better himself. Despite everyone's entreaties, he still hadn't checked into the hospital. He insisted that he wanted to "put this case to bed" before he took any time off.

Everyone resumed their places around the table.

"There's one detail we omitted," Mike continued. "When Fielder spotted Ben on the streets searching for Trixie, he went after him. He didn't find Ben at home, so he tore the place apart, just to send a message. Maybe he thought he might find the picture Ben and I retrieved from Hamel's attic. I don't know. He didn't find anything. But of course, that's because there wasn't anything to find.

"As you all know," Mike continued, "Fielder was killed in his fall. That concludes this investigation. Chief Blackwell has declared this matter closed"—he looked pointedly at Ben—"a fact that will no doubt come as a considerable relief to many of you."

Amen to that, Ben thought.

"I have a question," Chuck asked loudly. "I understand everything you've said, but what I don't understand is who cut Mr. Crichton's belay line? That's the creep I'd like to take apart."

Count on Chuck to be the one who couldn't keep his mouth shut, Ben mused. Especially when an opportunity to do some quality sucking-up presented itself. "I'd rather not go into that right now," Mike replied.

Chuck pounded on the table. "Damn it, I want to know. If someone's after our mentor, we need to take action."

Ben scanned the faces around the conference table. He saw a mixed array of reactions. All of them were uncomfortable, just in different ways.

"Well, Chuck," Ben said, spreading his arms across the table, "if you must know who cut Crichton's belay line—I did."

"*What?*" Mike almost rose out of his chair. "*You* cut his line?"

"That's what I said."

"Why the hell would you do that?" Chuck bellowed. "You just started here. What beef could you have against Crichton?"

"I was trying to flush out the killer. Everything was too relaxed, too pat. I wanted to stir the batter up, to throw a wrench into the killer's complacency and get himself to expose himself."

"So you tried to kill Mr. Crichton?"

"I wasn't trying to kill him. I was right behind him all along. The distance from the giant's ladder to Crichton was only about five feet—an easy jump, especially since I knew what was coming. He was never in any danger."

Mike and Chuck stared at him, mouths gaping. Ben couldn't tell who appeared more outraged.

"That is the most lame, bullheaded, irresponsible plan I've ever heard," Mike said, incredulous. "What if you had missed?"

"I didn't."

"You sorry sack of shit." Chuck was on his feet now, swaggering toward Ben. "I want this prick out of here, Mr. Crichton. I want him fired."

"We'll talk about this later," Crichton said, staring intently at Ben. "Does anyone else have any questions for Lieutenant Morelli?"

No one spoke. Chuck planted himself, arms folded across his chest like Mr. Clean, and glared at Ben.

"If there's nothing else," Crichton said, "then this staff meeting is adjourned. Mr. Kincaid, I would like to see you in my office."

"I have to meet a friend who's waiting for me," Ben said, checking his watch. "I'll drop by when it's convenient."

The other lawyers stared at him. He'd come see Crichton . . . when it was *convenient*? For *him*?

Crichton smoldered without comment. "As you wish, Mr. Kincaid. I'll be waiting for you."

* 53 *

About fifteen minutes later, Ben strolled into Crichton's office, a manila folder tucked under his arm. Crichton was leaning back in his chair, dictating.

"Glad you could make it," Crichton said, peering over his reading glasses. "Hope I didn't interfere with your plans."

"Don't worry about it. What did you want to discuss?"

"I've spoken to Harry Carter about your work on the new assignment. He's not pleased with your performance."

"Well, that's what he does best, isn't it?"

"Harry is a very important member of our staff. When he makes a negative recommendation, well . . . that's difficult for me to overlook."

Ben sat down in one of Crichton's chairs. "Let's not pussyfoot around, shall we?"

Crichton stiffened slightly.

"I've been talking to a friend of mine named Loving. He's a private investigator. At my request, he undertook a search for Al Austin, the long-lost member of the XKL-1 design team."

Crichton's feet dropped to the floor. "You did . . . *what*?"

"Loving had a long conversation with the man. He's a funny dude. Seems he didn't like some of the corporate policies being implemented here at Apollo, so he quit. More than just quit, actually. Disappeared. Seemed to think it would be best if no one at Apollo had any idea where he was."

"Austin was always a borderline crazy. Paranoid. Probably an alcoholic."

"Uh-huh. That's what he said you'd say. Anyway, he claims that after the XKL-1 was manufactured and distributed, a design defect was discovered. A defect that made any vehicle using that suspension system unsafe. Especially on rough or bumpy terrain." He looked directly into Crichton's eyes. "Such as the dirt field outside a football stadium."

"Austin was fired because he was accused of sexual impropriety by several female employees. We had no choice."

"Uh-huh. He said you'd say that, too. He said all four women who filed complaints disappeared before he or his lawyers could even talk to them. Apparently, they were bestowed with rather lucrative retirement plans."

"We had no choice. If we hadn't made them happy, they would've sued."

"I think you were creating a smoke screen, Crichton, just as you're doing now. The point is that the XKL-1 was and is unsafe."

"That has never been proven."

Ben reached into his manila folder and began withdrawing documents. "Loving had a heck of a time finding Austin. He was holed up in western Oklahoma—don't bother asking, I won't tell you where. Bought a chicken farm, and that's what he does for a living now. Says he's much happier. Which I don't doubt."

Ben passed the top document to Crichton. "I guess Al thought that since Loving had gone to so much trouble, he deserved to be rewarded. So Al dug up his personal copies of these reports, copies you didn't know he had."

Ben pointed to the top page. "I bet you've seen this report before, haven't you? Your initials are on it. After the first field reports came in suggesting there were problems with the XKL-1 design, Apollo ordered a series of tests. The testing was quite extensive. No doubt about it: the XKL-1 was unsafe. And you, and Bernie King, and everyone on the design team knew it."

"The testing was inconclusive. Improper control group, wild extrapolations from insufficient data—"

"Don't bother, Crichton. I've already read the report." He passed across the next document in his stack. "Here we have the minutes of a series of meetings held by the Apollo Board of Directors. It seems they learned about the safety problems, too. And they had to decide what to do about it."

Ben pointed to the bottom of one of the pages. "Evidently some of those meetings were a bit on the dull side—notice all the doodling in the margins. I particularly enjoyed that cartoon with the small child being mangled by the XKL-1 suspension system. You Apollo guys sure have some sense of humor."

"I see nothing incriminating about this," Crichton said unevenly. "On the contrary, this seems to me to be the work of a conscientious corporation trying to discover the truth."

"Trying to discover the truth? Yes. The question is: what did they do with the truth?" Ben tossed the final document in his stack to Crichton. "This document outlines the cost-benefit analysis performed at the behest of the Apollo directors. They determined that the cost of redesigning the system, implementing the new design, altering the manufacturing equipment, recalling the XKL-1 and marketing the new product would be almost two hundred million dollars. Not enough to sink Apollo by a long shot, but a sizable chunk of change nonetheless.

"As you can see, if you're reading along, Apollo then analyzed the costs attendant to retaining the current design. The only real cost item was the lawsuits that would predictably arise as people were injured by the defective system. They estimated that approximately twenty lawsuits a year would be filed, and that the average plaintiff could be bought off—excuse me, that a settlement could be reached for about a quarter of a million bucks. A quiet settlement, before any publicity got stirred up. In short, even if this went on for forty years, it would still be cheaper to retain the old design."

Ben looked at Crichton sharply. "Guess what they decided to do?"

Crichton cleared his throat. "The business of a corporation is to make money. If business suffers, everyone suffers."

"Spare me the trickle-down rationalization. This corporation decided that it would be cheaper to allow people to be mutilated and killed than to spend money implementing a new design. So they just sat back and counted their millions while people like Jason Nelson died."

"There's no need for sanctimonious—"

Ben flung the report into Crichton's face. "These ten pages are the documents you removed from the production to the Nelsons and their attorney. You misrepresented the contents of the documents to me, and based upon that misrepresentation, I got summary judgment against them. If the Nelsons had received these documents, as they should have, they would have blown me out of the water."

"Litigation is a cutthroat business. We play hardball at Apollo. We have a duty to our shareholders—"

"This is the most cynical, cold-hearted exercise in unrestrained greed I've ever heard of! Corporations should use their vast resources to help people. Instead, you let this anything-for-the-bottom-line mentality fester until it creates monsters like Rob Fielder and the XKL-1."

Crichton pushed himself out of his chair. "You're so goddamn naive. This is corporate America, Kincaid. Everyone does it! Why do you think soft drink companies still use those bottle caps that poke people's eyes out? Why do so few cars have airbags? Corporations don't exist to contribute to the common good. They exist to turn a profit."

"Well," Ben said, "since you feel so righteous about this, you won't mind if I take my information public."

Crichton folded his hands in his lap and settled down. "All right. What do you want?"

"First, I want you to go before the Board and tell them the XKL-1 has to be scrapped, and all existing models must be recalled."

"That would cost millions—"

"And you'll do it! Or I'll go public with these documents, and you'll have consumer groups, government agencies, and probably a class action suit breathing down your neck."

Crichton's teeth rattled together. "Very well. What else?"

"Five million dollars to the Nelsons. No strings."

"That lawsuit is over."

"That lawsuit is over because you lied to me. If you hadn't misrepresented the nature of the missing documents, we'd still be in court, and they'd be in line for one of Apollo's quarter of a million dollar Christmas presents. Five million won't make up for the loss of their son. But it's better than nothing."

"All right. What else can we do for you, Kincaid?"

"You can pay Gloria Hamel's medical bills. Including her plastic surgery. And give her some money to carry her through this period of mourning and recovery. Two hundred thousand ought to do it."

Crichton's eyes widened. "Surely you're not suggesting Apollo is responsible for what happened to her?"

"No, not directly. But she needs help and you can give it to her. Consider it compensation for all the misery you've inflicted since the XKL-1 was implemented."

"Fine." Crichton checked his calendar. "The Board

meets tomorrow morning. I'll present your package to them then."

"I'll be waiting to hear the result."

"And if they refuse?"

"Then I go public with the documents."

"You are a lawyer representing the Apollo Consortium. You owe us a duty of zealous loyalty. In fact, those documents are covered by the attorney-client privilege. It would be a gross ethical violation to disclose them to the general public."

"I don't give a damn. If the Board doesn't cooperate, I'll send copies to every newspaper in the Southwest."

"I'll see that you're disbarred."

"And I'll see that you're arrested. Negligent homicide. Aiding and abetting, at the least."

Crichton laughed, but the laugh sounded very hollow. "That will never stick."

"Do you really want to take the chance?"

There was a long silence as the two men stared at one another across a much too small expanse of carpet.

"Have you no sense of propriety at all?" Crichton asked. "No sense of loyalty?"

"To you? No."

"You were hired to assist the Apollo Consortium."

"I wasn't hired to be a patsy."

A hideous grin spread across Crichton's face. "You still haven't figured out why you were hired, have you?"

Ben raised his chin. "What do you mean? I was hired to work on your litigation team."

Crichton shook his head. "You stupid fool. Blinded by your own egotism. Surely you didn't believe all those nauseating compliments I paid you?"

"I . . . don't know what you mean . . ."

"You were hired because we learned you had represented the Nelsons on a prior personal injury matter. Period. We were searching for something we could use against them in their suit against Apollo—something to force an early settlement and ensure their silence thereafter. We learned from the court records that your lawsuit for the Nelsons involved mental injuries as well as physical. If we could find a doctor's report, or perhaps a deposition transcript, indicating that one or both of them had mental problems ... well, obviously, that would undermine their credibility. It would reinforce our argument that the Nelsons were paranoid, unbalanced people desperately searching for a scapegoat."

"Surely you didn't think I would give you access to any incriminating records from a prior lawsuit."

"No, I didn't. Not a self-righteous snot like you. Not if you knew. But you may recall, one of the first things Howard Hamel did after offering you this job was to arrange for the transfer of your files."

Ben pressed his fingers against his temples. "That's why your attitude toward me changed after I won the lawsuit."

"Did you think I would shovel out that nauseating crap forever? It made me sick, believe me. But we needed your files. Or so we thought. Little did we know, you were such a stupid, unquestioning soldier, so eager to please your new masters, you won the case on your own. You didn't need the medical files; you did it with some fancy legal footwork. No matter—the result was the same. But as soon as the case was over, I assigned you to Harry and put you on the track the hell out of here."

Ben could feel the bile churning in his stomach. "You're disgusting, Crichton. And the worst thing is, you're a perfect exemplar of this whole disgusting operation."

Crichton made a tsking noise. "Sticks and stones."

"I'll be calling tomorrow as soon as the Board meeting ends. And I'll be calling from the lobby of the *Tulsa World*."

"I'll be waiting with bated breath."

"You may consider this my resignation." Ben stood up and started toward the door.

"Fine. Of course, we'll give you the customary two weeks."

"Don't bother," Ben said. "I'll leave today."

* 54 *

"Sergeant Tomlinson, I'd like you to meet my friends Ben Kincaid and Christina McCall."

After Mike introduced them, Ben extended his hand to the lean figure lying on the St. John's hospital bed. He still had tubes attached to his nose and mouth, the lower half of his body was in a cast, and dark circles underscored his eyes. His coloring was fairly normal, though, and he appeared strong. "Glad to meet you."

"I want to congratulate you on that astonishing undercover work you did," Ben said. "You showed a lot of promise as a homicide detective." He nudged Mike. "Didn't he, Mike?"

"Huh? Oh, yeah. I suppose."

"I should be congratulating you," Tomlinson said. "I understand you found the creep after I let him get the best of me."

"You saved a girl's life by doing what you did." Ben kept his inevitable tag to himself: saved her life for another three days.

"How are you feeling?" Christina asked.

"Much better," Tomlinson replied. "Still sore in places. Legs ache when I try to move them. If you see my wife outside, though—don't mention it to her. Karen tends to worry."

Imagine that. "I saw your daughter outside," Ben said. "She's a cutie. How's she taking it?"

"Oh, Kathleen is fine. Except she keeps wanting to crawl around on my cast and stitches. The doctor doesn't approve."

"I can imagine. So, Mike," Ben said pointedly, "wasn't there something you wanted to tell Sergeant Tomlinson?"

Tomlinson's eyes perked up.

"What?" Mike said. "Oh . . . er . . . well . . . I guess I wanted to say . . . you did all right, Tomlinson."

"Oh. Thank you, sir."

"Not perfect, of course, but certainly not bad. You showed a lot of guts out there."

"And that's what you wanted to tell me?"

"Yes. That's it."

"Oh." The gleam faded from his eyes. "Thank you."

Mike turned away, then stopped. "Oh yeah. One other thing. I approved your transfer to Homicide."

"You—" His eyes ballooned. A vivid smile spread across his face. "Why—thank you, sir. Thank you very much. Very very much. I won't disappoint you, sir. I promise. Thank you very very much."

Mike grinned. "My pleasure. You earned it, kid. Say, if you get bored, you can swap notes with Buddy, the guy who hid the girl. He's in a room just down the hall. We found him in a warehouse off Eleventh. He was seriously torn up, lost a lot of blood, but I think he's going to pull through."

"That's great," Tomlinson said. "I'm glad someone else came through this alive."

Yeah, Ben thought. Someone.

"Don't kid yourself, Tomlinson. If Fielder hadn't been stopped, he would've killed every name on the Kindergarten Club list. You've saved a lot of lives. Right, Ben?"

Ben was no longer standing by the bed. He was facing the window, staring out at the sun setting across the western horizon.

Mike saw something glistening in Ben's hand. It was a golden necklace, a half-heart with a jagged tear down the center.

Mike and Christina exchanged a meaningful look. If there was something they could do, they'd do it. But there was nothing. It would just take time.

A nurse came through the door pushing a wheelchair.

"Who's that for?" Mike asked.

"You," she said briskly.

"Now wait a minute—"

"Don't bother arguing, Mike." Christina steered him into the chair. "You've been putting off these tests since you tangled with Fielder. For all we know, you could be hemorrhaging in a hundred different places."

"But—but—"

"Save it." She waved at the nurse. "Take him away."

The nurse pivoted by the door. "Oh, Mr. Kincaid?"

Ben turned his head a fraction from the window.

"There's someone outside who would like to speak to you."

Ben returned his gaze to the window, then, a few moments later, left the hospital room.

He found Shelly in the visitor's lounge. She was dressed in a formal business suit—probably came straight from work. She was holding a baby girl in her arms, trussed up in blue ribbons and a white frock.

"This must be Angie," Ben said.

"Yeah. I just picked her up at day care. Isn't she beautiful?" Angie rubbed her little fists in her eyes and peered sleepily at Ben. "Can we talk?"

"Sure, Shelly. What's on your mind?"

"I just . . . wanted to thank you."

"Oh?"

"Yes. I know you know."

Ben took a paper cup from the water dispenser and

poured himself a small drink. "Want to tell me about it? I promise it'll remain confidential."

She sighed, then pressed her baby against her chest. "I've been with the Apollo legal department for six years now."

Ben was surprised. Judging from her position, he would've guessed she had been there a year, perhaps two.

"They always say corporations are the best places to work when you want to have a family as well as a legal career. Nine-to-five days, no billable hour demands. I didn't want any special favors; I just wanted some common decency." She inhaled sharply. "Common decency. Now there's an oxymoron.

"I learned right off the bat that everything I'd been told about corporate legal staffs was a lie—at Apollo, anyway. The corporation worked its employees just as hard as the firms, maybe harder. Crichton always acted as if he owned me. And there was no outside client to prevent him from exercising complete control over his department—his private kingdom. He did anything he wanted. Crichton and the other men called me *honey* and *sweet young thing*. They asked if I was *getting any* and when I was going to start making babies—and if I wanted any help. If I complained, they said I didn't know how to take a joke.

"Anyway, so I've been here six years, and I'm still in an Attorney One position. Herb's been promoted. Chuck's been promoted. Even Doug has been promoted, for God's sake. Every man in the department has been promoted. But not me."

"You should file a complaint," Ben said.

"Oh, they're way ahead of me there. They've been papering my file since day one. You know, I wasn't always the quiet, mousy, pathetic nonentity you've known. When I first came here, I could belly up with the best of them. And on my very first review, they complained that I was too aggressive. Strident. Can you imagine them ever telling a male attorney that he was too aggressive? But that's what they told me."

"Crichton, I assume."

"Yeah. The thing is, I'm not even sure he realizes that there's anything wrong with that. I don't think he's intentionally discriminating against women. I think he's oblivious to it. I think his sexism, his different standards and expectations, his preference for working with other men, is so deeply ingrained that he isn't even aware of what he's doing.

"Anyway, it was clear that if I continued behaving as I had—actively, aggressively—I was going to be out on the streets."

"So you . . . changed?"

"Of course. I didn't feel I had any choice. It was a real compromise—but you know how bad the job market is in the Southwest right now, and it would be even worse if I were fired, or if I quit after receiving a negative review that every subsequent employer would read. So I did what they wanted. I did my work, and I did it quietly. But as you may have noticed, I still haven't been promoted."

"Perhaps you should file a Title VII lawsuit."

"I threatened to do just that, when Crichton started giving me grief about taking maternity leave. So what did they do? They promoted Candice. Not far—certainly not as far as her male peers, but they did give her a token promotion. And we both know why they chose her—she only got that tiny promotion after she gave Herb what he wanted.

"The point is, if I claim Apollo engages in systematic sex discrimination, they're going to haul out Candice, their token female attorney with a promotion, and deny everything. The only reason Shelly wasn't promoted, they'll say, is her poor work performance. And then they'll haul out all these bullshit evaluations they've been writing to prove it."

"That's insidious," Ben said quietly. "You should fight them. Surely some judge would listen to you."

"Ben, I can't afford to lose my job. Who's going to hire me now—a single mother with a three-month-old baby? Forget it. They know I'm helpless. As Crichton himself said, 'Screw you—where are you going to go?' " She pressed her free hand against her forehead. "And then Chuck started doing his junior supervisor routine on me, threatening to get Crichton to fire me. I was so scared. I guess you know Howard was Angie's father."

"I suspected."

"And then he was killed, and I didn't know what we were going to do."

Ben kept his personal opinion to himself—that she was better off without him.

"It all welled up inside me at that retreat at Camp Sequoyah. Crichton was complaining that I was spending too much time with my baby, and Chuck was threatening to get me fired. You probably remember that big scene at Crackerbarrel, when Chuck said he was going to get Crichton to can me. The next day, I'm sure you also saw him huddled with Crichton on the High Course. I knew I was the topic of conversation. And Crichton looked like he was buying every lie Chuck told him."

"So you cut Crichton's belay line."

Shelly nodded. "How did you know?"

"Well, after I didn't find the knife up on the high course, I realized my initial theory was wrong. So I just kept thinking about that morning, where everyone was sitting, what everyone was doing. And I finally remembered you, spreading mayonnaise on sandwiches. With a knife."

"Just a kitchen knife. But it was sharp enough. When I was done, I put it back where it belonged with all the other lunch paraphernalia. It was the Purloined Letter principle—since it was in plain sight, exactly where it was supposed to be, the cops overlooked it." She smiled faintly. "Thanks for covering for me at the staff meeting."

Ben tossed his paper cup into the trash. "No problem. I didn't figure you were the hardened criminal type."

"If Crichton knew, he'd fire me. It would be just the excuse he's been waiting for. And he might have me arrested as well. I don't know what Angie would do if I went to prison." She kissed Angie on the cheek. "But taking the blame onto yourself like that. You could get into some big trouble. Crichton might bring charges."

"I don't think so. I have a bit of leverage over him at the moment. I also have a friend, Clayton Langdell, who could probably give you a job—outside Apollo. Or I think I can ensure that you keep your present job for some time. Whatever you want."

She paused for a moment. "Let me think about it. I'll get back to you. I can't stand that place, but I hate to just give up."

"I understand. It's a hard fight, but it's fighters like you who are going to make the world a better place"—he poked Angie in the tummy—"for people like her."

Angie grabbed Ben's finger. He reached out and took her into his arms.

"You've been so kind to me," Shelly said. Her eyes were welling up. "And I don't even know why."

Ben bounced the little girl in his arms. "Well," he said, "we all do what we can."

Angie clapped her hands together and cooed.

"A buddy doesn't move in
on another buddy's girl. **Ever.**
After all, chicks come and go;
buddies are forever."

Also by
William Bernhardt...

THE CODE OF BUDDYHOOD

Published in trade paperback by Available Press.

Bobby and Mark are University of
Oklahoma undergraduates, dorm dwellers
in the seventies, who invoke "The Code of
Buddyhood" and test it to the limits. After
eleven years of estrangement, the two
reunite in Dallas to assess the past and
patch up old wounds. This is a dazzling
novel about growing up and apart and coming back together.

Look for
THE CODE OF BUDDYHOOD
at a bookstore near you.